Faraway
CHILD

ALSO BY
AMY MAIDA WADSWORTH:

Silent Witness

Shadow of Doubt

Faraway
CHILD

———— ✦❁❁✦ a novel by ❁❁✦ ————

Amy Maida
WADSWORTH

Covenant Communications, Inc.

Cover image © Comstock Images.

Cover design copyrighted 2005 by Covenant Communications, Inc.

Published by Covenant Communications, Inc.
American Fork, Utah

Printed in the United States of America
First Printing: April 2005

11 10 09 08 07 06 05   10 9 8 7 6 5 4 3 2 1

ISBN 1-59156-817-X

—— ❈ Dedication ❈ ——

This book is dedicated to Maida, Jessica, Russell, and Kira—my
teachers, comforters, and rays of light.

Acknowledgements

Since this novel is truer to life than any other I've written, there are more people to thank. Thanks to family and friends who loved us and supported us and helped us through our times of trial by babysitting, listening, and crying with us. Thanks to readers and critiquers. Thanks to Arnold and Barbara Grundvig, Gwen Jefferies, and the rest of the Brighton Third Ward for putting up with our noise and loving us anyway. Thanks to Camille Bradstreet for being my eye into Catholicism and enhancing the Christian nature of this novel. Thanks to the teachers who helped our daughter make so much progress over the years, especially Glennys Sabbucco, Lisa Coleman, and their wonderful staffs. And also appreciation to Lynne Harris, the best bus driver of all. Special thanks to Angela Colvin Eschler for encouraging me to write this novel.

But most of all, thanks to my Lord and Savior, who healed my heart, bore my grief, and gave me everyone in this list. Truly, we are never alone.

Chapter 1

THE RACK

A golden chicken turned on a rotisserie spit in the deli, the sharp smell of aged parmesan filled the air, and the pierce of Kaye's scream made me want to crawl into a hole.

The woman in line behind me tried to be sympathetic. "I never bring my children shopping. It's just too hard."

I nodded and looked at Kaye's face. Her mouth opened wide in a loud—almost inhuman—scream, but her eyes were completely dry. How nice that the woman behind me had a choice whether to bring her children shopping or not.

"What does she want?" the woman asked.

"She wants to stand in front of the book rack, I think." Mention of the book rack increased her scream by at least two decibels.

I'd tried to give her several different books when we first got to the store—it was the routine, and Kaye was all about routine. We normally entered the store, went to the book rack, Kaye picked out a book, and we shopped. It always ended in screaming when I took the book away at the check stand since I couldn't afford to buy it. At least we got through the shopping without difficulty that way. Well, we usually did. Today, she wouldn't pick a book, and she stood before the rack, staring, smiling, and singing to herself. Apparently she didn't understand I had come to the store with a mission, and a limited time in which to fulfill it. Dinner depended on this shopping trip. And the lady in front of the line at the deli couldn't choose between crab and pasta salad.

Kaye's face turned a deeper shade of red, and she started to stand up in her seat. I put my thumbs against her hipbones and grasped the metal bars behind her back to hold her in place. She screamed directly in my ear.

The woman behind me shifted her weight. I glanced back at her as I rubbed my ear with my shoulder, and I saw her scrutinizing the way I was holding Kaye in the cart. Realizing it probably didn't look very good for me to force Kaye to sit, I looked ahead at the deli menu and ignored the woman's stares. I wasn't doing anything wrong, and the alternative was much worse. If I let Kaye out of the cart, she would streak to the book rack, I'd have to chase after her, I'd lose my place in line, and our shopping trip and the stress accompanying it would be extended.

"It's almost our turn," I whispered in Kaye's ear. "We're almost there."

My four-year-old, Marie, looked over the different cheeses and specialty meats in the refrigerated case. What a jewel she was. Quiet, polite, and obedient, she was almost the exact opposite of her little sister, even though only a year and a half separated them.

"I love you, Marie," I said.

She smiled at me. "I love you more!"

The woman in front of me changed her mind again, and I sighed. My arms ached as I continued holding Kaye in place. I wouldn't be able to hold her there for much longer. I'd planned on buying roast beef for Adam—a little splurge for his lunches—but maybe the splurge would have to wait.

I veered my shopping cart out of the line, still holding Kaye in place. The woman behind me watched me move. I nodded my good-bye and called for Marie.

Diapers were next on my list. I let go of Kaye just long enough to grab the jumbo pack and throw it in the cart, then we rounded into the cereal aisle. A policeman stood at the end of it. It wasn't the best part of town, so it didn't surprise me to see a policeman in the grocery store. I just wasn't sure what he was doing in my aisle.

Kaye still squirmed and let out an occasional scream. I held firm and let go of her only to put items in my cart. Each time I let go, she tried to stand up. One time she almost made it out of her seat belt, and I sat her back down sharply just as the cart began to roll.

The policeman walked down the aisle toward me. He walked casually, but didn't take his eyes off of me. I wondered if he'd followed the screams, or if the woman in line at the deli had tipped him off.

"Cute kids," he said.

"Thanks." I loosened my grip on Kaye a little, and she fought hard to get up. I had to tighten my grip again.

"She's having a hard day, huh?"

I nodded. "She always has a hard day. She's a tough one." I finally let go of her hips and tried to hug her. She pushed me away.

The policeman looked Kaye over—I could only assume he was looking for bruises, which made me grateful Kaye hadn't been accident prone that week—and then his eyes fell on Marie.

"How are you today?" he asked.

She smiled her sweet, beautiful smile. "I'm fine. We're having chicken for dinner."

He smiled back. The sight of Marie seemed to ease his mind. "Well, you ladies have a good day."

I nodded. "We will."

The officer walked past us and turned down another aisle.

I knew I'd done nothing wrong, but the scrutiny itself upset me. Images flashed in my mind of a woman I'd seen on television, slapping her child silly as he sat quietly in his car seat. I pushed Kaye's hair out of her face. There was a big difference between that woman and me. By the looks of that video, she didn't have any reason to lose her temper. I had reason to lose mine, but I refused.

When we had everything on our list except the roast beef, I turned to pass the deli again. If there weren't a line, maybe I'd buy it after all. In my haste, I turned down the wrong aisle and the book rack came into view.

If I hadn't been in her way, Kaye would have jumped out of the cart and headed straight for the rack. Instead, I caught her, pushed her back into the seat, and tightened the belt as much as I could without hurting her, then resumed my vice grip on her hips. She screamed louder than she had previously, and I knew that trip to the deli wasn't going to happen.

I turned the cart around and took a different aisle to the nearest cashier. The line wasn't long, but my arms were aching so bad that any line was almost a curse. When we reached the cashier, Kaye was still screaming. I smiled briefly, kissed Kaye's cheek, and tried to look her in the eye to comfort her. "It's okay, honey. We're almost done."

She turned her face away from me and screamed louder. I shrugged at the cashier. "She's two."

The cashier nodded and gave me a saltwater taffy. "Will this help?"

"Maybe. Thank you." I let go of Kaye, unwrapped the taffy, and broke off a piece of it for her. She sat down to receive her candy. Sucking on it stopped the crying for a second, then she gagged on the candy and started screaming again. Sticky pink drool dripped down her chin.

I grimaced. "Well, we tried."

The cashier gave me a wan smile along with my total. I lifted Kaye from the cart, held her with one arm, and wrote the check quickly with my free hand. Kaye tried to twist out of my grip, turning her body toward the book rack and pushing against me with all of her strength. Heavy stillness accentuated Kaye's scream, and I could feel several pairs of eyes staring at me, but I focused on the task at hand and scribbled my name. It didn't look like my signature. I hoped the cashier wouldn't ask for ID. But she was efficient and did her job as she'd been told to do it. I fished through my purse for my wallet and pulled out my driver's license. Thankfully, she didn't question the scrawl any further.

"Thanks, Mrs. Young. Have a good day." She handed me my receipt.

I raised my eyebrows at her and forced a smile. "Oh yeah, we're off to a good start."

With my groceries bagged and reloaded in the cart, I gratefully left the store, passing the policeman as I headed for my car. Kaye continued to scream and tug at the belt across her stomach, and it seemed like I couldn't get to the car fast enough. When I did reach the car, I realized I'd left my keys on the checkout counter where I'd written my check. I looked back at the store. The policeman stood near the doors, watching me.

My eyes burned. I prayed some kind bag boy would bring the keys to me. As I turned the cart around and headed back for the store, I cursed the grocery chain for not having enough employees, or not training them in customer service. I tried to smile at the policeman as I passed, and thought to myself, *Serve and protect!* Every eye flew to us once more and watched us all the way to the check-stand, where I claimed my keys. I felt their eyes on my back as I left, and felt their sense of relief that I was finally gone.

Angry tears wet my cheeks while I put the girls in their seats. I couldn't look at Marie, but I knew she was crying too. I opened the trunk and loaded it with the paper bags full of food. When the cart was empty, I lifted its front wheels onto the curb and climbed into the sanctity of my car.

Kaye stared contentedly out the window, a slight smile gracing her now-serene face. Her big blue eyes were the only dry ones in the car. The change in her amazed me. How could she scream for an entire shopping trip, and behave perfectly only seconds after it was over? It didn't make sense. She didn't make sense.

If only the people in the store could see her now, I thought. The looks on their faces flashed through my mind, along with the judgments I thought they were passing: *Why can't she control her child? What a brat! She must spoil that baby if she's screaming like that just because she can't have a book.* Deep in the back of my mind was the fear that those judgments might be correct. What if I wasn't a good mother? What if I got lucky with Marie, and Kaye was the product of poor, permissive parenting?

I rubbed my eyes one more time and took a deep breath, then drove home.

I navigated on autopilot, taking the shortest, easiest way to our townhouse. When Kaye screamed again, I jumped and felt my heart begin to race.

"What's the matter?" I asked, turning quickly to discern what was bothering her.

Kaye craned her neck and tried to slip her arm from under the straps of her car seat. She succeeded in freeing her right arm.

"Kaye, hold still!" I reprimanded.

With her right arm free, she was able to shift her weight and get her left arm out too. She twisted her body and looked out the back window, screaming. The scream reverberated in my small Metro, and I felt a headache coming on.

I glanced in the side-view mirror, and the catalyst for her latest tantrum glowed in the reflection—golden arches.

"I don't have any money, Kaye. We can't go to McDonalds."

She screamed louder at the mention of her favorite place to eat.

I sighed and kept my eyes on the road. *Just get home. We're almost home. Get home and roast that chicken. It will make great drippings . . . a lovely gravy.*

I felt like I'd been roasted on a rack that day—had my juices cooked out of me. After I set the timer for dinner, I lay down on the couch and tried to rest before Adam got home.

Torture is tiring.

Chapter 2

SOLUTIONS

That night, I dreamed again of my perfect place—the place I imagined for my perfect self and perfect family. Kitchen floors you could eat off of, soft, toe-curling carpet, wide rooms with high ceilings. Even the yard was perfect, especially on that perfect day.

In a moment, she had ruined everything. I followed the screams to the back of the lawn and lifted Kaye's purple party dress from the garden. She had wiped mud across her bare chest.

I wondered how I'd save the perfect afternoon—the happy children running around the beautiful three-tiered birthday cake I'd decorated myself, the aspen trees shimmering like glitter in the breeze behind our house, the stack of gifts I couldn't wait for Kaye to open. Maybe saving the afternoon was beyond me, and maybe it didn't matter anyway. The birthday girl certainly didn't seem to care.

"Let's get you cleaned up, and then you can get back to your party," I said, and I picked up Kaye and shook her dress off over the dirt.

"I tried to play with her, Mommy." Marie tugged at my pant leg as I headed for the house.

"It's okay, Marie. Just let me get her dressed." I pushed past two olive-skinned sisters, the same ages as Marie and Kaye, and they chased each other happily into the sunlight.

"Mommy," Marie said. Her voice wavered and her bright blue eyes filled with tears.

"What, sweetheart?"

"Why won't Kaye play with me?"

* * *

Kaye's scream woke me with a start and remnants of my dream clung for a moment before I realized I was awake. Marie had been asking a painful question in my dream, and I felt a dull ache in my chest. It was a hot night. I'd kicked my covers off to Adam's empty side of the bed. The red digital glow of the clock read one in the morning. I hated it when Adam worked nights.

Kaye jiggled her doorknob and screamed again. I longed for the day when she would learn to open the door herself so that I could get some sleep. As it was, I had to let her out to avoid upsetting the neighbors. We'd already been dragged into the apartment office once because of complaints about screaming at one in the morning, and though we tried to explain that our daughter just didn't sleep well, we were still threatened with eviction. Our three-bedroom townhouse was a steal—the best bang for our buck—and we weren't about to let ourselves get evicted. So, I got up with Kaye every one A.M. like clockwork.

By the time I got to her bedroom, Kaye's little mouth was near the crack at the bottom of the door, and I could hear her scream again, much louder than before. "I'm right here, Kaye," I said, and I jiggled the doorknob.

She backed away as I opened the door. Kaye seemed to have a map in her head and didn't need me to turn on the light for her to find her way down to the television. Marie still slept as if she were in hibernation; she drooled on her pink pillow. No doubt she could sleep through a rock concert.

I followed Kaye downstairs and turned on the television. The blue glow filled the dark room, and Kaye rocked back and forth in front of the screen, smiling and singing wordlessly as I played the movie on top of the stack next to the television. She sat flat on her bottom as the FBI warning came on, and her wide grin reinforced my whipped feelings.

"Who's the mother here, anyway?" I asked. Then I flopped down on the couch. "Well, I may be the mom, but you're the boss."

She hummed along with the music, not quite singing the words. I slipped into sleep before Cinderella woke her wicked stepmother.

When I woke up again, it was almost four in the morning. Kaye slept on the floor in front of the television, and the video had rewound on its own. Adam should have been home by then. I got up and looked out the kitchen window to see if his car was in the parking lot, but it wasn't there. On my way back to the couch, I picked Kaye up and let her snuggle with me as she slept.

I lay in the dark, looking at the kitchen door, wishing that Adam would open it soon. He delivered newspapers to paperboys, and he was always home before three. He didn't have a cell phone, and I wasn't even sure what part of town he was working in that night. All I could do was wait.

Sleep began drifting across my consciousness again when I heard the key click in the doorknob. Adam's figure was a dark shadow silhouetted by the streetlamp in the parking lot behind him. He shut the door, tossed his keys on the kitchen table, and took a few steps forward until he was standing just inside the television's glow. I felt relieved to see him there, until his face came into the light.

"Hi," I said.

"Hi." He took his baseball cap off and hung it on the hook inside the coat closet. Then he collapsed in the recliner. His heavy eyelids and the down-turned corners of his mouth tipped me off that something was seriously wrong.

"You're late. You okay?"

"No." He leaned his head back, and I could tell by the pitch of his voice he was near tears.

The feeling of dread I'd been suppressing began to climb to the surface. He rarely cried. "What happened?"

"I messed up, Jen. I really messed up this time." He buried his face in his hands.

I wiggled out from under Kaye and went to Adam. I'd never seen him so upset. He seemed afraid to tell me what had happened, which made me afraid to hear it. It wasn't like Adam to be so discouraged. I knelt next to him and absently traced the fraying hem of his jeans.

"I loaded the truck, right?" he began. "But I was really tired."

I nodded.

"I didn't check the tires," Adam continued. "They're always fine. I didn't think about it . . . I just wanted to get out on the route." He took a deep breath and let the air out slowly. He wiped his eyes with the palms of his hands.

"Well, I don't blame you for that," I tried to comfort him.

Adam shook his head. "The guys who do maintenance didn't tighten the lug nuts on the back wheel, and while I was on the route, the wheel came off."

I tried to picture it. "The whole wheel?"

He nodded. "The whole wheel. I hit a dip in the road. It had probably been wiggling its way off for a while."

As I imagined the large newspaper truck falling on its axle while in motion, I started examining Adam for cuts and bruises. When I didn't find any, I wondered if he wasn't feeling well, and things weren't as bad as they seemed.

"I'm okay. I wasn't going very fast because I'd just gone over a dip, but the truck is wrecked." He sighed.

"So, were you in the hospital getting checked out or something? You're almost two hours late." As I thought about it, I was grateful I'd slept through most of the two hours.

"No. I was with my supervisor getting reprimanded."

Reprimanded? I thought. It sounded to me like Adam was lucky he wasn't hurt. "Why reprimand you? It wasn't your fault the lug nuts were loose."

"But it was, Jen. I'm supposed to check the truck over before I leave the dock."

I sat back on my heels, feeling a slight chill.

"They're talking it over with their lawyer in the morning, and with their insurance people. But I'm pretty sure they're going to fire me."

I looked up at his face. He was avoiding my gaze, and he stared at nothing in particular. His eyes were hollow in the blue light of the television, and his face was gaunt.

I knew how hard it was for him to find a job that paid a decent wage and fit the hours he had available. If he didn't have a well-paying job, we'd have to take out more student loans for him to finish school, and we were already looking at twenty years of debt. The thought nauseated me. It had taken him weeks to find the job at the newspaper, and two more weeks before he was able to start it. That job had sustained us the entire previous school year, and we were counting on it. The likelihood of him finding a deal that sweet again was almost nonexistent. My throat ached, and I fought the burn of coming tears. There had to be a simple solution. He struggled through school anyway, and I didn't want him to have to deal with pavement pounding as well. I hated watching him shoulder all the stress of financial responsibility.

"Maybe I can get a job," I ventured. My hours were probably easier to work with than his were.

"What about the kids?"

"I could work nights."

He shook his head. "I don't want you going out alone every night. This isn't the best part of town."

"Adam, I'd be fine."

"No." He looked at me as though the subject were closed, and I relented. I didn't particularly want to go to work anyway, especially because of the girls.

"Well, then, what are we going to do, Adam? We're barely making ends meet as it is."

"I know," he said. He put his face in his hands again and leaned his elbows on his knees.

I could have kicked myself for stating the obvious. We needed solutions, not reminders of the problem.

"We'll figure something out," Adam said, and he reached for my hand. "We'll just have to have faith."

"Yeah," I agreed. It was the type of thing that needed faith. But I doubted the Lord would arrange for us to win a million-dollar sweepstakes, no matter how much faith we had.

"I'm tired. I'm going to bed." Adam stood and plodded up the stairs. He left Kaye and me in the front room—Kaye snoring, and me plotting. Adam made a little money at his other job as a bank teller, but since that was only part-time work, we had to come up with something else. We needed a solution, and I was going to find it.

Chapter 3

PLANS

I did some research before I called my little sister, Brienne. Kosy Kitchen was still in business, and their website said they were always looking for new representatives. I didn't have many skills, since I'd married young and had kids right away, but the skills I had were practical. Everyone needed to cook.

Brienne's phone rang once before someone picked up.

"Barclay residence, this is Russ."

"Hi, Russ," I said.

"Jen! Long time no see." He was being sarcastic. He'd seen me the day before when he'd come home to find Brienne and me working on scrapbooks.

"Yeah, Russ. Since you saw me last, I've sprouted three gray hairs." I wasn't sure I was exaggerating.

"You old lady," he laughed.

"Yeah, well you'll always be older than me." Five years older, I recalled, which made him seven years older than Brienne. I loved teasing him about robbing the cradle.

"We're only as old as we feel," he retorted. "And I don't feel thirty."

I felt thirty. Maybe even forty. Maybe I was older than him after all. "Hey," I changed the subject, "Is Bri there?"

"I'll get her." He put me on hold.

Brienne had a bubbly voice—not squeaky, but high-pitched enough that it was noticeable. She didn't squeak until she got excited about something. She'd been a cheerleader in high school, and had curly hair and a cute figure, which didn't change much after she'd had her first child. She did yoga and Pilates every day. People were surprised when she'd married the older, intellectual Russ Barclay. But they both had hearts as big as the Rockies.

"Jenny!" Brienne said as soon as she picked up the phone.

"Hi, Bri." I smiled. I could still picture her in her cheerleader outfit.

"What's up? You never call me on Saturdays."

"Well, I was wondering if you could do me a favor."

Within minutes of hearing my situation and my solution, Brienne had a list of fifty people she could invite to a cooking show, and I'd come up with an impressive menu.

"We could do it on a weeknight, so people aren't too busy," Brienne said.

"Sounds good." I got out my calendar and looked at the dates. My calendar was completely open, so I let Brienne pick the date.

"How about June seventeenth? That's a Thursday. It will give me enough time to make invitations, deliver them, and shop. Just get me a list of the stuff we'll need."

I grinned. "Can I do anything?" Brienne loved planning parties. She had all the paper, ink, stamps, and fancy scissors to make the invitations. I was certain she'd come up with something cute enough to frame.

"We can make the invitations and shop together. I'm excited!" She squeaked just a bit.

Adam came downstairs. His sandy hair was disheveled and dark circles shadowed his eyes.

"I'll call you back, Bri. Thanks." I hung up the phone and looked at Adam with concern. "Are you okay? You don't have to work at the bank today. You could have slept in."

Adam shrugged. "I couldn't sleep. I've got to find another job. We're going to fly through our savings—my car is acting up, the rent's due in two weeks, we barely have any food." He opened the cupboard to find some cereal. We had more food than he thought, but I knew it wouldn't last long. With a slight shake of his head, he closed the cupboards again without getting something to eat.

"I can do cooking shows again," I said. "I've already got my first show booked with Brienne in two weeks."

Adam nodded. "I hope I'll have a job by then. I don't even care what it is, really. Just as long as it's something I can do until I finish my degree." He sighed. "One more year, a couple of tests, and I'll be a CPA. I can't wait."

I put my arms around him. One year seemed like an eternity. I knew we'd have student loans to pay back after he graduated, but at least we'd have a steady income. It was hard to run a household as a student.

"But we'll be okay." Adam turned and kissed my forehead. "Let's keep a long-term perspective here. We'll be better people because of our struggles—more compassionate."

"Can't we learn compassion without struggling so much?"

Adam shook his head. "I don't think life works that way."

"Hmm." I grunted and wondered how deficient in compassion I was, and how many hard lessons I had to learn.

"Listen, I've got a plan too."

"Okay."

"At church tomorrow, I'll try to meet with the employment specialist. Maybe he can help us find something that will work."

"Does the Church have night jobs?"

"Well, the employment specialist knows about jobs outside of the Church, too. Maybe he'll have something. If not, I can go to job services."

I nodded. "Sounds good." I doubted it would help much, and figured Adam would end up going to job services after all. At least we both had a plan. At least we were doing something.

* * *

Our meetings started at nine in the morning, but since we were focusing on attending sacrament meeting that day, I slept through Relief Society. Kaye had a hard time going to sleep the night before, and I was the one that paid for it.

We snuck into the back of the chapel and found seats in the overflow, right behind an elderly couple. Kaye started her drone-like singing almost immediately. I hated going to church and spending the entire time in the foyer—it seemed a little pointless.

The white-haired man in front of us cupped his hand over his ear and glanced back at Kaye. I watched him lean over to his wife and whisper something, and I pressed my finger against Kaye's lips to try to get her to be quiet.

It didn't work, of course. Kaye pushed my finger away and sang even louder.

The man in front of us looked back at Kaye again, his hand still cupped over his ear. Then he took his wife by the arm and stood up. They gathered their things and went to sit on the opposite side of the chapel.

They sat in front of another family with well-behaved children who sat there coloring and minding their own business.

Kaye giggled.

"I wonder who the employment specialist is, anyway," Adam said, looking around as if he expected the man he looked for to be wearing a badge of some sort.

"You'll probably have to ask the bishop," I said as I tried again to get Kaye to be quiet. She squirmed off my lap and began crawling on the floor toward the end of the aisle.

"Okay. I guess I'll wait till after the meeting, then."

Kaye had reached the end of the aisle and was standing up, almost ready to bolt, when I grabbed her arm. I took her out to the foyer, where another tired-looking mother paced with her young child. We gave each other a sympathetic smile.

I thought of waiting for Adam after the meeting, but Kaye was squirming and Marie was tired. So I took the girls and began a lazy walk home. By the time Adam pulled over to pick us up, I knew his plan had failed.

"He doesn't have anything right now," Adam said. "But he said he'd keep his ears open."

I nodded. "So, what are you going to do?"

He shrugged. "Check with job services. Plus, I'll check with the bank tomorrow and see if they can extend my hours."

It would help—a little.

Chapter 4

BITES

The phone rang a week later. Brienne's cooking show was that Thursday, and I was brushing up on my skills while Marie played with her dolls and Kaye watched *Cinderella* again. I wondered if she'd ever get sick of that movie.

It was the employment specialist from the ward with a message for Adam. He'd found just the type of thing Adam was looking for, and he'd set up an interview for him the same night as my cooking show. It figured that the beginning of my plan's execution would coincide with the one night Adam would be away from home. I needed to find a sitter.

The last time I'd hired someone to watch my girls, I picked a young woman from our neighborhood at the U. She was about thirteen. We'd left her the phone number for the restaurant and the movie theater, and she called before they'd even brought us our food. She was sitting on the couch crying, almost as hard as my girls, when we got back. Kaye was still sitting by our front door, screaming—just as she'd been when we left.

I knew other people in the Salt Lake valley—people I'd grown up with who probably babysat me at one time. Most of my friends had moved on, or we'd kept in such limited contact that it would be rude for me to call them up and say, "Hey, I know it's been six years since we talked, but can you babysit for me this Thursday?"

The thing that was missing from those old relationships was intimacy—not the kind they talk about in magazines, but the comfortable, trusting kind, ensuring that no matter what disagreements we might have, we'd still be tight. Instead, these people were mere acquaintances. I knew them just well enough that I wanted to impress them, and their watching Kaye for one night would probably do just the opposite. I had that comfortable kind of intimacy with Brienne, with my parents, and with Adam's Aunt Olive. Really, there was no one else I could trust with Kaye. No, that was the wrong way to think of it—there was no one else I could leave my children with and know they'd still like me after the babysitting job was done. No matter how much Kaye screamed while Brienne watched her, Bri would still love me when I came to pick Kaye up. And she'd still love Kaye, even when her little face turned red while she screamed at fifteen decibels.

Brienne was hosting the show, so she couldn't babysit. My parents were serving a temple mission—starting their second year—in Washington D.C., and Aunt Olive lived clear out in Alpine. There was no one to call.

The thought of contacting the Relief Society president to ask for help made me feel sick. But backing out of the show clearly wasn't possible, and Adam had to go to his job interview, so asking for help from some stranger in the ward was my final option.

The Relief Society president's name was printed on the back of the program I'd stuffed into my diaper bag the previous Sunday. Calling the number made me so nervous, I had to start the dishes as her phone rang so I'd have a distraction.

"Hello?" The voice was young—probably a boy who hadn't hit puberty yet.

I cleared my throat. "Hi, is Sister . . ." I forgot her name and had to look on the program I'd just dropped to the counter. "Sister Nulman there?"

"Just a minute." The phone clattered, and I heard him yell, "Mom!"

After a moment she answered the phone. "Hello? This is Shauna."

"Sister Nulman, you don't know me, but I'm a member of your ward."

"Well, if you're a member of my ward, and I don't know you, then I've dropped the ball, haven't I?" She tried to make a joke, but she was obviously embarrassed.

The last thing I meant to do was lay a guilt trip on her, so I rushed to fix the problem. "No, I didn't mean it that way. I just . . .

it's fine that you don't know me. It's my fault that you don't know me. Don't feel bad."

I sighed. I'd called to ask a favor. Now, I was sure to get one—just because I'd started our conversation off wrong. It was a good example of why I was tight with family and basically no one else—no one understood my intentions until they'd known me for a number of years and they could see through my faulty communication.

She ignored my attempts at smoothing things over. "What's your name?"

"Jennifer Young."

"How long have you been in the ward?" I heard papers rustle on her end of the line and was sure she was looking for my Church records.

"A few months is all."

The rustling stopped. "It's been almost a year. Oh, Jennifer, I'm so sorry. You don't even have visiting teachers."

"Sister Nulman, that's okay. I don't need visiting teachers anyway. Everyone's busy with their own lives—no one needs to spend their time on me." It was getting worse. I needed a babysitter, but I would probably end up with plates of cookies dropped off at my door by smiling women who wanted to come in my messy home and have a heart-to-heart talk.

"Everyone needs visiting teachers," she said with conviction.

I shook my head. "All I need is a babysitter for Thursday night, but I don't know anyone in the neighborhood."

"Oh." She stopped. I could almost hear the gears shift in her mind. "Well, do you want a young woman from the ward? An adult with children?"

"I have a four-year-old girl, and another daughter who is two and a half and . . ." I almost said "difficult." "I think an adult with children would be better."

"Oh, I know who'd be perfect. Dani Stark—she's the nursery leader, and she has a two-year-old of her own." Papers rustled again. "Here's her number."

I wrote Dani's number down on a message pad near the fridge. "Thanks."

"No problem. Now, about those visiting teachers . . ."

"Really, don't worry about it."

"Well then, when can we come and see you as a presidency?"

My mother had been the Relief Society president for most of my adolescence. I'd seen her sacrifice time with her family almost every night of the week to magnify her calling, and I didn't want to make Sister Nulman spend time with me while her children grew up without her. "I'm fine, really. I promise I'll call if I need anything."

"Okay. We'll just drop in sometime, then." She laughed.

Somehow, I doubted she was kidding.

Dani seemed nice enough on the phone, and she agreed without hesitation to watch the girls that Thursday night. I wasn't sure how much to tell her about Kaye's strange behaviors. Sometimes people didn't even notice her quirks—it all depended on what would happen that evening. I didn't want to scare Dani off if it turned out that Kaye would pick that night to be normal.

Thursday night, Adam put on his best suit and left in his Saturn. I gathered the things I'd need for the show, fixed up the girls so they looked cute—although Kaye wouldn't let me do her hair—and we piled in my Geo. Dani's house was small, but clean. The yard was beautiful and green, and there wasn't a weed in sight. I parked the car and got the girls out. Marie clung to my hand, and I clung to Kaye's.

Dani was short and stocky, like me, but she had a wide, dimpled smile. Her house was as immaculate as the yard, and the first thing I saw when she opened the front door was a picture of the Savior with his arms open wide. A scented candle burned somewhere, and the sweet, woodsy smell tingled my nose as I brought the kids inside. A little boy with big brown eyes and a bowl haircut clung to Dani's leg and sucked on two of his fingers. Marie went straight to him and said hello.

"This is Steven," Dani said to Marie. "And what's your name?"

"Marie." She smiled at Steven.

I hadn't let go of Kaye yet, but she started to squirm away from me. I reluctantly released her, and she ran into the middle of the room to look around.

"That's Kaye," I said. "She likes to explore, but she won't hurt anything."

Dani smiled. "She can explore all she wants. We're baby-proof."

That much was certain. Nothing below my shoulders looked breakable. Plastic protectors plugged all the outlets and strips of foam padding lined the corners of the coffee table, which was covered with children's books. Dani's life seemed to rotate around the Church and her little boy. The thought eased my mind a bit.

I held out a lunchbox. "Here's a tuna sandwich for Kaye. She won't eat anything else. There's a bologna sandwich for Marie if she wants it, but she ate a little before we left."

"Well, I'll be fixing dinner soon. They can eat with us."

"Thank you. I doubt Kaye will eat anything but the tuna. She's a little picky. And she doesn't really like to play with other kids."

Dani's eyebrows shot up.

I shrugged. "She's a bit of a loner. She's a good kid, though."

Kaye was kneeling beside the coffee table. "She'll probably want to look at those books all night," I said. "She loves books."

"I'll keep that in mind."

"Here's my sister's number if you need me. Adam's out tonight, so you won't be able to reach anyone at home." I'd almost told her he was at a job interview, but I didn't want to let her know we were broke.

Dani put Brienne's phone number on the hutch near the front door.

I knelt down and looked Marie in the eye. "I won't be too long, sweetie. I'll pick you up before bedtime. Help Sister Stark with Kaye, alright?"

Marie nodded and I kissed her.

I walked to Kaye and kissed her head. "Bye, Kaye. I'll see you later."

She didn't acknowledge me.

I waved at Marie one more time, then left the house with a prayer running in my mind.

* * *

Brienne's house looked gorgeous. She had a huge kitchen with a bar next to the dining area. She'd taken away the barstools and set up chairs facing the bar so I could cook in the kitchen with plenty of counter space between my audience and me.

The women filtered into the dining area and found seats. They all looked wealthy, with manicured nails and primped hair. Most of them were close to my age, around twenty-five, but a few of them were older. After most of the guests had arrived, I started the show by chopping vegetables. I was nervous—I hadn't been the focus of attention for years.

Kosy Kitchen had sent me brochures, and I'd found the manual that had come with the sales kit I'd bought in high school. It said the first thing to do in a cooking show was to set the audience at ease and make them like you. The cooking was easy. Making people like me was harder.

"Now that's a knife!" I said in my best Australian accent as I chopped green onions on the cutting board. In my nervous state, I noticed the stains on that cutting board from the time I'd made pomegranate jam—pink stains deep in the surface cuts of the white plastic.

The women chuckled at my movie reference, but they didn't laugh as much as I'd hoped they would.

"Okay," I continued, "now I'm going to fillet this salmon and we'll put it here in the aluminum foil."

"You're very good at that, Jen. I can't fillet worth a darn," Brienne said with a chuckle.

I winked at her, grateful for her willingness to make me seem more wonderful than I really was. "It's not that hard, if you practice. And a very sharp knife makes it so much easier." I filleted another salmon steak with ease.

"I'd be afraid to have knives that sharp in my home with kids around." A mousy woman on the back row wrinkled up her little nose at the woman sitting next to her, speaking quietly as if I couldn't hear her.

"Our knives come with a case that's sturdy and difficult to open. I've kept these knives in my house for years, and I have two small children. We've never had a problem with them getting the knives out. Of course, I keep them up high just in case." I spoke matter-of-factly, as if I hadn't heard the woman and it was all part of my sales plan.

I had six salmon fillets on six squares of aluminum foil, waiting for the fun stuff. "Now, I'll spread this topping on it that I made earlier—the cream cheese with a touch of dill and lemon."

"Cream cheese is awfully fattening," the mouse whispered to her neighbor again. Apparently she still thought I couldn't hear.

I gave her a warm smile and finished spreading the cream cheese mixture across the salmon. "It may be a little fattening, but it's so good," I said. "Oh, and by the way, all the recipes I'll make tonight are in our cookbook. I love to cook, but I have to use recipes so I know it will be right every time."

Brienne laughed. "Not like Mom. She just throws everything together."

I laughed too. The catch was that Mom somehow managed to "throw together" magnificent meals. I tried to make homemade gravy once, per my mother's estimated directions, and it tasted like paste. I didn't like guessing.

As I reached for the cut vegetables, Brienne's phone rang. The women were finally interested enough in the dish I was making that I could almost see them salivating. I glanced at Brienne.

"We'll let the machine get it," Brienne said.

The machine beeped and Kaye's scream pierced the room. I couldn't hear what Dani was saying, but she sounded stressed.

Brienne gave me a quizzical look.

"I'll just return that call in a minute," I said with a smile. The apprehension was back with a vengeance, so I meticulously centered the salmon, mentally measuring the shiny tin foil around the fillet like a perfect frame.

I cleared my throat and continued with an agitated voice. "We top the salmon with a handful of our chopped zucchini, yellow squash, and carrots. Then we sprinkle on these green onions."

I folded the aluminum foil around each fillet, leaving enough room for steam to collect and cook the food. "Then we'll put these nice little packages in our patented steamer. No more cooking fish in the dishwasher!"

"You can cook fish in the dishwasher?" A different woman on the back row spoke up, her eyebrows raised until they were invisible beneath her bangs.

"Sure," I said, hurrying to get all the salmon in place and concentrating on keeping my voice level and calm as concern tugged harder at my mind. "Our mom used to do it all the time, huh Brienne?"

Brienne nodded. "The house would smell for weeks."

The mouse wrinkled her nose.

"Okay, ladies," I said with a smile. "I'm going to let you look over our brochure while I return that call. Excuse me, please."

I counted out brochures and handed them to the women at the end of each row, encouraging them to pass the remaining copies.

Brienne got up and followed me to the other room with her cordless phone. When I was out of earshot, I called Dani.

"Jen?" Dani skipped the friendly greeting.

"What's wrong?"

"Kaye is freaking out. She's been screaming like this for an hour now. I can't get her to calm down. What do I do?"

"Did you give her the tuna sandwich?"

"That's what caused the problem. She took off the top piece of bread then dropped the sandwich face down. I couldn't let her eat it off the floor, so I threw it away. Then she tried to get it out of the garbage and I stopped her. I finally had to take the garbage out to the dumpster and she's been sitting by the door ever since, screaming her head off."

"Have you got any tuna?" I asked.

"No. If I did, I would have fixed some by now." She sounded insulted.

"I'm sorry, of course you would have."

"I tried to hug her and she just pushed me away. Then Steven tried to hug her and she bit him."

"She bit Steven?" Kaye had never bitten anyone before. I couldn't imagine where she'd learned to bite.

"He's okay. She didn't draw blood. But he's in his room crying because he doesn't want to get anywhere near her. I think he's scared of her now, not that I blame him. And the noise really bothers him. I can't take this anymore, Jen. I've tried everything I can think of, and she won't stop. You have to come get her."

I looked back at the kitchen. The women were looking at the brochures, but I could tell a couple of them were getting restless. "I haven't even finished cooking the meal yet, let alone dessert. And the dessert shows off the neatest products."

Dani groaned.

I didn't know what to do. I felt for Dani. I knew how hard Kaye could be. But I needed to do well with this show. I needed money.

"What's wrong?" Brienne whispered.

I stared at her and listened to Dani.

"Jen," Dani said, "if you don't come get her, I don't know what I'll do." I could tell she was close to tears by the pitch of her voice.

"Okay, Dani. I'll be right there." I ended the call and handed the phone to Brienne.

"Well?" Brienne asked.

"I have to go get Kaye. She's throwing a fit."

Brienne knew what it meant when Kaye threw a fit. She'd witnessed many of them. "But what about the show?"

"Um . . . I can't exactly come back, not with Kaye." I untied my apron and handed it to Brienne. "Could you take over?"

Brienne's expression fell. "I can't cook!"

"All you have to do is take the salmon from the steamer when the timer goes off. There's nothing to it! They can do without dessert, I guess. Maybe the catalogue will be enough to make them buy something."

"The dessert's the best part."

"Well, it's too fattening for *Miss Mouse* anyway."

"Miss Mouse?"

I shook my head. "Never mind. I can come back later, after Adam gets home."

Brienne nodded and tied the apron strings behind her back, her face twisted with a nervous look.

"You'll do fine, I promise." I kissed her cheek and dug in my purse for my keys. "Make my apologies?" I pleaded. Then I was out the door.

I was halfway to Dani's house before I realized I'd forgotten to set the timer. *Poor Brienne,* I thought. *She's going to hate me.*

* * *

I heard Kaye's scream as soon as I got out of my car in front of Dani's house. Dani would probably hate me too. At least I knew Brienne's frustration would be short-lived.

Before I had a chance to knock on the door, Dani had it open and she was shoving my diaper bag at me. Kaye was kneeling on the floor in front of the door, and as soon as she saw daylight, she headed right out on the porch, looking around as if she'd lost something. Marie followed Kaye out the door, waving at Dani. Dani's face was streaked and her eyes were red. She waved briefly at Marie, but glared at me. The door was shut before I had a chance to say thanks. I turned to look for Kaye. She was running away, and was almost at the sidewalk.

"Kaye! Stop and wait for Mommy!" She didn't stop. I ran and caught her just before she reached the road. As soon as I had a firm grip on her hand, she sat down, jerking me as she dropped to the ground.

"Stand up, Kaye," I said.

She continued to scream and sit.

I set down my purse and carried Kaye to her car seat. As soon as I set her down, she was arching her back, tightening her gluteus, and thrusting her body out of her seat. She looked toward Dani's house and screamed.

With my hand pressed firmly against her chest, I held her in while I pulled a strap over each of her shoulders. I pressed my forearm against her chest and clicked the buckles in place as quickly as I could, then I tightened the straps.

When she was finally strapped in and I was satisfied she couldn't wiggle her way out, I closed her door and leaned against the car with a sigh. Why was she so difficult? I'd never seen a child so strong-willed.

I picked up my purse and keys and went around to the other side of the car where Marie waited patiently on the sidewalk, clutching her doll. How could Adam and I have two children so completely different? Marie stretched up her arms, and I hugged her close. When I pulled away, her little chin was quivering.

"Mommy, why is Kaye so sad?" Big tears welled in Marie's blue eyes and she sniffed.

I ran my fingers gently through her wavy hair and leaned my forehead against hers. "I wish I knew, baby."

Kaye had stopped screaming for a moment and was staring out her window. I knew two-year-olds were hard. Marie hadn't been easy at that age, and she was probably the sweetest child I'd ever known. But Kaye was so stubborn that once she got her mind on something, she wouldn't let go. Like with that stupid tuna sandwich.

I'd hoped to call Brienne from Dani's house, but that obviously wasn't going to happen. I drove the few blocks to my townhouse and hurried inside.

Brienne picked up as soon as it started to ring.

"When is the timer supposed to go off?" she asked.

"Oh, Brienne," I said with remorse, "I forgot to set it."

Brienne sighed. "Well, do you think it's done?"

I glanced at my watch. "I'm sure it is. It's probably overdone."

"What should I do?"

I shook my head and sighed. "Taste it and see if it's edible."

"You know, I've never really liked salmon. I just thought it would be sort of fancy."

I groaned. "If it's not edible, toss it."

"Well," Brienne finally said, "I'll take down the names of anyone who wants to order and you can pick up the list when you come to get your things."

"Do you think anyone will order?"

"Most of them left already," Brienne admitted.

So much for money to get us through the week. Maybe Adam would come home with good news. "Okay. Thanks for your help."

I looked at Kaye, trying to hide my frustration with her, though I doubted she'd even notice if I gave her the silent treatment. Knowing she was probably hungry, I fixed her a tuna sandwich, but she left it on the kitchen table.

* * *

Adam walked in later as I slammed the dried-out sandwich into the garbage can.

"How was your evening?" I grumbled.

"Oh, about as good as yours, it seems." He flopped down in a dining chair and loosened his tie.

"Was it a bad interview?"

He shook his head. "More like a bad company. I couldn't stand working there and don't know if I'd accept if I were offered a job. How did you do?" Adam asked.

"I had to leave and pick up Kaye halfway through the demonstration. I didn't make a dime."

Adam stood up and pulled me to him. "I'm sorry. Next time I'll arrange to be home with the girls."

I nodded. It felt good to stand there with his arms around me. I missed him. I was too tired to pick up my things that night, so I called Brienne and told her I'd see her in the morning. She told me I had a couple of orders—one was Brienne's—and I thanked her, but I knew it wasn't enough to make a difference financially.

We sang "I Am a Child of God" with the girls before we tucked them in bed. Marie fell asleep almost before we shut the bedroom door. It took a bit longer for Kaye to drop off.

Both of our plans had failed. I snuggled with Adam and tried to devise a new plan. I could try another cooking show since Adam still didn't have a night job. I could check with Brienne and see if she knew of anyone who would watch my kids while I worked retail, but since she lived on the other side of the valley, as did most of the people she knew, I'd end up spending more money on commuting than I'd earn. Not to mention the cost of the child care itself.

I couldn't come up with another plan. I thought, calculated, schemed, and added projected figures until I slipped into sleep.

I dreamt of my perfect house again—three stories with white siding and hunter-green shutters and a vinyl fence around the big yard with aspen trees—and Marie and Kaye played with each other the way Brienne and I had played when we were young. Suddenly, in my dream, Kaye leaned over and bit Marie. Marie wailed and pulled away, cradling her bleeding arm. As I looked at Marie, her face turned slowly into Brienne's face, and she held her arm close to her body as her wounded eyes looked at me.

When I woke at one in the morning, jolted from sleep by Kaye's scream, I felt the need to apologize to Brienne, but I wasn't sure why.

Chapter 5

PHASES

I hated being broke. The failure of my first cooking show tugged at the back of my mind and filled me with nervous energy, as if poverty and the humiliation of destitution were waiting around the corner for me. What I needed was a vacation. Adam was just as stressed. He read the want ads every day, circling potential jobs and phoning personnel managers only to discover the position had been filled, or the hours wouldn't work with his school schedule in the fall. He worked at the bank, then came home and paced the floor, or sat in his recliner and changed the channels on the television until I was dizzy from sensory overload.

So, even though we had to spend some of our grocery money on gas, we packed up Adam's Saturn and headed for our annual campout near Mount Timpanogos. We always met Adam's Aunt Olive there the last weekend in June. Kaye's behavior was better the previous year—she was much less like a two-year-old, and much more compliant. This year, however, she was running everywhere and getting into everything. It was getting hard to go anywhere with her, and I had no idea how she would do in the mountains. Marie giggled as we loaded her bedding in the car, but Kaye didn't like the fact that her pillow and blanket were off of her bed. She kept grabbing them and racing upstairs with them in hand. Finally, we put her in the car then tossed her bedding on the floor at her feet. Once I gave them to her, thinking she'd like to snuggle with them and take a nap or something, but she tried to push the blanket out the open window.

"What does she want?" Adam asked.

"I don't know what she *wants,* but she *doesn't* want her blanket in the car."

"Well, it's something new to her. It's not like we travel much."

"I know. She hates change." I pulled the blanket to my lap and stuffed it at my feet, hoping that if the blanket was out of her reach, she might forget about it.

I was wrong. She screamed the whole way to the campsite, and didn't calm down until we set up the tent and laid out her sleeping bag, blanket and pillow, then set up the other bags next to hers. Marie lay down on her bag and snuggled into her blanket. Kaye watched her and followed suit.

"See," Adam said, "she'll have fun. Everything will be fine."

Olive wore khaki capris and a plaid camp shirt with a white T-shirt underneath. She had a scarf tied around her curly hair, and looked far younger than fifty-five.

"How're my kids?" she asked, and she threw her arms around me.

"We're doing fine," I replied.

"Yeah, now that we're here." Adam zipped the tent's net door closed and tied the nylon flaps open so we could see Marie and Kaye playing hide-and-seek in their blankets.

"They've sure grown," Olive said. "I can hardly tell them apart."

"They wear the same size," I said as I watched Kaye pull the blanket from over her head. Her light hair stood on end. "There's an easy way to tell them apart, though. Marie's the one who talks."

Marie pulled her blanket away, and her hair stood on end too. She laughed and held her hand up to feel the static electricity. "Look at my hair, Daddy."

"Looks great," Adam said with a smile.

"Kaye doesn't talk yet?" Olive asked. "How old is she?"

"Well, she talks a little. Sometimes she repeats what we say. She likes the word 'juice,' but she doesn't say it when she wants juice, so I'm not sure what she means by it. She'll be three in August."

"Really?" Olive smiled at the girls' antics. "Have you talked to your pediatrician about it?"

"At her checkup last August. He said she's developmentally delayed. No surprise there. He also said it's probably just a phase."

Olive shrugged her shoulders. "He's probably right. Have him look at her again, though. It can't hurt." She watched Kaye play with the blanket and laughed. "No matter what, she's still our Kaye. We'll love her just the way God made her."

We all watched Kaye for a minute as she copied Marie. It occurred to me that Marie was the only child I'd ever seen Kaye really play with. Marie laughed at the charged halo around her head. Kaye laughed at Marie's laugh, which made Marie laugh harder. Eventually, they both got the hiccups.

"Well, I've got to finish setting up camp." Olive smiled, then turned and walked toward her car, calling for her husband. Her hair was short and curled at the nape of her neck. A white scar peeked up from the top of her blouse. She'd been in a car accident long before I'd met her, and after three back surgeries and extensive physical therapy, she still walked with a limp and had little use of her left hand. It didn't stop her, though—she hiked and kayaked with the best of them.

She stumbled slightly on a stone and gripped her lower back as if she'd felt a spasm of pain.

"Are you okay, Olive?" I asked.

"I'm ready to hike!" Olive called over her shoulder and raised her fists in triumph.

"Did you see that?" I asked Adam when Olive was out of hearing range.

He nodded. "She's hurting."

"Maybe we shouldn't hike."

"We'll hike," Adam assured me. "She lives for this stuff. Besides, she knows when to quit."

* * *

We got halfway to the caves when Olive needed to rest. She sat on a fallen tree near the path while Adam hurried behind Kaye. I had worried about whether Kaye would be able to handle the hike, but in all the open space, Adam just aimed her in a direction and off she went. She had such good balance that we weren't too worried about her twisting an ankle or anything, and Adam was getting a good workout. Uncle Scott hung back with Olive, and I could see the worry in his eyes.

"Olive, we don't have to go all the way to the caves," I said. "We've seen them before."

"Oh, I just need a breath, is all. I'm in that phase of life where your body falls apart, even if your mind is more collected than ever." She rubbed her left arm.

"Olive?" Scott sat next to her on the log and rubbed her back slightly.

"I'm fine, sweetheart." She took a deep breath. "I'm fine." She reached up and patted Marie's arm.

"How are you, Marie? Do you like the mountains?"

Marie nodded, then scratched her leg where a fly had landed. "I don't like bugs."

"Well, I can't blame you for that." Olive touched Marie's face briefly. "You're a beautiful girl, you know? And I bet you're a big help to your mommy."

Marie nodded.

Olive smiled. "Very good. Can you make it to the cave?"

Marie nodded again.

"Alright, then. Let's go to the cave." Olive stood again, though slowly. Scott reached for her with a hesitant look.

"I'm fine, Scott. Let's go." She leaned on her walking stick and headed for the caves again. I looked at Scott, but he kept his eyes glued on Olive's ascending back.

* * *

It had been an unusually dry spring, so campfires were against the rules. Kaye took off her clothes as soon as she was bored and started walking in her diaper along the brick edge of the cold fire pit. Marie was singing and watching the men cook hamburgers on the propane grill Scott and Olive had brought.

Olive was rubbing a lotion insect repellant on her legs as we watched Kaye walk in circles. "So," she said, "how is Blanch?"

It felt odd that Olive would have to ask me about her own sister, but they'd had little contact since Adam had joined the Church back when he was eighteen. Presumably, Blanch had blamed Adam's change of heart on Olive, since it had occurred during the summer Adam spent in Olive's home.

I sighed. "She's still Blanch."

"That good, huh?" Olive grinned.

"The last time we heard from her was Christmas. She called and talked to us for about ten minutes. I talked to Tim for a while, and that was the best part of the day. At least Adam's dad loves us even if we didn't follow in his religious footsteps."

"Yeah, Tim's a jewel. The best thing that ever happened to Blanch as far as I'm concerned. Did she send you any gifts?"

I nodded. "Dolls for the girls and a gift certificate for us. At least she's not sending anti-Mormon literature anymore."

Olive chuckled. "I can't believe she ever did. That's some Christmas present."

"Did she call or send you anything?" I asked.

She shook her head. "She gave up on that long ago."

I couldn't imagine being so angry with Brienne that I stopped speaking to her. It was unfathomable.

"It's been twelve years now. I won't give up, though. I'll haunt her. And she believes in ghosts."

Blanch was the most superstitious person I'd met in my life. She loved cats but refused to buy a black one. She wouldn't set foot on a construction site because she was so afraid of ladders and broken glass. The word "witch" sent her into a tizzy. She didn't even like *The Wizard of Oz.*

Olive beckoned for Marie and started spreading insect repellant on Marie's legs. "She's nice to Adam, and that's the most important thing. Although, she could be nicer to you."

"I don't care how she treats me," I said with more contempt than I intended.

Olive moved on to Marie's arms and smiled. "Blanch really is a good woman. She's generous, and strong, and lots of people love her."

"She's generous to causes of her choice. She's downright stingy if you don't fall in the right category. To put it bluntly, if you're a Mormon, you'll never be a recipient of her 'generous' side." I'd never experienced persecution because of my religion until I married Adam. It was a new experience for me.

"You wait and see," Olive said. "She'll come around. She'll set foot in an LDS church again. At *least* before I'm six feet under."

I was wondering when Blanch had set foot in an LDS church before, and was just about to ask when Olive said, "Where's Kaye?"

I looked up at the fire pit, but there was no sign of her.

"Adam, where's Kaye?" I asked.

"I thought you were watching her." Adam turned to me with a spatula in his hand.

I frowned. "Well, I was. But I got talking."

I scanned the campground and couldn't see Kaye anywhere.

Fear crept into my throat. There was a stream close by—I could hear the water gurgling over thousands of smooth rocks. The water was low that year, but it was still a danger. I sent Adam to look in the water's direction. Olive went to the restroom area, Scott went to the tents, and I went down the sidewalk toward the gravel cul-de-sac and the winding canyon road.

I looked back at Marie, who sat on a picnic bench under the pavilion, watching the adults walk away. "Stay there, Marie. I'll be back in a minute." If any of us did find Kaye in a bad position, I didn't want to scare Marie.

She nodded, looking very small in the big wilderness around her.

It wasn't quite dusk, but I knew if Kaye had found her way to the road, she'd be in a precarious situation. Someone could take a corner just a little too fast and not even notice my two-year-old crouched down playing with rocks.

Father, please help us find her, I prayed silently. "Kaye!" I called. I heard everyone else calling her name.

As I neared our cars in the cul-de-sac, I saw Kaye's blanket bunched near the Saturn door. When I was close enough, I heard the muffled sound of Kaye's voice.

"I found her!" I yelled as relief punctured the tight, tense balloon that seemed to have filled my chest. "She's here, by the car." I picked up the blanket to see her sitting on the dirt in a slightly worn diaper. Her feet were filthy, and her blanket was just as bad. When she saw me, she stood and gathered her blanket, then stared at the door handle to the car like she was waiting for me to open it.

Soon Adam was by my side. "I think she wants to go home."

I sighed. I needed this break from reality, even if it was just for the change of scenery. Kaye spoiled a lot of things for me, but she wasn't going to spoil the weekend. "Well, we're not going home. So she'll have to be disappointed. Come on, Kaye." I grabbed her hand. "Do you want to eat?"

She pulled her hand out of mine and stared at the door handle, her nose less than an inch away from it.

"Go fix her a plate and bring it here," I suggested to Adam. "If she sees food, maybe she'll join us."

Adam nodded and went back to the grill. Olive pulled side dishes from our coolers and they blessed the food, then Adam came to us with a full plate in his hand. He showed it to Kaye, but she wouldn't budge. I tried to grab her hand again, but she yelled at me incoherently and gripped the door handle with both of her small hands.

"It's okay," Aunt Olive said as she walked to us with a large, clean blanket in hand. "If Kaye won't come to us, we'll come to her." Olive unfolded the blanket and spread it out on the gravel. She went close to Kaye and held out her arms.

Kaye looked Olive in the eye for a split second, then tugged on the locked door handle again.

"Scott, honey, will you bring my plate over please?" He took his plate in one hand, and Olive's in the other. Soon he was sitting on the hard ground next to his wife and my little Kaye, who had let go of the door handle and was eyeing Olive's hamburger.

"Thank you for the idea, Kaye," Olive said. "I love a picnic at sunset."

I didn't like the idea. The gravel poked up under the blanket and there was dust everywhere. I was sure my backside would be bruised and filthy by the time I was done eating.

Kaye was finished long before the rest of us—she picked at her hamburger and drained her can of pop. She stood and focused on the car door again, and when no one moved to open it, she started tugging at the blanket under us. Since it was obvious she was more than ready to go, we broke camp and packed up our car.

Olive pouted as she saw my morose expression. "Oh, is life really that bad?"

I couldn't help but grin. "Yes, it is!" I whined. "I want to stay and play."

Olive took me in her arms and squeezed. "Olivejuice," she said. It was a family joke. When you said "olivejuice," it looked like "I love you" to someone reading your lips, and it was Olive's favorite way to express her feelings. She always said she wanted to live her life so that the only thing hardship could squeeze from her would be love.

"Olivejuice too." I smiled.

As the mountains faded into the background and city lights assaulted my eyes, I thought about what Olive had said about getting another appointment with the pediatrician. Maybe something was wrong with Kaye. We'd had health insurance with Adam's job at the newspaper, because it was full time. So losing that job not only hurt us financially, it made it much more difficult to get medical help. I wondered how much a visit with the pediatrician would cost without insurance.

"Do you think she'll just grow out of this?" I asked.

"Grow out of what?"

"Her . . . control issues. Her weird behaviors. I mean, she has to have everything her way, or she makes everyone miserable." I felt miserable at that moment. I'd been looking forward to staying up late in the night, talking with Olive as crickets chirped outside the tents. Instead, I would sleep in my bed until I got up with Kaye at one.

Adam didn't reply. Then, he glanced in his rearview mirror. "Look at her. She's so pretty."

She was pretty. She'd been pretty since the day she was born—perfectly shaped head, denim-blue eyes, apple cheeks, and long black eyelashes. I'd never seen a newborn with such perfect eyelashes.

I looked at Marie. She was of slighter build, and her complexion wasn't as rosy as Kaye's, but Marie was just as beautiful. And her mind was sharp. She slept, looking like a weary angel in the backseat.

"They grow up so fast, Jen. We've got to enjoy them while they're little, because it won't last forever."

I would miss little Marie, but silently I wished that Kaye would grow up just a bit faster, and leave the self-centered phase she was wrapped up in.

Chapter 6

INDEPENDENCE

"Have I done anything to hurt you?" I asked.

Brienne pulled the previously tossed green salad from her fridge. "Not that I can think of. Why? Do you think you've done something to hurt me?"

I shrugged. "I don't know. It's just a feeling I've had lately. I feel guilty, and I'm not sure why."

"Are you suffering from female guilt syndrome?" Brienne asked.

"What's that?"

"Women invent things to feel guilty about when everything is going well."

"I wouldn't say everything is going well. Adam's still out of work. We're broke. Kaye is difficult. Marie is bored. Shall I go on?"

"Okay, then, you're feeling guilty because nothing's going well. Knowing you, you've taken personal responsibility for everything." Brienne's smile made me feel a little better. "Quit blaming yourself. Life doesn't always go the way we plan. Some things you just can't control."

As we joined our families on Brienne's deck, I thought how easy that must have been for Brienne to say. She didn't seem to have any problems.

Emily, Brienne's daughter, came to me with a Barbie doll in one hand and a small, frilly outfit in the other.

"Hewp, pwease," Emily said.

I took the doll from her and slipped the long, unrealistically shapely legs and hips into the dress. After fastening the Velcro at the neck, I gave the doll back to her.

She smiled and said, "Tank you."

"She's talking so well, Bri. I can't believe she's Kaye's age. Kaye won't even call me Mommy."

"Yeah, she's precocious." Brienne set a bowl of potato salad on the checkered tablecloth and sat down across from me. "Russ has taught her the state capitals already."

"You're kidding!" Adam said.

"No! He's obsessed with geography. Emily, come here sweetie."

Emily came to her mother with the doll still clutched in her hand. "Ask her a capital. Any state."

"Okay, let's think of a hard one . . . Texas." I watched as Emily's green eyes looked around for a moment. I thought I'd stumped her.

"Authtin," Emily said, like it was no big deal.

"Wow!" Adam said. "How does she memorize that stuff?"

"Russ quizzes her," Brienne responded. "And he's put a map up on her bedroom wall with all the states and capitals on it. She can't even read it yet."

"Exposure to the written word sinks in even before children speak," Russ said. He brought over one plate full of New York–cut steaks and another plate full of hot dogs. "Children learn to read because they've been exposed to words. We leave the captions on our television, no matter what's on. She already reads basic words, doesn't she?"

"Dog, cat, that sort of thing," Brienne said with a humble nod.

"Marie likes books too," I said, though I didn't want to elaborate. She wasn't reading by herself yet, and she was a year older than Emily. "I wish I could get her in a good preschool."

"They're so expensive, though." Brienne shook her head.

Money wasn't an issue for Brienne. Russ had served his mission in Russia then studied foreign relations in college. He'd finished his doctorate and written a dissertation on building democracy in ex-totalitarian states. It had turned several heads in D.C. Everyone expected big things out of Russ. He made good money in the meantime, working real-estate with his father.

"Yeah," I said. "I hate money—or the lack of it."

Russ nodded at Adam. "Things will look up for you when you finish that degree. Wait and see, you'll have jobs lined up within the year."

"I hope so," Adam said.

"Everybody needs a good accountant. I'll send you my taxes as soon as you're ready to do them. That'll be a good initiation." Russ rolled his eyes and looked at Brienne. "All the investments and deductions and stuff we've got make my head spin."

I tried not to look dumbfounded. I barely had an idea what it meant to invest, since it was something we couldn't afford. Besides, I doubted there was anything that made Russ's head spin. He was just being nice to us.

"So, how are things going on the job front? Any prospects?" Brienne asked.

Adam sighed. "I'm still working at the bank, and I think I'm going to continue that because they'll work with me when my schedule changes in the fall. They'll let me work part time. But, it's just not enough money. I've got to find something else."

"What about your cooking shows?" Bri asked me.

I rolled my eyes, feeling a little stung about my attempt at earning an income. "I've had one since yours. It wasn't much better, but Adam was able to watch the girls, so at least I finished the show. I didn't make any money, though." It seemed like I had disappointing news to share no matter what we discussed.

"Have you talked to your ward employment specialist?" Russ asked.

"Yep," Adam said.

"No luck, huh?"

Adam and I both shook our heads.

"How's your ward anyway?" Brienne asked. "Mom asked about you in her last letter, since you don't tell her much when you write."

I shrugged. "I don't want to worry them. Besides, our ward is just fine." I thought about the disaster with Dani, but didn't say anything.

"I wish we knew more people," Adam said. "We have a hard time going to church. We try to go, but we end up going home early most of the time. And Church activities never seem to fit with our schedules."

"When we go, we spend most of the meetings in the hallway with Kaye," I asserted.

"That's true," Adam said. "We always make it for the sacrament, but we usually leave right after the ordinance, so we never hear the talks. Anyway, I don't *feel* like I go to church."

Brienne set a bowl full of steaming corn on the cob in front of me. "You can't get much out of church when you spend all your time in the hall. Don't you have any help?"

I shook my head. How could anyone help us when they barely knew we were there? Of course, they knew we were there well enough to move away when we sat near them. Besides, I didn't want help. It was our burden to bear.

"You don't have home teachers or anything?" Brienne asked.

Adam shook his head. "At least, none that have shown up."

"Well, you need to call your bishop and get that fixed right away. I'm amazed at that. We've got such a great ward."

I tried not to glare at Brienne. Everything in her life was perfect, and I didn't want to hear about it anymore.

We sat in silence for a moment as I straightened the paper plates and cups in front of us.

"Well, shall we eat?" Brienne asked.

"Sounds great!" Adam and I said in unison.

We called Marie, Kaye, and Emily to the table. Marie and Emily came. Adam went to get Kaye.

After we'd blessed the food and Brienne had served her family and I had dished up plates for Kaye and Marie, Brienne sat next to me and sighed. "I'm worried about you," she whispered. "You don't seem like yourself lately. You're not just feeling female guilt syndrome, you seem depressed."

"Well, you worry too much."

"Oh, no I don't. I know you. You're usually cracking jokes all the time and playing with your kids. What's going on?"

"It's just hard with Kaye."

"Well, Jen, every parent has a hard kid. You can't let that make you go inactive."

"I'm not inactive. I'm just not so involved that I don't have time for anything else. And my testimony is as strong as it's always been."

"Are you a visiting teacher?"

"How would I go visiting teaching with Kaye? Answer me that!" I didn't want to talk about it anymore. "Just drop it, please."

Brienne closed her mouth tight and I took a big bite of potato salad. She picked at the food on her plate.

"What else did Mom mention in her letter to you?" I asked in a much kinder tone.

Brienne's tone was subdued. "She told me about a man they met in the temple."

"Who?" I asked.

She answered with a light in her eye. "The man who was just called to be a stake president in Nigeria, and his nephew had saved up money for years to bring him to D.C. so he could attend the temple there. Imagine, a stake president who's going through the temple for the first time."

I nodded. "It's pretty cool."

"Our world is sure changing," Brienne said. She looked around at her backyard, her eyes not really focusing on anything. "It's so wonderful. Such an exciting time to be alive."

I nodded again. We sat in silence for a moment, looking around at the mess our families had made while they ate.

When Brienne spoke again, her voice was distant and thoughtful. "You've never really liked change, have you?"

"What do you mean?" I asked, trying to figure out why she would make such an observation.

She looked at me, then Emily came up to her with a newly stripped doll and its dress. "Hewp, pwease."

Brienne seemed grateful for the distraction. I looked around the yard to check on my kids while Brienne dressed the doll, and I spotted Kaye standing next to the giant sunflowers that lined the back fence. They were taller than she was, and Kaye stared at the huge brown center of one flower. It was almost as big and round as her face, and she looked at it so closely, the tip of her nose was covered with brown pollen. Tenderly, with a light enough touch to barely move the flower, Kaye traced the outside of one of the petals. She touched the prickly stem, stared at her fingers, then got on her tiptoes to put her face next to the heavy flower. It seemed to dip its head to kiss her cheek.

"Look how beautiful that is, Jen. She sees things none of the rest of us see." Brienne sighed, then rose from her seat to start clearing the table without answering my question.

* * *

As the sky grew dark, Russ pulled a huge box of fireworks from the shed and led us down the long driveway toward the cul-de-sac. From their house on the east bench, we had an amazing view of the valley, and fireworks bloomed over several locations below us.

"Ever seen fireworks below you?" Russ asked.

"They look so small from here," I said.

"Well, these will look bigger." He ripped the plastic from the box of fireworks like a kid opening a Christmas present. There had to be two hundred dollars' worth of fireworks in that box.

Russ lit them for an entire hour, even with Adam's help. Kaye squirmed in my lap as if she couldn't get close enough to me to feel safe from the flying sparks. She laughed when Russ lit a screamer, and she screamed when he lit a quiet fountain.

Brienne leaned close to me. "I'd better answer your question, Jen. About things that are changing."

I wondered what she was talking about and suddenly thought she might be pregnant again.

"Russ got the call we've been waiting for." She didn't look totally enthusiastic.

Her expression made my stomach flip as I grasped what she was talking about. "He did?"

She nodded and looked at her husband. "We'll be moving to Washington D.C. We'll get to see Mom and Dad, so that's a definite plus."

I felt my eyes sting. It wasn't unexpected news, but it was certainly unwelcome.

"When do you leave?" I asked.

"He starts work on August ninth, so we'll be moving around Kaye's birthday."

I nodded. At least we had one more month together.

Russ lit the last of the fireworks—three fountains at once. "Happy Independence Day!" he shouted over the pops and crackles of the gunpowder.

I wasn't sure I wanted independence.

"So, will you be okay with the changes that are happening?" Bri asked.

I nodded. "Sure. I'll be okay." I smiled and tried to think of something funny or at least sarcastic to say, just to make her feel like I was the "old" me. "Are you kidding? I won't have to live in my pretty little sister's shadow anymore. Whew! Now the world can see the real me!" I hooted and punched my fist in the air.

Brienne grinned, but I could tell she didn't believe me.

It took all my willpower to keep from crying until we got in our car and headed home. My parents were gone and wouldn't finish their mission for another year. Brienne would soon be gone, and my closest connection to the world outside my townhouse would be severed. The family I'd grown up with would be gone. I held Adam's hand as tight as I could, feeling that he and Aunt Olive were all I had left.

"Jen, I think we need to work harder at going to church and getting something out of it. We need to start going to activities, get involved . . ."

I nodded, keeping my face toward the window so he wouldn't know I was crying.

"We need something, Jen. Life can't go on like this."

I steadied my voice. "I know."

"You're worried about Bri." He squeezed my hand. "It will be okay. Besides, don't be sad about it yet. They won't leave for another month."

A month wasn't enough time with Brienne.

He chuckled. "Kids—including your little sister—grow up and go away, so we have to enjoy them while we can, before they get a little independence."

I hated growing up.

Chapter 7

CHURCHGOERS

It was barely nine the next morning when a knock sounded on our back door. A woman who looked vaguely familiar stood on my doormat. She had wide brown eyes and a toothy smile, and her long, frizzy hair was as orange as tiger lilies. She was tall, with strong, freckled forearms and looked like she could beat up Adam if she wanted to.

I opened the door to her.

"Hi," she said in an alto voice. "Are you Jennifer Young?"

I nodded.

"You don't know me." She smiled and extended her hand.

I shook my head and took her hand.

"You must not go to church much," she gave me a sly smile, like she had caught me.

I didn't respond. Since I could still taste my conversation about religion with Brienne, I didn't want to bite the challenge this strange woman extended to me. Adam had already decided we would go to church the next Sunday, and stay for the whole three-hour block, no matter what.

The woman cranked my hand and smiled so wide I could see most of her teeth. "I'm Cathy Clark and I'm your new visiting teacher."

I'd been warned.

"Can't talk long," she said with another over-achieving grin. "On my way to work. I work at Welfare Square downtown during the summer. They sometimes let me bring home overstock in-season vegetables for people in need. Are you in need?"

"Not right now." It was true. Brienne had sent home lots of leftovers from Independence Day. We had enough food for another day or two.

"Ah, but you must be in need sometimes!" She looked over my shoulder into my kitchen, which was embarrassingly messy.

"Aren't we all?" I noted, trying to close the door enough to hide the dish-filled sink.

Her face softened. "That's so true. I like you, Jennifer!"

I smiled and felt myself blush a little. "Call me Jen."

She finally let go of my hand and started toward her small Toyota pickup, which was parked crookedly next to Adam's Saturn.

"I'll see you at church, Jen," she said over her shoulder. She grinned and waved happily as she got in her truck.

I shut the door and peeked out the kitchen window as she pulled away. She was different from any other woman I'd ever met. Obviously the kind of woman who spoke her mind regardless of tact, dropped in whenever she felt the need, and saw through whatever facade of complacent perfection I might erect. She was the ultimate visiting teacher. She irritated me already—in a good way, like something my mother called "productive guilt."

I also noticed she seemed completely different from Dani. A definite plus.

I spent Saturday afternoon getting ready for church because I knew I'd have enough stress without having to deal with ironing little dresses and packing books and cereal in time for our nine o'clock meeting. As I ironed a dress that I hoped would still fit Kaye, I wondered if the whole process was worth it. In the pit of my stomach, I knew we'd have to leave church early, as usual. People would stare at us or ignore us or get up and move to the opposite side of the chapel to get away from us. I was so nervous about going to church the next day that I barely slept, and by the time I finally did drift off, Kaye was already wiggling her bedroom doorknob. Adam kissed me softly and told me to stay in bed. Sounds of Kaye's Cinderella movie drifted up the stairs, along with Adam's voice, trying to sing Kaye back to sleep.

* * *

I pulled the tightish pink dress over Kaye's snarled hair. She fought me, but once her arms were in the sleeves and the buttons were done, she calmed down a bit.

"Should we try to put Kaye in the nursery?" I asked as I spritzed Kaye's hair. She squirmed and I had to sit on the floor with my legs wrapped around her to get her to hold still. That was why I always got ready last.

"I think so. The worst that could happen is they'd come and pull one of us out of class, then we'd be in the same boat we've been in all along," Adam said as he tied the bow at the back of Marie's dress. She held her scriptures in her hand and beamed at me, looking closer to fourteen years old than to four.

"You look so pretty, Marie," I said.

Her smile brightened.

Kaye squirmed between my legs as I pulled her hair back in a crooked ponytail, which she pulled out as soon as she was out of arm's reach.

"It's okay," Adam said. "Go get ready. She looks fine."

I got up obediently, but felt that she looked more like an urchin than a child going to church.

When we entered the building at five minutes after nine, most people were already in their classes. I took Kaye to nursery while Adam dropped Marie off at Primary on his way to elder's quorum.

I opened the door slowly in case a child was sitting near the door. Kaye pushed past me and shot toward the stacks of books. I looked up to see a familiar face, and immediately wished I had stayed home.

Dani watched over the children with a mild smile. Her son, Steven, stood next to her.

Dani saw Kaye run to the books, and she looked up at me. Her smile faded.

I waved at her sheepishly. "Hi, Dani."

She returned my halfhearted wave then gazed warily at Kaye.

"Hi. I don't think we've met." A woman who sat near the door extended her hand to me. "Are you new in the ward?"

I took her hand and returned her smile. "Not really."

"Oh. Well, welcome," the woman said. "This little one is yours, then?" She indicated Kaye.

I nodded. "Her name's Kaye."

"She bites," Dani chimed in. "We'll want to watch her with the other kids."

I felt suddenly defensive and wanted nothing more than to take Kaye home. I glared at Dani.

"It's better she know the truth up front, to protect the other children," Dani said, putting her arm around Steven. He turned his dark eyes toward Kaye and wrapped his arms around his mother's leg.

I vaguely remembered the Relief Society president stating that Dani was the nursery leader, and I silently kicked myself for forgetting that little detail. It wouldn't be long before they came and took me from class. If I'd thought I could bear being in the same room with Dani, I would have stayed in the room to watch over Kaye, but Dani radiated mild contempt as she looked between Kaye and me.

The other nursery leader's kindness would hopefully be enough to sustain Kaye for the few minutes she'd be in their care. "I'll be in Relief Society," I said, and I left the room. Kaye's attention was focused on her row of books, so I didn't tell her good-bye.

They were just starting the Relief Society lesson when I sat down. I looked around the room for Cathy's orange hair, but she wasn't there. So, no one would notice or miss me when I left to care for Kaye.

It took ten minutes before Dani opened the door enough to stick her head in and look for me. She gave me a condescending, "I knew this would happen" look, and I followed her to the nursery.

Kaye had taken off her dress and was streaking through the room. She wasn't causing any problems that I could see, except that the other ten children in the nursery were also taking off their clothes. Kaye did look like she was having fun. I smiled and suppressed a snicker.

Dani's face was grave. "We can't have these kids taking their clothes off."

I covered my smile with my hand.

"It's not funny. We tried to get Kaye dressed again and she ran away from us and screamed. It upset the other kids. We can't have her in here."

The other nursery leader had two dresses in her hand and was chasing two little girls, asking them which dress belonged to which girl. Several loose white socks and little black shoes were strewn across the floor as well. By the looks of things, the children had stripped at about the same time, probably while the leaders had been chasing Kaye.

"What are these parents going to think when they come to pick up their kids and we don't know which clothes are theirs?" Dani asked in disgust.

"Maybe tell them you had a lesson on modesty—showed them what not to do?" I suggested as I walked to Kaye's side and pulled her pink dress over her head one more time.

"Very funny," Dani said. She held Steven on her hip. He, at least, was fully clothed, but he looked like he was eyeing the other children with envy.

When Kaye was dressed, I picked her up and headed for the door. Dani stood in my way.

"Listen, Dani," I said, figuring she wouldn't be able to say anything if I was already talking. "I'm sorry Kaye bit Steven. She's never done that before, and if I had known she was going to do that, I would have warned you at least. And I'm sorry she threw a tantrum at your house . . ."

"A two-hour tantrum," she clarified. Her face flushed, and I could almost see her biting her tongue. "I've never seen a tantrum like that," she added, altering her tone as if she were trying to show sympathy. "You poor thing."

I wondered if she was laughing inside. She cast her eyes to the carpeted floor. Maybe she just felt guilty for letting her thoughts slip past her lips. Guilt wasn't necessary. I could tell she didn't like me, and that was fine. I didn't need her good opinion. "With her, they don't come any other way."

"I don't know how you deal with it. It's just too much for me," she said. She took a deep breath and let it out slowly as if she regretted what she was about to say. "In fact, I don't think it's a good idea for me to babysit her anymore." She locked her eyes on mine. "Ever."

I wondered if that meant nursery as well. That was fine, too. I didn't particularly want Dani watching her anyway.

"I won't ask," I said, and I left the room without another word.

I was seething, my face hot with anger. I tried to take a deep breath and calm myself down while I decided where to go. Kaye was squirming in my arms, trying to head back to the nursery and its pile of books. It was too much. The only things that kept Kaye entertained were books, videos, and a place to pace—a curbside or a playground edge. She liked walking back and forth along my washer and dryer as well. The easiest place to keep her entertained was at home.

The Relief Society and priesthood meetings were excused, and the hall filled with people. I readjusted Kaye on my hip so I had a better grip on her and went to look for Adam. I'd take his keys and go home, then I'd come back to pick up him and Marie at noon. It was too hard to stay.

On my way toward the door, I saw Cathy's hair above the mass of people clogging the halls as they moved to Sunday School. She was walking with a group, but I could tell she was alone. Her large eyes darted among the people in front of her, and finally they rested on me. She flashed her toothy smile.

"Jen. I'm glad you're here," she said over the heads of the others. Some of them looked at me, but most just filed into the classroom without giving me a glance. Cathy walked past the room and met me in the foyer.

"I'm glad you're here too. I didn't see you in Relief Society."

"Oh, I teach the Mia Maids."

I felt somewhat relieved. I didn't like the idea of her giving me a hard time about Church attendance, then skipping out herself.

"Are you coming to class then?" she asked.

I shook my head. "I'll probably be out here with her." I couldn't very well leave after Cathy saw me.

"She doesn't like nursery?" Cathy asked.

"Nursery doesn't like her."

She looked incredulous. "Well, I doubt that."

I shrugged. She might not believe it, but it was true.

"Here, let me take her and you go in to class."

The offer surprised and warmed me as her handshake had done the day before. But I shook my head. "She's a pretty hard kid. I'm afraid you'll never speak to me again after an hour with her." I laughed as if it were a joke, but after seeing Dani, it wasn't funny to me.

"We'll find a room and I'll read her some books or something. Or we could go for a walk." She smiled.

"Won't your husband miss you?" I asked.

"I don't have a husband," Cathy said, and I regretted making the assumption. She saw my look of dismay. "But I'm cool with that. I have other things to do with my life." She looked at Kaye, who was squirming so hard I almost lost my balance.

"Are you sure?" I asked.

She nodded as she held out her arms to Kaye and gave her the broadest smile I'd seen yet.

Kaye didn't reach out for Cathy, but she let Cathy take her from my arms. It was a miracle.

"You're sure?" I asked again. "You can come and get me if you change your mind."

"Go," Cathy said. "You're going to be late. What's her name?"

"Kaye."

"Hi, Kaye," Cathy said. She tried to look Kaye in the eye, but Kaye turned her head and flapped her hands, wiggling her fingers up at the lights in the ceiling.

"Is she autistic?" Cathy asked.

I'd heard the phrase before, on a news report about the recent rise in diagnosed mental illnesses. "No," I said, feeling offended.

"Okay." She smiled. "You go to class." She looked at me with her velvet eyes. They looked so sincere, as if she were inviting me into her heart simply by looking at me. "Feel the Spirit, okay?"

"Okay," I said with a grin, and I handed her my diaper bag. No one had ever said anything like that to me before—it was such a direct invitation to be spiritual. My parents had made similar statements, but not so casually. Cathy took Kaye and walked toward the overflow area between the chapel and the cultural hall. There were no chairs or people in there, and I figured it would be a perfect place for Kaye to run around and strip if she wanted to.

For a moment, I wondered if I could trust Cathy. I really didn't know her after all, and I'd handed my child over without a second thought. But there was something unmistakable about her that made me trust her, and when I thought of her, my heart felt full in my chest and tears pricked my eyes.

I took a deep breath and headed for Sunday School, feeling better than I had in weeks.

Chapter 8

TEMPORARY

It had been a long time since I'd attended a Gospel Doctrine class. Adam sat on the back row and looked at me with surprise when I sat next to him. I told him about Cathy, then held his hand and waited for the class to start.

A man with a kind face, deep happy dimples, and dark hair stood at the front of the class. He opened his Bible and asked us to do the same. "I am so grateful to stand before you today, brothers and sisters. We'll be talking about the Beatitudes today, so if you'd open your Bibles to Matthew . . ."

I opened my scriptures on my lap. Every few minutes I glanced at Adam's watch, expecting Cathy to open the door and ask me to rescue her. But she didn't come to the door. I had nearly an hour of quiet, just listening to people discuss the gospel. It left me with a calm, sweet feeling that I hadn't had in months.

When the class ended, I was the last person to stand. I didn't want to go back to my reality. I wanted to stay there and study the scriptures and let someone else endure my day-to-day trials. Adam took my hand and gave me a soft smile, as if he knew what I was thinking. Then he led me out of the classroom to get Marie and Kaye.

Cathy had pulled Kaye into the foyer and was dressing her again. Probably for the hundredth time. Cathy looked up at me with wary eyes as I walked to her side and took the diaper bag from her.

"Was everything okay?" I asked.

"Yeah, she was fine." Cathy's brow furrowed, and I sensed that there was a "but" following. "Are you sure she's not autistic? I've got a niece who's autistic, and Kaye sure reminds me of her."

I couldn't look Cathy in the eye. Kaye was different, but she wasn't disabled. "Well, you know what, Cathy? I don't think people should be labeled just because they act different."

My words obviously stung her. She blinked and leaned away from me just a little. "I'm sure it's hard to hear," Cathy said, almost under her breath. She wasn't stunned for long. She pulled a small planner from her bag and started writing something on a piece of paper for me. "Here, this is the name of my niece's doctor. I've taken her a few times. His name's Dr. Suriya. He's good, and he knows what he's talking about."

She tore the paper from her planner and held it out to me. "Please take it, Jen. The earlier these kids are diagnosed, the earlier they can be treated, and the more progress they make."

I took the paper with a scowl on my face. Kaye wasn't disabled, I was sure of it.

Adam and Marie joined us. They both looked so happy, but Adam's expression fell as soon as he saw me.

"What's wrong?" Adam asked.

I looked at Cathy. "Nothing's wrong."

Adam looked back and forth between the two of us, then said, "Okay. Well, here. Take Marie and Kaye and find a seat. I'm going to ask the employment specialist if he's heard anything yet."

He slipped into the chapel.

"You need a job?" Cathy asked.

"No," I said. "Adam does."

Cathy looked at me like I had betrayed her. "Why didn't you tell me? I would have brought you some food."

I shrugged my shoulders. I didn't tell her that our savings was all but gone, or that our fridge and cupboards were nearly bare. The fact was, I didn't want her to know. And Adam had a credit card without a balance. I could buy a few things the next day, just to get us by until Adam got a job—hopefully in the next week. I didn't want Cathy to do anything for me because I didn't want to owe her anything.

Cathy shook her head a little, then tried to smile at me. "I can't help you if I don't know you need help. Don't let your pride get in the way of your family's needs."

It was my turn to feel stung. I wasn't being prideful. I just didn't want to be a burden to anyone, least of all someone I barely knew. All my life I'd been taught to be self-reliant, and I wasn't about to give up on that just because we were unemployed.

"Thanks for watching Kaye," I said quietly. Even if I didn't like her suggestion that Kaye needed psychiatric help, Cathy had given me a much needed service that day, and because of that service, I'd had forty minutes of being carefree and feeling the Spirit. I needed to thank her for that.

"You'll be in my prayers." Cathy's words faded into the buzz of the crowd as I left her standing in the foyer and took the kids to a bench near the back of the chapel.

I looked at the name and phone number scribbled on the piece of paper Cathy had given me, and folded it into my scriptures. I doubted I would call the number, and I thought of throwing the paper away, but there wasn't time—a member of the bishopric was standing to start the meeting, and Adam was hurrying toward our bench with a piece of paper in his hand.

I sat Kaye close to the wall and started pulling out books and crayons, but she was restless by the time the opening song was over. It was always a bad sign when the container of cereal was empty before the sacrament even started.

We left before the first speaker had reached the pulpit.

* * *

Adam and I lay in bed that night, listening to Kaye and Marie singing themselves to sleep.

"What was that little tiff with Cathy today?"

"Nothing. Just me being an idiot. She hurt me, so I lashed out at her."

"She hurt you?"

"Yeah. She thinks Kaye is autistic," I said.

"She does?" Adam sounded thoughtful.

I rolled to my side and looked at Adam. "Do you know much about autism?"

"I studied it a little in my psychology class. It's been a few years, but if I remember right, autistic kids sometimes have seizures and they like to rock back and forth a lot, and they lack emotion, or they don't like to be affectionate or something like that. Kaye isn't like that, but maybe they only talked about worst case scenarios in school."

"She gave me the name of a doctor to take Kaye to. She said he's good."

"Well, maybe we should take her, then. Better safe than sorry, right?"

I nodded. "We need insurance first. I'm not dropping a hundred and fifty dollars to have some quack tell me my daughter's got a 'different personality.' Besides, it's just like your dad said when we talked to him at Christmas—kids talk when they need to."

Adam looked at me and started to say something, then he seemed to think better of it.

"What?" I asked.

He shook his head. "Nothing."

"No, don't do that. If you've got something to say, say it."

"I think it's more than a 'different personality.'"

I felt my jaw drop with surprise.

"When dad told us she'd learn to talk when she needs to, he was basing his idea on me. I had an older sister who did everything for me. I really didn't need to talk till I was almost four. Marie does stuff for Kaye, but not like that."

I looked away. I wanted to believe his father.

"I think we should see this doctor as soon as possible," Adam said quietly.

I stared at him for a moment, then rolled to my back and changed the subject. "So did the employment specialist find a job for you?" I didn't want to talk about seeing Dr. Suriya. I didn't even want to think about it.

Adam sighed. "One. But it still might not work."

"Why not?" I asked.

"The hours. I don't think you'd like it." He stared at the ceiling.

"If it brings money in, I'll like it. You know I'd go get a job if I could, but without a degree . . ."

"I know, Jen. You wouldn't make enough to pay the sitter."

"So tell me about this job."

"It's making telephone reservations for a hotel chain. They need a night manager who speaks French."

"Night manager, huh? So what are the hours?"

"From 4 P.M. to midnight," he said with a heavy voice.

"Would you get enough sleep?"

"I won't get much sleep if we lose our townhouse because we can't pay the rent anymore," Adam said.

I sighed heavily. I was alone with the kids all day, and with that job, I'd be alone with them most of the night. Brienne would get sick of me calling her all the time just to have an adult conversation. Of course, she'd only be around for a few more weeks anyway—I couldn't afford to call her often once she moved.

"So, what do you think?" Adam asked.

"I think we need a job, Adam."

"Then I'll call tomorrow."

He rolled his back to me and was soon sleeping soundly. I looked at the clock. Eleven. Two hours left before Kaye's internal clock woke her up—not much time to sleep. Adam was lucky. Unless he was still awake, he never heard her wiggle the doorknob at night and scream until I let her out of her room. And I never woke him to ask him to watch her during her midnight playtime.

I closed my eyes and thought of the calm, sweet, forty minutes of bliss I'd had during Gospel Doctrine. How quickly that wonderful feeling had faded. Were all my joys meant to be so temporary?

Chapter 9

RUNAWAY

It took one day for Cathy to make me feel indebted to her. At three o'clock, Monday afternoon, Cathy's hair glowed just outside my back door. Several white plastic bags hung from her forearms, and the faint outline of her biceps showed through her white T-shirt. I opened the door mostly out of curiosity about what she was carrying.

"I haven't called that doctor yet, if that's what you're wondering," I said. I knew it was rude, but it got the question out of the way, and it kept with the tone of our recent conversation.

Cathy smiled. "I still like you, Jen. Even though you're mad at me. Can I put these down?"

I backed out of her way as she entered my kitchen, and I took a bag bulging with groceries from her hand. She'd brought me groceries, a couple of weeks' worth by the look of it, and the first thing I had done was insult her.

She unloaded seven grocery bags from the lengths of both of her arms then held up one finger at me. "Hang on, there's more."

"More?" I asked, and tears blurred my vision. The bags were full of kid food. Three large bags of frozen chicken nuggets, a large box of cheese crackers, a bag of sugar-free fruit snacks, several kinds of cereal, all of them low-sugar but kid-friendly. There were even several cans of tuna. She was killing me with kindness.

Cathy came back with a paper bag in one arm and two huge zucchinis in the other. A smile spread across her face. She was having fun serving me, I could tell. I stood before her, surrounded by the groceries she'd bought for me. I refused to cry, and tried to focus on the fact that this meant I owed her something. But it didn't work.

Her smile showed me she wanted absolutely nothing in return—she seemed happy enough at that moment to make any payment paltry.

She couldn't stop grinning, even while she spoke. "There's a couple dozen eggs on the bottom of this bag, and about four loaves of bread. Do you have freezer room? I wanted to make sure you had enough food to last until you and Shauna can get together and fill out a food order for the storehouse. She's out of town this week, but she'll be back next week and I'll make sure she calls you."

"Well, hopefully she won't have to. Adam's at another interview right now."

"Even so. I just want you to know that if you need help, it's here." She smiled at me. "I hope I bought the right size diapers. I didn't buy the biggest size, but from what I remember of watching her streak around yesterday, she's got a bit of a booty. I bought size four."

"That's perfect," I managed to say. I wanted to tell her I was sorry, to say thank you, but I couldn't say what I was feeling at that moment.

"Cathy, I . . ." I sniffed as my nose began to tingle.

She held up her hand. "Let's put these away, shall we?"

I nodded and smiled weakly.

She loaded the top shelf of our fridge with three gallons of milk. "I wasn't quite sure what to buy, 'cause I wanted it to be a surprise. I figured you wouldn't turn me away if I showed up at your door with food."

I shook my head and stacked the twelve cans of tuna in my nearly bare cupboard.

"And you told me you didn't need anything. I can see you weren't completely destitute, but you were close. What were you going to do if the food had run out?" she asked.

"We have a credit card. I was probably going to use that."

"Oh, don't buy food on a credit card. Jen, promise me you'll never do that. Today's bread isn't worth tomorrow's enslavement, and that's all a credit card is."

I nodded.

"Do you promise?"

"I promise."

"Okay." She looked satisfied, and she pulled a large bag of cereal from the last grocery bag. "Where do you want this?"

I pointed at the small pantry.

She put the cereal away and began to gather up the empty grocery bags.

"Why are you being so good to me, Cathy?" I asked. "I was terrible to you yesterday."

"Yes, you were," she smiled.

"Do you really think Kaye's autistic?" I asked with a lump in my throat.

She nodded, though her eyes looked pained to admit it. "Every autistic child is different, so it's kind of hard to tell. But Kaye seems to have a lot in common with my niece."

I finished stacking the last of the vegetables in my pantry and sat at the kitchen table.

"Even if she is autistic, it's not the end of the world." She joined me at the table and sat close enough to look me in the eye. "You know what's really neat about my niece? She doesn't make much progress, but every bit of progress she makes seems . . . miraculous. It makes you grateful for the simple things in life—the things everyone else takes for granted."

I couldn't think of anything to say. I still wasn't sure she was right about Kaye. There were moments when Kaye seemed completely normal. Sure, she didn't play with dolls the way Marie did—Kaye had more fun lining up blocks or toy cars. She liked organizing things; there was nothing wrong with that. Kaye laughed like any normal child. She loved to be tickled, and when she laughed, everyone joined in because her happiness spread through the room until they had no choice.

Cathy slapped her legs to jumpstart herself into motion. "Well, I have to run. I'm babysitting my niece tonight, as a matter of fact. So you know I'll be thinking of you."

I was grateful for her kindness, but it also made me kind of mad. If I hadn't needed that food, I would have turned it away. I didn't want to need anyone's help. I wanted to provide for my family on my own. Part of me wanted to run and hide, but I accepted her generous gift and said, "Thank you so much."

"Hey, don't mention it. Oh, and I'll babysit for you sometime, too. Just call me."

Fresh tears came to my eyes. "Don't offer if you don't mean it."

Cathy smiled. "I mean it."

As she pulled out of the parking lot in her little truck, Adam pulled his Saturn into our empty space. He was barely through the door when he burst with his news. "I've got a job!"

I smiled as relief relaxed me. I wouldn't have to get a food order from Shauna Nulman. "Your interview went well?"

"Yeah. My boss served his mission in Belgium too. We spoke French to each other for a while. Man, am I rusty." He chuckled. "But he seemed to like me. He hired me on the spot and I start a training program next week. I'll have to quit the bank, but we'll have health care, sick days. Benefits, Jen! You can take Kaye to that doctor."

That knocked my happiness down a rung or two. Just because I could take Kaye to see Dr. Suriya didn't mean I wanted to.

"The question is, how are we going to get by until then?" Adam opened his empty wallet.

I stood and showed him the full fridge, cupboards, and pantry.

"Wow. How did that happen?"

"Cathy," I said.

Adam smiled. "I knew I liked her."

* * *

I'd been getting up with Kaye for so long that my body's clock had adjusted to hers. I woke up at one the next morning and lay in bed, waiting to hear Kaye pull books from her shelves.

Finally, I climbed from bed as quietly as I could, and walked down the hall to her bedroom. Her door was already open.

Marie was sound asleep, and so was Adam. Kaye had been playing with doorknobs, and had opened her bedroom door a couple of times during the last week, but I doubted she could figure it out in the dark. I slipped downstairs to see where Kaye was, wondering what she might be into. None of the lights downstairs were on, but moonlight streamed through the kitchen door onto the linoleum.

Our townhouse apartment had two doors, one leading from the front room to a busy street, and the other connecting the kitchen with a small back patio and the parking lot. Smaller, stacked apartments rose behind the parking lot, and in the center of the buildings sat the complex office and the swimming pool.

I thought of that swimming pool as I looked at the open kitchen door, and the open gate to our patio. Panic hit me, but I tried to calm myself with logic. Kaye had never opened the back door before, and I couldn't imagine her knowing how to unlock the deadbolt. The gate was impossible for her to open. I'd seen her try and fail several times. She couldn't have opened her bedroom door, unlocked the back door and opened it, opened the gate, and slipped into the night. Logically, it didn't make sense, but little about Kaye made sense to me anymore.

The alternative was that a stranger had entered my home and taken Kaye. But somehow, I knew that wasn't what had happened. The back door and patio gate stood open before me, moonlight showing the path to the pool that we had walked many times that summer. I was sure Kaye knew the way. I didn't know how she did it, but I knew Kaye was heading for the pool.

For an instant, I thought of rousing Adam, but I knew there wasn't time. Visions of Kaye slipping through the bars of the gate to the pool flashed through my mind. She had no fear. She would jump in, completely unaware of the danger, and for a few moments, she would thrash in the water.

"Kaye!" I called, though I knew it would do no good. She never responded when I called her name.

I was past the gate, looking at the cars around me, trying to catch a glimpse of her running among them. "Kaye!" I called again, feeling my desperation rise.

As the pool came closer, I looked at the surface of the water, half expecting to see ripples where she had been splashing. The spaces between the bars of the gate around the pool were narrow, but not too narrow for her to fit through them. There was a hot tub just out of view, and I wouldn't be able to see it until I pressed my face against the fence.

"Kaye!" I called again, but my voice cracked and her name came out as a squeak. I reached the fence and tried to look at the hot tub.

"Is this your daughter?" a voice asked.

I turned to see a woman walking toward me with Kaye in her arms. "Yes!" I said with relief.

"She was heading toward the pool. I caught her though. I was wondering what to do with her when I heard you calling."

I took Kaye from the woman's arms. "Oh, thank you so much. I can't explain why she's out here. I didn't know she could open the back door and the gate."

"She's autistic, isn't she?" the woman said.

I looked at her with wide eyes.

"I'm a nurse. I've seen a few autistic kids in my line of work." She looked at Kaye, who was trying to squirm her way out of my arms.

"Thank heaven you were out here," I said. "She might've . . ."

"Well, she didn't. I just got home from work, actually. The timing was good. You might want to find another way to lock your back door, though." She smiled.

"Thank you," I said.

"I'm glad to help," she said, and then she turned and headed toward the east apartment building.

I was too happy holding Kaye in my arms to think of how indebted I was to this total stranger.

Kaye reached for the pool over my shoulder.

I kissed her forehead. "We can't go swimming right now, Kaye. The pool is closed." She kept reaching as if she had no idea what I'd just said to her. It occurred to me that maybe she didn't know what I'd said. I was sure she'd heard me, but what if the words meant nothing to her? She didn't respond when I called her name, but she'd had hearing tests and I knew it wasn't because she couldn't hear me. What if it was because she didn't know what the word "Kaye" meant when I said it?

Understanding came to me in a flash. Two people had asked if Kaye was autistic in less than three days' time. I was in denial, and it would only hurt us in the long run. It was time for a professional opinion.

When we were back in the townhouse, the television on and Kaye planted in front of it with a juice box in hand, I opened my scriptures and found the note with the doctor's name and phone number on it. I decided I'd call him in the morning, and we'd find out for sure.

I spent the rest of the night in the hallway between the front room and the kitchen so I'd feel her if she made her way toward the back door again. I was grateful we'd never used the front door that led out to the busy street. Even at that late hour, if she had gone out that door she could have been killed in an instant.

It occurred to me how amazing it was that a nurse had come home from work just at that time and seen Kaye walking toward the pool. It was too perfect to be coincidental. I knew I'd witnessed a miracle that night, one I might never have witnessed had Kaye been more receptive to me. Her apparent fault had allowed me an opportunity to see the hand of God. As I leaned against the wall, watching Kaye play as if it were two in the afternoon instead of two in the morning, I prayed. I thanked God, silently, for returning my runaway to me, for giving me a miracle. And I prayed for the strength to call Dr. Suriya in the morning.

Chapter 10

A KICK IN THE STOMACH

I couldn't dial the number. I stared at the phone in my hand, noticing the buttons' soft, green glow, and the slight, dirty crust forming around each of the buttons. Before I could dial the number, I had to clean the crust from the phone.

Finally, I dialed all but the last number and looked over at Kaye sleeping soundly on the couch. Remembering the panic I'd felt when I noticed the open kitchen door, I pressed the last number and held the phone against my ear.

The receptionist was kind, but I was certain she had no idea how hard it had been for me to make that phone call, and when she told me she couldn't fit me in for three months, I felt my stomach tie in knots. Three months of waiting. She said she'd call if there were a cancellation, but I counted on ninety days of agony. Or would it be ninety days of bliss? Did I want a definitive answer? Did I want to know if Kaye had autism? I realized I had to know. If I didn't know, I wouldn't be able to solve the problems we would encounter, and there would always be the question nagging at me.

Adam quit his job at the bank, and the following Monday he started the training program for his new job. The training program had banker's hours, but when his job actually started in the first week of August, he would manage a swing shift from four in the afternoon to midnight.

The day after training started, Brienne called and invited me to go shopping. Their new home just outside of Washington D.C. was a red brick colonial with hardwood floors. Russ told her to pick out new furniture, and they'd have it sent to the house so everything would be moved in when they got there in a little over two weeks—Bri would only have to set everything up. I agreed to go shopping with her, but only for the companionship. Our time was running short.

She met us in the parking lot of a posh furniture store where they sold new, stylish furniture as well as antiques. Russ had a thing for antiques. He had a family heirloom—a high-backed, armless chair sitting in the corner of his study—that dated back to the turn of the twentieth century. It was the most uncomfortable chair I'd ever sat in.

Marie had her favorite dress on, and Kaye was tugging at her shorts and T-shirt like they were chafing her. I took a firm grip on Kaye's hand, and we joined Bri and Emily at the furniture store entrance.

"Hey, you!" Bri put her arm around me and gave me a squeeze.

"Hey." I tried to smile. She didn't buy it.

"Okay, what's wrong?"

I told her about Kaye's adventure into the night and the phone call I'd made that morning.

"Wow. I didn't even know she could open doors."

I shrugged. "Until a few days ago, she couldn't."

"Well, she keeps you on your toes, at least," Bri said with a smile.

"Yeah, but I've got flat feet. I like my heels on the ground, too."

Bri laughed. "You're making jokes! That's a good sign."

I didn't feel like laughing.

Emily and Marie took each other's hands and walked just in front of us. As soon as we entered the store, Kaye began tugging in the direction of the chairs that looked a lot like the one in Russ's study. Kaye liked walking on seats—planting her feet in the center and walking along a line of chairs as if they were stepping stones in a pond.

"What does she want?" Bri asked.

"Oh, probably to walk on that line of chairs. What do you think the clerk would do if I helped her up there?" I raised my eyebrows.

"Don't you dare! Troublemaker."

We watched Kaye head over to the furniture, just so I could prove to Bri that I could predict something my child would do, but I caught up to Kaye before she could climb up the first chair. I couldn't afford to buy any damaged antiques.

I tried to get a firm grip on Kaye's hand, but she pulled away from me. I grabbed her wrist so she couldn't wiggle her fingers enough for my grip to slip, and she sat on the ground. I refused to let go.

If I had known the battle I was starting by holding onto her that way, I may have found an alternative. She started screaming as loud as she could, and since flopping to her backside wasn't enough, she lay down and kicked at my hand, which was still wrapped around her wrist like a vise.

It didn't take long for a clerk to come over to us. "May I help you?"

Bri looked at me. "It's okay. Just let her go."

I did as Bri had asked.

Kaye went straight to the chair at the end of the line and climbed up on it, then stood up. She sang her single, sustained note, then started saying, "Juice, juice, juice."

The clerk stretched his hand out. "Please don't let her put her feet on the furniture. That's an antique."

"I know it is. That's why I didn't want to let her go." I looked pointedly at Bri as I grabbed Kaye's wrist again. She screamed so loudly that time that all motion seemed to stop in the store, and it felt as if every eye focused on us. It was like the still air surrounding a lightning strike.

The clerk looked around at the many eyes on us, and I thought he might have a coronary, judging by his pained expression. "Please, you're disturbing my customers."

I wrapped my arms around Kaye's waist and lifted her from the chair. She kicked me in the gut, and the shock of it made me release my hold on her. She dropped to the ground. Without hesitation, she was back up on the chair and on her feet, bouncing lightly on the chair, making the old cushion creak.

"I'm going to have to ask you to leave," the clerk said as he reached protectively toward the antiques.

"Come on, Kaye," Bri said as I rubbed my lower abdomen. "Let's go bye-bye. I think you've had enough of this store." Bri tried to pick Kaye up the way I had done, but instead of keeping Kaye at her waist, Bri flung Kaye over her shoulder like a sack of potatoes and headed straight for the exit.

Kaye's kick hurt me more than it should have. It took me a second to shake it off. "Marie, Emily, let's go," I said. The girls had been looking at a four-poster bed with sheer hangings. They came to me obediently, and we followed Bri out the store doors. Kaye looked at me over Bri's shoulder and screamed. It was the closest thing to eye contact Kaye had given me in months.

"I'm sorry, Bri," I said as we loaded Kaye in her car seat.

"I've never been kicked out of a store before." Bri's face was flushed, and red splotches had bloomed on her neck—she was embarrassed.

I laughed. "I have. I've been kicked out of two restaurants and three hair salons."

"You're kidding me! Why?"

I pointed at Kaye.

Bri scrunched up her nose with worry. "Do people look at you like that all the time? That clerk looked like he thought we were—I don't know."

"Unworthy of shopping in his fancy establishment?" I suggested.

Bri nodded.

"I get the same look at the grocery store, and McDonalds, and the video store. Pretty much wherever I go, I'm not worthy to be there." My smile felt weak.

Bri's eyes dropped as she looked at me. "I'm sorry, Jen. I had no idea it was this bad."

I shrugged. "How could I tell you? 'Kaye had a really bad tantrum today, and I can never go back to Denny's'?" I shook my head. "You kind of have to experience it to know."

"So, why did you agree to meet me if going out is so painful?"

I smiled at her. "You know why, you geek. We've only got two more weeks together. I wanted to be with you before that's not an option anymore."

Bri hugged me, and I returned the squeeze.

"Well, if they treat you this way at this store, my money will be spent somewhere else." She glared back at the store.

I grinned. It was pointless for her to protect me, but it felt nice.

"Hey," Bri said, "How about we get some food at the drive-thru, my treat, and we'll go back to your place. Then, after we wait an hour, we can go for a swim. That seems like something Kaye likes."

"Sounds good. Thanks."

Bri and Emily got in her car, and Marie and I got in mine. Kaye was already strapped in her car seat and looking tranquil. I felt a sharp pain in my abdomen as I fastened my seat belt. I took a deep breath and wondered what Kaye had done to me.

When we got home with three Happy Meals and a couple of salads, I noticed my message light blinking. I pressed the button to play back the message.

"Mrs. Young, this is Dr. Suriya's receptionist. We've had a cancellation on July twenty-third. I know it's the day before the holiday, and it's this Friday, which is probably why we've had a hard time filling it. But if you can take the appointment, please call us." She left the phone number again, then ended the message.

"Is that the autism doctor?" Bri asked.

I nodded.

"Well, are you going to call them back, or not?"

I picked up the phone. "I guess I'm going to call them."

My ninety-day wait had been shortened to ten days, and it filled me with nervous energy. I sat down to eat my salad, but realized I wasn't hungry.

"It will be better to know," Bri said.

"I know it will," I replied, but the pain in my abdomen returned. I pressed my fingers in near my hipbone, hoping to ease the stitch.

"Are you okay?" Bri asked.

"I'm just stressed."

"This seems like more than stress to me."

"Maybe Kaye ruptured something when she kicked me today," I said with a smile, hoping Bri would take it as a joke. "Don't worry about me. Eat."

Bri took a reluctant bite of her salad, never taking her eyes off of me.

By the time Adam got home, I was doubled up with pain. Bri offered to watch the kids while Adam took me to the hospital, and I didn't object. The only other times in my life I'd felt that bad, I'd left the hospital with a newborn in my arms.

They took a blood test first thing, and that was how I found out I was pregnant. Stress had caused me to skip periods before, and since I was feeling more stress at that time in my life than ever, I figured it was the culprit again. The baby growing inside of me was already at eleven weeks gestation, and Kaye had nearly kicked him free of the warmth of my womb. I had almost lost the baby I didn't even know was there. The doctor prescribed bed rest, and I laughed at him. Adam smiled and smoothed my hair back from my face. He kissed my forehead and told me he loved me.

"How do you feel?" Adam asked.

I grinned sarcastically. "Like I've been kicked in the stomach."

Adam laughed and kissed me again.

Then I cried into the flat, white, sterile hospital pillow.

Chapter 11

D-DAY

When we got home from the hospital, Russ had installed chain locks on both of our doors, high enough that Kaye couldn't possibly reach them. We were hoping that I wouldn't have to spend the night in the hall anymore.

Brienne spent the night with me while Adam was at his training sessions. She chased Kaye and got her dressed over and over again, held her down while she changed her diaper, and I gave her sympathetic looks as I lounged on the couch. It made me feel guilty to watch her struggle, but she wouldn't let me get up unless I had to go to the bathroom.

Most of the time I lay there thinking about the baby inside me. I knew it was a boy. The pregnancy was so different from what I'd experienced with Marie and Kaye. Despite the bruise near my hip and a dull ache in my back, I felt great—hardly any morning sickness. I wasn't surprised that I hadn't even known I was pregnant. My physical condition was pretty good, but my mental condition was lacking. It also explained the strange dreams I'd been having. I couldn't get the question from my mind: Would this child be more like Marie, or more like Kaye?

The morning of July twenty-third came. Brienne and Emily showed up on my back porch as they had every morning all week, but that morning I had a hard time getting out of bed to let them in the apartment.

Bri gave me a sympathetic look as soon as I opened the door. I grinned and let her in.

"You okay?" she asked.

I shrugged.

"Kaye hasn't figured out the chain locks, has she?"

"No."

"So do you sleep better?"

I shook my head. "I can't help but think it's just a matter of time before she figures something else out. She's so bent on running away, doing her own thing . . . I don't know. I can't help but think that if she wants to get out of the house bad enough, she'll find a way."

Bri chuckled. "She is a smarty."

I didn't know that "smart" was a word I would have used.

"Well, at least she's pretty easy to deal with at home. Besides her desire to be nude all the time, that is. She entertains herself."

"Yeah," I said. "That would be great if I was content to stay at home. I get depressed here. But I don't want to take Kaye anywhere because that depresses me, too."

Bri walked up to me and gave me a hug. She held me for a while before she took a step back and looked me in the eye. "Do you want me to take her to the appointment today?"

I shook my head. "She's my daughter. I'll go."

By the time I pulled onto the street where Dr. Suriya's office was, I wondered if I should have let Bri take Kaye after all. I didn't want to go to his office. I knew with a deep sense of foreboding that nothing would be the same after my visit with this unknown man with a strange name. That sense tightened my chest and the pain returned to my abdomen; I thought I might hyperventilate or start hemorrhaging as I turned into the parking lot of the white stucco strip of doctor's offices. I wanted to run—anywhere but through those doors.

With a deep breath, I released Kaye from her car seat, held her hand firmly, and led her into the unknown.

The office was impeccably clean, and there were no dumb details for me to focus on for distraction, just a few children sitting in the waiting room at the feet of their mothers. One child moved his hands like Kaye did, looking up at the fluorescent light through dancing fingers.

The receptionist handed me a clipboard with paperwork on it. There were at least seven sheets, only three of which were new-patient information. The other four looked like some kind of questionnaire.

Question one asked: "Did your child reach for you from his/her crib?"

Well, of course she did, I thought. All babies do that. They want out, they reach for you. But just to be thorough, I thought back a couple of years to when Kaye was in a crib. There were days when I'd put her down for a nap. Unless she was already asleep when I laid her down—and the act of lying her down didn't wake her—all she did was play in her crib, much like she was playing now as I filled out the questionnaire. She'd looked through the crib bars at nothing, singing to herself as if she liked the sound of her voice. She'd played like that for hours, never crying, just content with the buzz in her head.

She only reached for me after I reached for her. I searched my memory for a time when she initiated the reach. I couldn't remember one.

Question two: "Does your child prefer a rigid schedule?"

Yes. I checked the appropriate box. She couldn't go to bed at night without a prayer and a bedtime song, unless I was okay with her screaming for an hour or more, which I never was. In fact, it was the main reason I dreaded Adam's new schedule. Daddy wouldn't be there to sing with Kaye at night.

Three: "Does your child arch his/her back when he/she is upset?"

Yes. I had the bruises on my chest and abdomen to prove it.

I whispered the next few questions to myself as my heart rate increased. "Does your child point at things that interest him/her?"

No. She'd never pointed at anything. It took a lot of guesswork to figure out what she wanted, but we'd worked out a system for some of the important stuff. She'd grab my hand and drag me to the fridge when she wanted a drink. If she wanted to watch a movie, she dragged me to the TV. Sometimes she'd cry for hours while I tried one thing after another until I figured out she was upset about a video put in the wrong place, or a box of cereal left on the kitchen table. It was sort of like caring for a newborn in a three-year-old body.

"Is your child's speech delayed?"

Yes. Her third birthday was ten days away and she still didn't call me Mommy.

"Does your child play well with other children his/her age?"

No. She preferred to be alone.

I looked back over my answers and got that eerie feeling again. I'd always thought of Kaye's quirks as part of her personality. Not all people were easy to get along with. Some children were more demanding than others. I figured she'd grow out of a lot of the problems she had. I thought the phase would pass.

A nurse tapped me on the shoulder and led me from the waiting room, telling me to get my child and bring her to Dr. Suriya's office. I obeyed.

He sat there in his leather chair and looked at my daughter. He didn't say anything, just observed, writing a scribble or two on his little notepad like a scientist observing a rat.

It went on like this for a few minutes before he acknowledged I was in the room.

"See, I may as well be a chair," he said, trying to get my daughter to look him in the eye.

"What do you mean?" I asked.

He looked at me as though the answer was obvious, and I must have been dense to not see it. "According to the way she treats me, I may as well be a chair. Any piece of furniture. She doesn't see me as a person. I'm just an object. Does she run into people often?"

"Run into people?"

"Yes, as if she doesn't even see them." His voice was impatient.

I had to think about it. "She does, sometimes."

He nodded. "See how she won't look me in the eye?"

It was true. He tried to get her to look at him, but she turned her face away every time.

Maybe you intimidate her, and that's why she won't look at you. Maybe it's your fault, not hers. I didn't say what I thought, and I kept my gaze on Kaye's face.

"Your daughter is autistic." The words slipped easily from his lips. It didn't pain him to speak them, and he seemed unaware of how I felt hearing them. "Do you have any questions?"

Gee, a few. Like who do you think you are? He seemed to think that just because he spent loads of money to read a bunch of books and hang a piece of paper on his wall, he was some sort of authority on my child. I'd lived with her for nearly three years by then. She wasn't rocking back and forth all day. She didn't hit her head against the wall, have seizures, drool, or injure herself. After glancing at a questionnaire and watching her for a few seconds, he could say four words that would turn our lives upside down.

"No," I said, "I don't have any questions." I thought about it. There was one thing I had to know, and it couldn't wait. I needed some sense of hope. "Except, what does that mean for her future? Will she ever talk to me? Will she always be . . . autistic?"

"It's hard to give a prognosis. We're learning more about autism all the time. We know these children can be helped through diet, parent education, and behavioral therapy. But each child is so different, it's hard to say what kind of progress your child will make. But, yes, she will always be autistic."

I nodded and felt my first wave of morning sickness, so I swallowed hard and grabbed Kaye's hand for support. She reached for the door.

He pulled an empty file folder from his desk and proceeded to fill the file with papers. "I'm giving you some literature about the disorder, as well as an address for the best preschool in the area for children with autistic spectrum disorder. I'll call and make sure Kaye is put on the waiting list to be evaluated. It may be another year before she's able to attend the school, though. The waiting list is quite long."

I was barely aware of his mumbling voice.

"I'd advise you to go to the parent-support group at this school. If your daughter's on their waiting list, you're eligible to go to the parent group. Some of the teachers run a daycare during the meetings, so you can bring your children with you. You'll probably gain your greatest support from other parents."

"How is all this paid for?" I asked as my practical self kicked in.

"It's a state-funded program, subsidized by your mental-health insurance plan."

I didn't even know if we had mental-health coverage.

Kaye turned the doorknob and started opening the door. I shot from my seat and closed it before she could sneak out.

"Is that all, then?" I asked. "Kaye's ready to go." Kaye wouldn't mind if I used her as an excuse to leave before I lost my breakfast on Dr. Suriya's shoes.

"I'll call the school and see what I can do to get you bumped up on the waiting list since she's fairly severe and she's almost three."

What does "fairly severe" mean?

"I'd also like you to arrange for some tests up at Primary Children's hospital—an MRI and an EEG. Here's the name of a neurologist you should make an appointment with." He wrote all the information down, then handed me the file folder containing his instructions and at least twenty photocopied pages of information.

"I suggest you call the neurologist and the school as soon as possible and see when they can set up an appointment for evaluation. If they have an opening this year, it would be to Kaye's advantage. This is a preschool, and they can only serve her until she's five." He nodded at me with a slight smile and I sensed he was through with us, so I let Kaye open the door.

Kaye led me through the building and out to our car. I strapped her tightly in her car seat so she couldn't Houdini herself out of the straps. The drive home was long and slow, and when I got home, I couldn't remember a mile of it.

I had wanted to find out the truth about Kaye. After Cathy's suggestion of autism, then the nurse in the parking lot the night Kaye ran away, I had to know. The news didn't really surprise me. Deep down, I'd known for a while.

I parked the car in my space, next to Brienne's Honda Odyssey. After the engine was off, and the keys were lying in my lap, I looked in the rearview mirror at Kaye.

Suddenly I realized why I'd been avoiding the diagnosis—this was a problem I couldn't fix. I was the mother of a disabled child. One who would likely outlive me. In an instant of despair, I felt sure I would never see her date, fall in love, or marry. She would never bear children. My hopes of spending time alone with Adam, traveling or serving a mission after his retirement, faded. Kaye would always be there, and we would care for her until our dying day.

And then came thoughts of Marie. She would miss the things that sisters so close in age should share. In an instant, we'd been denied the life we should have had. Adam, me, Marie—all of us had lost the Kaye we thought we knew. Kaye's future died on that day of infamy.

Now I didn't have *a* question, I had too many to name them all. Even if I could ask them, Dr. Suriya would be the last person who'd hear them. He was too cold for me to open up to. He may as well have been an antique chair, high-backed and stiff with no arms and scratchy upholstery.

Brienne opened the back door and looked right at me, but all I saw was a blurry image of her. I felt more alone at that moment than I ever had in my life, with a mind full of questions I couldn't ask and a beautiful little stranger in the backseat.

Chapter 12

STORMS

Brienne offered to take us to the Days of '47 Parade, but I wasn't in the mood. We spent the day at home, watching the parade on TV, and I did laundry and made bread. The girls didn't realize it was a state holiday, so they didn't care that we'd missed the celebration. Adam caught up on some sleep. After helping me with the laundry he buried his nose in a book.

That night in my dreams, I played over the diagnosis again and again. Distorted music drifted in the background, as if I were watching a silent movie. Kaye played in a room full of toys, except she wasn't really playing. She was just wiggling her fingers together, looking through them at the light above her. Suddenly, I was looking through her dancing fingers too, and the fluorescent light strobed through her flesh. It gave me a headache.

Kaye's scream woke me up. I was actually grateful to hear it, because that way I knew she hadn't figured out how to unlatch the new lock on the door and run into the night. I went downstairs to find her crouched in front of the television. It wouldn't turn on. I checked the plug and tried it again, but the television was dead. I tried to turn on a light, but it didn't work either. A huge clap of thunder nearly scared me out of my skin, and I realized the electricity was out.

I sat on the couch and tried to hold Kaye to comfort her, but she squirmed away from me and stubbornly tried to turn on the TV again. She screamed when it wouldn't work.

Soon, Adam came downstairs to see me sitting in the dark. "The electricity out?" he asked.

"Yes. Kaye doesn't like it."

"We have a flashlight somewhere."

"It's in the pantry." I wanted to go back to sleep, but another clap of thunder made my heart thump against my ribs. There would be no sleeping with thunder like that. I hated late summer storms—they unleashed too much anger and animosity and didn't yield enough rain.

Adam found the flashlight and shone it on the wall where the battery-operated clock was. It was three in the morning.

"Kaye woke up later than usual," I said with a derisive chuckle.

Adam gave the flashlight to Kaye to play with and hurried to the window behind the couch, where he parted the curtains and stared outside at the storm.

"Close those drapes! Are you trying to scare me to death? You know I don't like storms."

"I'm not opening them, just sticking my head through. You may not like storms, but I love them."

I shook my head and got off the couch to move farther from the window. If lightning struck, I didn't want to be there when the window shattered.

Adam watched me as I sat on the bottom step on the opposite side of the room. "You're being paranoid."

"Yeah, well life seems to be out to get me anyway, so I may as well expect lightning to strike."

"Life is not out to get you. You see things so much worse than they really are sometimes."

Kaye shone the flashlight on the television and started to pace in front of it like a caged animal. She peered through her wiggling fingers at her shadow reflected in the blank TV screen.

"Okay, then," I said. "Life is out to get my daughter. It may as well be out to get me."

"I don't know if you've thought of this, Jen, but Kaye may be the luckiest of us all."

I scoffed at him. "Oh, yeah. She's lucky to have doctors poke her and prod her for the next few months, running their EEGs and their MRIs. I called the neurologist Dr. Suriya referred me to, and she's on vacation, so we'll have to put the tests off for now. Besides that, Adam, Kaye's been labeled. She's been pushed in a nice little corner with her diagnosis, and now she can never really go anywhere. She'll probably never marry or have kids. We'll take care of her until we die. What happens after we die? Who will take care of her then?"

"She'll probably be able to take care of herself."

"Right."

"Did the doctor give you a definite prognosis that you haven't told me about?"

"No."

"So, you're assuming the worst." He looked at me with disdain, and lightning flashed through the curtains, highlighting the side of his face.

I sighed. He was right, of course. I was being negative. But I wasn't sure what else to do at that point. I didn't feel anything positive.

"Each of these kids is different, right? That's what the doctor said."

"Right."

"So how can you know anything until Kaye shows us who she is?"

"Adam, how can she show us who she is?" My voice rose. "She doesn't talk. She doesn't play with other kids. She can't sit still. What do we teach her, Adam? How do we teach her anything? Why take her to church even, when she doesn't understand anything we say!" I didn't mean to yell at him, but I grew more upset with each word I said, and my emotion got away from me. Soon I was crying, and the noise coming from my mouth didn't sound like my voice anymore.

Adam looked out the window as rain start to pelt the roof. "It's really coming down now," he said quietly. "Water's running down the gutters."

I took a deep breath and tried to stop sobbing, but all my efforts were worthless.

"You know what I like most about storms?" Adam asked. He didn't wait for me to answer. "The smell. And how clean the air is after they go by."

Lightning brightened his face again. His eyes were turned heavenward, as if he could see the source of the storm and feel the energy in the clouds above us. He seemed to love that awesome, raw power in the sky.

He closed the curtains and walked over to Kaye, who was still agitated. "You want to come snuggle with Daddy?" Adam blew on her bare belly and she giggled.

I scooted on the step so he could go past me. He stopped just above me on the stairs, and in a confident voice, he said, "Don't worry, Jen. The storm will pass."

I let him go upstairs without me, knowing it wouldn't be long before Kaye was back downstairs, expecting the TV to work so she could return to her midnight routine. I understood what Adam meant, but I didn't believe him. As long as Kaye had autism—which would be for the rest of her life—the storm would rage, and I'd be helpless against its power.

Chapter 13

SUNDAY

"Come on, honey. Get up. It's time to get ready for church."

I pried my eyes open. Adam hovered over me, tightening the knot in his tie. Birds were chirping outside, and the sun peeked through the large window behind the couch. I'd spent the night in the recliner, waiting for the storm to pass.

And the storm had passed. Adam opened the drapes to reveal a clean, glistening blue sky.

"See," he said. "Get up. It's a beautiful day."

I had a kink in my neck.

Adam had obviously bathed the girls. Marie's hair was pulled back in a clip, and it hung in damp curls to her shoulders. Kaye's hair was wild, sticking up as if Adam had dried it with a towel and given up.

"I don't want to go," I said.

Adam looked at me and smiled, then whispered. "Yes, you do."

I really didn't want to go. I wanted to sleep late into the day and let Adam deal with the girls. If he wanted to go, that was fine. I shook my head.

He knelt next to me and rested his hand on my belly. "How's my baby today?" he asked.

I had almost forgotten I was expecting again. "I can't feel him yet, so I don't know how he is."

Adam sighed. "Jen, please."

"Please what? Please pretend? Pretend that I feel good? Pretend that I can handle this?" I began crying softly, hoping Marie wouldn't see me. I felt a deep ache inside of me, like an open wound where my heart used to be.

He searched my face as if he were trying to understand me. I looked away. If he couldn't understand what I was going through, no one could.

"Please come to church with us." He rubbed my belly softly, then wiped a tear from my cheek.

"What's the point? I won't learn anything because I'll spend the whole time in the hall. I'm not taking Kaye to nursery, that's for sure."

"I'll spend the whole time in the hall."

"Then why don't you stay home?"

"Will you go if I stay home?" he asked.

I thought about it, then shook my head. I didn't feel well. I needed time to get better.

"Alright, then."

Adam had proven his point.

I rubbed my eyes.

"Should I lay out your clothes for you?" Adam asked.

I groaned and pushed myself from the recliner. All I wanted was a day off. I wanted to cry without anyone seeing me. I wanted to sit around in sweats all day and eat. Was that so bad? God would understand. The last thing I wanted was to run into Dani and her judgment, or Cathy and her questions. But since Adam wouldn't let it drop, I picked out my frumpiest dress and pulled it on, then flipped my hair back in a ponytail. That was the best I could do.

Adam took Kaye during Relief Society, and I sat in the back of the room looking around at all the women who didn't know me. I was distracted during the lesson, and when it was over I still wasn't sure what it had been about.

During Gospel Doctrine, I took Kaye outside immediately in an effort to avoid Dani. My efforts were in vain.

Dani led the nursery children on a nature walk around the church. Actually, it was more like a nature march. Her son, Steven, stood at the front of the line with one hand gripping the handle of a jump rope, and his other hand in Dani's grasp. The other nursery children lined up obediently behind Steven, holding to the rest of the jump rope. They looked horribly bored, though the sun shone bright around them and the grass beneath their feet was green and thick from the rain we'd received the night before.

"Okay, children. Let's keep the line, now. Steven's our leader today." She looked around with a satisfied sigh.

Kaye walked barefoot along the curb, keeping perfect balance as she placed one foot in front of the other. Adam had been smart enough to put a bodysuit on her that day, and she couldn't unsnap the clasps at her crotch, so she wasn't naked for a change, though her dress was folded in my lap.

"Don't get too close to the parking lot," Dani said, glancing at Kaye. "The parking lot is dangerous."

I looked around. We had the early schedule, and everyone who had to come to church that early was already there. If cars had been moving in the area, I wouldn't have taken Kaye out unless I'd wanted to hold her while she kicked and screamed, and since I was still supposed to be in bed as much as possible, I didn't want to carry Kaye unless absolutely necessary.

"Stay on the sidewalk until we get to that tree," Dani continued.

She gave me a too-perfect grin as they walked past. "Beautiful day, isn't it?"

"Yes, it is," I replied. "Taking the kids for a nature walk, huh?"

"It's the perfect day for it, don't you think? The sky is clear, and last night's rain has already dried up."

I nodded. I debated on voicing my thoughts about Dani's ducks all in a row, but I bit my tongue. The child at the end of the line looked back at Kaye as she paced along the curb, her bare toes clutching the cement. The poor little girl looked envious.

I couldn't keep it in anymore. "You should let them take their shoes off and run around in the grass. Let them experience nature, not just look at it."

She stopped and turned to me. "Very funny. I'm not about to let these kids take their shoes off."

I'd forgotten about the children taking their clothes off and streaking around the nursery, all because of Kaye's example. I tried not to grin.

"We had a terrible time figuring out which shoes went with which child, and we're not about to repeat that mistake." She looked at Kaye, as if to say it had been a mistake to let Kaye in the nursery in the first place. Her expression hurt me. Thankfully, Kaye was oblivious.

"You see, children, we should all learn from our mistakes and try our best not to repeat them. That's what Heavenly Father wants us to do. Come on. Follow me."

She resumed her walk toward a tree at the corner of the lawn. I could almost hear the whip crack over the little ones' heads. She was a prude, but I hoped she meant well.

I watched Kaye and thought of what Adam had said the night before. Maybe Kaye was better off. She seemed to be enjoying her life more than the other children. Kaye sang her trademark, sustained note, and smiled as she rotated her feet on the curb and walked back in the direction she had just come from. She was completely content walking back and forth on that curb—pleased by the simplest of things.

Of course, I remembered she was upset by the simplest of things, too, and I looked at the nursery children as they each picked a blade of grass to examine. Kaye loved being outside, and she loved being barefoot, but she hated the feel of grass on her bare skin. Kaye was easy to please as long as you followed her rules.

Soon, Dani looked at her watch and made the children stand and line up again, their little hands clutching the jump rope. They marched back into the church.

"Your parents will be coming soon. Let's go have singing time until they come." Dani didn't look at me as she walked past again, and I didn't mind.

When I figured it was time for sacrament meeting to start, I put Kaye's dress and sandals back on. Cathy was waiting for me in the foyer.

"How are you doing?" she asked.

I smiled, trying to look like all was right with the world. "I'm fine."

"That's not what Adam told me."

My smile faded, and I felt a bit betrayed. I looked into the chapel for Adam.

He was sitting on a pew at the side of the room, near the back, with his arm around Marie. His expression was resolute as he looked over his shoulder and his gaze met mine.

"Well, what did he tell you?" I let go of Kaye's hand so she would stop tugging me.

"He said that in the last ten days, you've found out you're expecting and Kaye's been diagnosed." Cathy grabbed my hand. "How are you holding up?"

I tried to be subtle as I wiggled free of her grasp. "Kaye got away from me. I've got to go find her."

"I'll go," Cathy offered.

"No," I said. "I'll get her."

I turned and walked in the direction I thought Kaye might have gone. Cathy followed me.

Each classroom we passed was empty. I began to wonder if Kaye could push open the outside door, even though it was quite heavy. When I reached the end of the hall, I turned around to head back to the foyer and start down another hall. Cathy was right there.

"Do you want to look down that hall, and I'll try the other side of the building?"

"I can find her by myself," I insisted. "I don't want to bother you."

"You'll find her faster with my help."

I felt pressure building up in me again until it came out in a barely restrained emotional burst. "Why won't you leave me alone?" I whispered through gritted teeth. Her brown eyes searched my face. I shifted my weight as she looked at me, and tried to ignore the spotlight that seemed to shine on me. I felt immediately apologetic. Cathy didn't deserve any lashes, but I'd scarred her twice. I tried to be firm, and explain my position as quickly as possible. "I can handle this alone."

Cathy took the hint and stepped back with a forlorn look. "Okay. But when you need me, you know where to find me."

I looked at the floor, feeling an odd twist in my stomach.

She turned and walked away, and I headed for the foyer again. The congregation in the chapel started singing, "Lord, I Would Follow Thee," and as Cathy entered the chapel, I turned down the hall. The music faded behind me.

By the time I found Kaye, I was crying again. Kaye had slipped into an empty classroom and was walking along the chairs, singing. I sat at the end of the row and looked around for a clock, but the walls were bare and white. If I'd had my scriptures with me, I might have opened them, but I probably wouldn't have read anything. All I wanted was sleep, so I listened to Kaye's voice reverberate on the white walls until I heard people in the hallway. Then I took Kaye out to the car, strapped her into her seat, and waited for Adam.

Cathy passed me as she started her walk home. Her eyes met mine for a moment, but she didn't say anything. My stomach twisted again. I hadn't meant to be rude—I just wanted to handle things myself. I didn't want to be a burden on anyone. I wanted to be in control. And I felt control—of the situation and of myself—slipping away.

The sun shone so bright after the night's storm that I closed my eyes and wished for a calm rain, with no lightning or thunder. Either that, or a long, dark night that I could sleep through. I didn't want sunlight. I just wanted to close my eyes and make everything fade away.

After waiting long enough that I was beginning to sweat, I saw Adam leave the church. I rolled my window down to see if there was enough of a breeze to make me more comfortable, but it was just as hot outside as it was in the car. Adam had Marie by the hand, and he was talking to a member of the bishopric as he left. I heard him say, "Okay. See you at three."

Adam helped Marie into the car, then sat next to me. "Hey. How come you didn't come in for the sacrament?"

"Because I didn't want to go in and have to turn around and go back out."

"I would have traded you so you could have heard the meeting. It was wonderful. You missed out."

With a sigh, I asked, "What did I miss?"

"I had a spiritual experience. My testimony was strengthened. That's what you missed. Yours might have been strengthened, too. And you could use a little strength."

I tried not to resent him for pointing out my weakness. After all, he was right.

He drove out of the parking lot and headed for home. As we pulled into our parking space, Adam looked at me. "We have a meeting with the bishop today at three."

"What for?"

"I just want to talk to him, that's all. We're going through a hard time, and we need some help."

I looked out the window. "Nobody can help us with this, Adam. So why bother him?"

Adam sat back in the car and closed the door. "Is that what you think? That no one can help?"

"How can he help, Adam? What can he do? He can't take our problems away."

"Well, for starters, he can give us spiritual advice. He can give us priesthood blessings, especially since your dad's not in town right now. The bishop can help us."

The mention of my father stabbed me. I wanted my family around me. I didn't want Brienne to move.

Adam looked resolute, but I doubted the bishop could do much to relieve our situation. He couldn't give us back the Kaye I'd expected to raise. He couldn't turn back time and help me figure out what I'd done wrong to put us in that position in the first place. Was it genetics? Was it something I ate or drank or breathed while I was pregnant with Kaye? Was there any hope for the child growing inside of me?

When I didn't respond, Adam got out of the car and released Marie's seat belt, then Kaye's. I followed the three of them into the house.

"Do I have to go with you, Adam?" I asked.

He looked at me with drooping eyes. "I guess not, but I'd rather you did."

I sighed.

"How about you rest for a while, and see how you feel?" Adam tried to grin.

I agreed to his proposal, and slipped into bed as soon as I could. I'd only have a couple of hours before the appointment with the bishop, and out of guilt I decided I would go. Those two hours of rest had to count.

I fell asleep thinking of Dani and her smug expression as she led her little ducks into the church, and I was vaguely aware of my gratitude that Kaye was my little duck, not Dani's.

* * *

Adam and I entered the bishop's office with Marie and Kaye in tow. The nap had done me some good, and I wasn't feeling as obstinate as I had that morning. But the second I walked into the bishop's office, I wondered why we were there. That doubt filled me again, and I felt like we were wasting each other's time.

Bishop Hean was young, with a full, clean-shaven face, and broad shoulders. His eyes were a tender light brown, and he looked at me with such sympathy that I felt an instant urge to confess my slightest sins. I wondered if that was part of his personality, or if it was because of his calling as bishop. I couldn't imagine why I hadn't paid attention to him before, even though I'd been in the chapel and seen him sitting on the stand several times.

He reached out and shook my hand, then offered us a seat.

"What can I help you with today?" He laced his fingers together on his desk. His hands were clean and his nails well groomed. I wondered what he did for a living.

Adam lifted Kaye onto his lap, and tried to hold her still. "Well, we're just going through a hard time right now, and we'd like some guidance."

"Okay." He smiled gently, as if to encourage us to give him more information.

"A couple of days ago, out little daughter, Kaye, was diagnosed with autistic spectrum disorder." As if on cue, Kaye squirmed and fought against her daddy's grasp.

Bishop Hean looked at Kaye and smiled again. "This little one?" he asked.

Adam nodded.

"Okay, and what can we do to help you with this?"

It was a good question. I looked at Adam with an expression that said, *I told you he couldn't help us.*

"Well, I've been thinking about it, and there are a couple of things that might make a difference." Adam finally let Kaye down, and Kaye went to the metal folding chairs lining the back of the room. She climbed up to walk along them. I stood to go and get her.

"She's okay," Bishop Hean said. "She can't hurt them."

I sat back down. Kaye's Sunday shoes clattered on the chairs, but the bishop ignored the noise and focused his attention on Adam's face.

"Go ahead," Bishop Hean said.

Adam nodded. "Well, we've lived in this ward for a year and we've never been contacted by home teachers. I work nights now, so my schedule will be difficult to work with, but I'd still like to have someone try, you know?"

Bishop Hean nodded. "Absolutely. I'm sorry you've gone that long without home teachers. That's not as it should be."

Adam nodded. "The other thing I've been thinking of is the possibility of getting Kaye her own Primary teacher. Nursery doesn't seem to be working for her."

The bishop looked a little concerned over that suggestion.

"See," Adam continued, "Jen and I miss our classes a lot because we're out with Kaye." Adam leaned forward as Kaye started singing as she walked along the chairs again. "I think we're starving, spiritually, and we need to go to our classes."

Bishop Hean's face softened again, and he nodded. "I'll talk to our Primary president. Do you know who she is?"

Adam and I shook our heads.

The bishop pulled out a ward list from the top drawer of his desk. "Do you have one of these?"

We shook our heads again.

He slid the phone list across the desk with a slight shake of his head. "I'm sorry you've fallen through the cracks. I've noticed a lot of this lately—many of our ward members have become complacent and stuck in their grooves. So I'm going to encourage you to attend all of your meetings. Shake the members up. Provide them with a challenge."

His pep talk made me chuckle. Was it a compliment to name us the ward challenge?

Adam was beaming. The bishop had apparently said just what Adam wanted him to say.

"We'll pray about you, and we'll find just the right person to work with your daughter."

"Thank you, Bishop." Adam took the bishop's extended hand and shook it vigorously. I shook his hand too, though with less enthusiasm. Adam took Kaye in his arms and I took Marie's hand.

The bishop opened his door for us, and we left. Adam had a wide smile on his face. "I feel better, how about you?"

"Well, that depends on who they find to be Kaye's Primary teacher. There's no guarantee she'll even be able to handle it, and we may end up pacing the hall anyway." I immediately thought of Cathy. She would be ideal. She'd already proven that she was willing and able to watch Kaye, and I felt comfortable with her, even though I didn't show it very well.

"The bishop said he'd pray about it, so they'll find the right teacher. I'm not worried." He loaded the girls into the car, unable to wipe the smile from his face.

Adam was so happy that he fixed dinner that night and let me relax on the couch. I had to admit he made good spaghetti.

When dinner was through, I called Brienne. It was her last full week in Salt Lake, so I planned to go to her house and help her pack, promising that I'd take it easy and not lift anything too heavy. We decided to plan a party to say farewell to Bri and her family, and to celebrate Kaye's third birthday, the next Tuesday afternoon, before Adam had to go to work at four. They would head out for D.C. following the party. So much change in such a short amount of time, and yet, the day had dragged by, one blistering hour after the other. As the sun finally set, I thought about what the bishop had said about us falling through the cracks, and I resented it. Why had we fallen through the cracks? Why, when we needed just as much as anyone else, had we become transparent?

I also thought of everything Adam had said. We were starving spiritually. I felt nothing positive, even with the bishop's offer to help us. Even though the day had been sunny, the storm had not passed for me. I felt like I was experiencing the winds before the storm. The front was just approaching.

Chapter 14

SISTERS

I dreamed that night. Steven clung to his mother, a bruise on his arm. She screamed at me about what a horrible mother I was—she said that I'd let my daughter bite her son and felt absolutely no remorse. But Dani didn't know how I felt. She couldn't know. Kaye didn't bite anyone else. I tried to get her to bite me, but she wouldn't. She kissed my arm gently. When Kaye wouldn't bite me, I decided to bite myself. It would be my penance for Steven's bruise. So I held my arm out and sunk my teeth in until the pain was almost unbearable. When I pulled away, my teeth marks were in Cathy's arm, not mine.

Sweat dampened my back when I awoke. I felt extreme guilt about what I'd done to Cathy. All she had ever tried to do was serve me, love me. Why was I pushing her away with such force? I knew myself well enough to know that I resented that I needed help, but why bite the hand that fed me?

* * *

I cleaned my house the next day and did a more thorough job than I'd done in months. I had too much energy, and no way to spend it that would satisfy me. Even when I was finished, the floors weren't clean enough. And Kaye had messed up the front room to nearly the state it had been in when I started cleaning. I looked carefully at the mess and found that she'd put the toys exactly where they had been when I picked them up. I'd left the room messy long enough that Kaye had come to believe that the toys were in their proper places—strewn across the floor. I was afraid she'd never let me clean again.

I called Brienne and apologized for nothing—just said I was sorry. Even as I spoke, I knew that Brienne wasn't the sister I needed to apologize to. She wasn't the sister I had hurt. I'd apologized to Dani, but she had ignored my peace offering. There was nothing more I could do with her. I didn't even know where to begin with Cathy. I thought of her most of the night, remembering the look on her face as she walked past me on her way home from church. With just a few words, I'd wounded her, maybe irreparably.

If I'd had a tail, it would have been between my legs when I called Cathy's phone number. But no one answered.

Chapter 15

GOOD-BYE

"I hope she'll like this," Bri said as she handed me the huge package.

"Bri, what did you do?" I hoped she hadn't spent too much money. We'd been together all afternoon, celebrating Kaye's birthday and torturing ourselves with a prolonged good-bye. Kaye wasn't interested in anything except blowing out the candles and eating the cake. Even the presents I bought for her—with money I didn't really have—didn't hold her attention for long. All the gifts had been opened except for Bri's, and I knew it was only a matter of minutes before my sister and her family loaded their Odyssey and began their four-day journey to Washington, D.C. I carried on normal conversations, but all I could think about was how far away Bri would be, and how alone I would feel.

"Kaye, come here." I said the words out of habit, hoping that someday they would mean something to Kaye. She was playing in the laundry room, walking back and forth along the top of the full-sized washer and dryer. "Get down, sweetie. Aunt Bri has a gift for you."

I lifted Kaye from the dryer. She eyed the gift as we went in the front room. I wondered if she liked the geometric shapes on the wrapping paper, or if she was more concerned about what was wrapped inside.

With a little help from me, Kaye tore the paper and opened the plain, brown box. Inside was another box with a bounce tent and balls to fill it with. Kaye glanced at the box, but played with the paper.

"Oh, Bri. She'll love this!"

"I have a pump in the car, but I didn't want to bring it out until you knew what the pump was for. It would spoil the surprise." She looked giddy as she ran to her van and got the pump. She plugged it in, and in a few minutes the front room was half filled with a five-foot-tall plastic tent with a huge air mattress on the bottom. The tent fascinated Kaye even before the balls were inside.

"How long do you think before she wears a hole in that thing?" I asked.

"You may have to let the air out and blow it up again in their bedroom, so you can see your TV." Bri laughed as she tore open the bag of balls and threw them in. Kaye squealed and her face lit up as the balls bounced with her. She sang and bounced until Marie and Emily couldn't resist anymore and joined her.

"They'll never leave the bedroom, then," I said.

"Well, that's not a bad thing. Maybe you can get some stuff done. You know, do something for you." Bri focused on me with a concerned expression. "I'm worried about you, you know."

"Don't be. I'll be fine," I lied.

We sat and watched the girls jump until they started to tire. At least, Marie and Emily got tired. Kaye kept jumping with fervor.

"Bri, she loves it."

"Good. I wasn't sure what to get her."

"Well, this was a stroke of genius."

Russ looked at his watch, then said, "It's already three. We'd better go."

Russ hugged me, then Marie, then gave Adam a solid slap on the back. Emily gave us all hugs, and Marie had a hard time letting go of her. I wondered if Marie understood just how long it could be before she saw her cousin again.

I walked Bri to the door, avoiding her glance. When I finally looked up at her, her eyes were wet. "We'll figure something out. We'll at least come here to visit you."

My vision blurred as I nodded.

"Will you be okay?" Bri asked.

I sniffed and took a deep breath, willing the tears in my eyes to dry. "Stop worrying about me. I'm supposed to be the big sister here. I should be worried about you going off to a new place."

Bri threw her arms around me. "We'll worry about each other, okay?"

I nodded because I couldn't speak.

Russ leaned out of the open window of his van and waved an envelope at Bri. She took it, then handed it to me. "I want you to have this. But don't open it until we're gone."

I took the envelope and gazed at Bri's curly handwriting.

"Take care of that baby," Bri pointed at my belly. "He needs you to be happy, you know."

My chin began to quiver. "I'll never have the money to come visit you." I hated good-byes. In fact, I doubted there was such a thing as a good parting with someone you loved.

"You will. And even if you don't, we'll work something out. Maybe just you?"

"Right." I chuckled. It would be impossible for Adam to get away from his responsibilities long enough for me to go to D.C. And how would Kaye react if I weren't home to sing to her at night? Even if Kaye didn't call me Mommy, or tell me she loved me, I was part of the scenery and she would miss me if I were gone.

Bri hugged me again, then climbed in her van. They all waved, and I saw Bri take a deep breath as Russ backed the Odyssey out of the parking space. I watched until they turned onto the street and turned south to head for the freeway.

Part of me wanted to cry. The rest of me wanted to clean the kitchen again until there wasn't a dirty speck in any corner. I opted to clean.

Adam met me in the hall and gave me a hug. "I love you."

"I love you too," I said. But I wanted to clean before I started to cry, so I pushed him away gently.

"What was in the envelope?" Adam asked.

I shrugged.

"Well, you've got to open it. If you won't, I will."

I was curious, so I didn't stop him as he slid a knife in and cut the envelope open.

He pulled out the letter and unfolded it. A small piece of paper fell to the floor. I picked it up. It was a receipt to the best preschool in town, with Marie's name on it. The amount paid was scribbled out, but I noticed that tuition had been paid in full for the coming year.

I sat down and let the tears come. "I can't believe her," I choked.

Adam read the letter aloud.

Dearest Jen,

*I love you so much, and I can't tell you how much I will miss you.
I plan on still calling you every week, so be prepared to answer the
phone when you see a D.C. area code. This little gift I have for
you has to count for Christmas and your birthday for the next
couple of years, but I want you to know how happy I am to be
able to give this to you. There is one condition to you accepting
this gift. Since Kaye will qualify for special ed, and Marie will be
in school six hours a week, you have to promise me that you will
use that time doing something for you. Don't clean the house—
unless you really want to. Don't pay the bills. Don't pick up the
dry cleaning or run dumb errands you can do while the kids are
with you. Find something that interests you and spend six hours a
week on it.*

Adam's eyes watered as he looked at me. "What did she do?"

I handed him the receipt. "Just what you think she did."

"Oh, my." Adam inspected the receipt then turned back to the
letter.

"I'll check in with Adam," I read aloud, "and if I find out you're not
spending that time on yourself, I'll never give you another gift again."

Adam laughed and looked up at me. "I'll tell on you, too."

I tried to think of something I'd do with time to myself, but I
couldn't think of anything. Thinking made me tired. I couldn't believe
Bri had given me so much. And I couldn't believe she was gone.

* * *

Aunt Olive called to wish Kaye a happy birthday. Adam had told
Olive about the diagnosis on Pioneer Day, back when I could barely
say the word "autism." When he answered the phone, I knew it
would come up; and when Olive asked to talk to me, I was crying
before I said hello.

"It's not so bad, is it?" she asked.

"Olive, it's the worst I've ever dealt with. Dr. Suriya gave me a
bunch of papers to read about autism, and her life expectancy is the

same as mine, but there's no guarantee she'll grow out of it at all. She may never be able to take care of herself." I sobbed. "What am I going to do?"

"Pray a lot. Go to the temple."

I didn't want to tell her I didn't have a temple recommend and hadn't paid my tithing for months. I couldn't go in. Besides, I wasn't sure prayer would do much good.

"Jen, can I tell you something I learned raising my kids?"

I dabbed at my eyes with a tissue. "Sure."

"Every one of them was God's child before they were mine. They're still God's children, He just trusted me with them for a while. And you know what? As much as I love my children, God loves them more. He gave them to me for a reason."

"So, why did God give Kaye to me?" I asked.

"I don't know. Why don't you ask Him?"

Because He won't tell me. I didn't speak my thoughts. Instead, I took a deep breath and willed my tears to stop.

"Have Adam give you and Kaye blessings. You'll feel better." Olive sounded tired.

"Thanks, Olive. I'll do that." I wiped a few remaining tears from my cheeks and tossed the damp tissue into the garbage. I wasn't sure a blessing would make a difference.

"Jennifer," Olive said. She never called me by my full name. She took a deep breath as if she had something important to say.

I waited.

"Can I tell you something really personal?" she finally asked.

"You can tell me anything."

"When I was in the car accident, I thought I was going to die. I remember the car rolling, and I looked down at my legs, but I couldn't feel them. I couldn't move my arms. I knew I'd broken my back, and I thought about what my family would do with me if I was stuck in a wheelchair—if they had to do everything for me. For a second, I wanted to die so they wouldn't have to go through that."

I couldn't imagine life without Olive, and I was glad she hadn't died.

"But," she continued, "I thought about my family gathering at a funeral to say good-bye to me. Billy was twelve then, and he was particularly attached to me. The look on his face tore me apart, and I decided I wasn't going to die because Billy needed me alive, no matter what kind of difficulties we'd have to go through.

"My point is—life is precious no matter what form it takes. You have to enjoy Kaye while you've got her, the way you've got her, because you never know what will happen."

I turned and looked at Kaye as she jumped in the bounce tent Bri had bought for her. Kaye laughed as her hair kissed her bare shoulders, then lilted in the air again.

"You should see her right now, Olive. She's so happy."

"Right! And you wouldn't trade those moments for anything, would you?"

I shook my head and whispered, "No."

"Good." Olive sounded genuinely relieved. "Well, hon, I've got to go. I've been really tired today."

"Thanks so much for calling."

"I wouldn't miss Kaye's birthday. Give her a hug for me, will you?"

"Will do."

"Olivejuice."

"Olivejuice." I smiled.

"Good-bye, hon," Olive said.

I hung up the phone and went to the bounce tent. Kaye was laughing so hard she had the hiccups. I chuckled at her, then motioned for her to come to me. When she didn't come, I climbed into the tent with her. She jumped around me, balls bouncing everywhere. I threw my arms around her and hugged her, smiling and tickling her the whole time. She let me hold her for a few seconds, then she pushed me away and continued jumping.

Those seconds were few, but they were fun. "I love you, Kaye. Happy Birthday."

Kaye sang her favorite note, and bounced until it was time for bed.

After we sang with the girls, I thought of Aunt Olive and realized with a twinge of guilt that I had hung up the phone without saying good-bye.

Chapter 16

SUPPORT

Brienne had been gone for a week and Adam had started his second night at his new job when I attended my first parent-support group meeting. Despite the fact that I didn't want to go, especially alone, I packed the girls into my Metro and we headed to the building near the University of Utah, where Kaye would hopefully start full-time school in the fall. Adam encouraged me to attend the meeting, and I knew he'd be upset if I didn't go. He said I needed as much support as I could get. The girls and I entered the old building and looked around with apprehension.

A few steps into the main hall, I heard the familiar sounds of children singing sustained notes, or screaming as if they were being tortured. A sign pointing to the right was taped to the white brick wall in front of me, so I obediently followed the arrow.

The parents were meeting in a small school library filled with beanbags and child-sized chairs. The teachers at the school were in a gym across the hall, and several children played on the padded equipment there. Some of the children spoke to the teachers. Other children pushed themselves around in little cars or sat contentedly in wagons. The biggest hit of the gym, the thing I was sure Kaye would head for as soon as I let go of her, was a small trampoline with a horizontal bar next to it so the children could jump and have something to hang onto. A teacher hovered near the trampoline, making sure each child got a safe turn.

I let go of Kaye's hand, and she headed straight for the trampoline. But, instead of pushing the other children off and demanding her turn as many children would have done, Kaye stood just behind the teacher, sang her favorite note, and rocked back and forth, watching the children through her dancing fingers.

Marie wrapped one arm around my leg. The room was noisy, and some children cried and boxed their own ears as other children added to the cacophony. "I want to stay with you," Marie said.

I put my arm around her sympathetically. I couldn't blame her.

A young teacher with brown hair and soft green eyes came over to Marie and me. A nametag, which read "Julie Coltan," hung around her neck.

She extended her hand to me. "Hi. I'm Julie. Are you new here?"

I nodded. "Dr. Suriya told me to come. He says my daughter's autistic."

Julie looked down at Marie, who clung to me even more.

"What's you're name?" Julie asked Marie.

"Oh," I interrupted. "This is Marie. She's not autistic. It's my other daughter, Kaye." I pointed to where Kaye was finally getting a turn on the trampoline.

Julie nodded. "How old is she?"

"She just turned three."

I put my arm around Marie and held her close. I was feeling more and more uncomfortable in this room of screaming children. A little boy walked past us with a distant expression on his face. I looked at Marie, who had scooted behind me.

"Austin, hands out, please." Julie touched the boy's right arm near his elbow, and the boy quickly obeyed. "Each of these kids has a repetitive behavior," she said to me. "Some of them are more embarrassing to us than others. I'm sure your daughter does something repeatedly to calm herself down or show you when she's excited."

I nodded in Kaye's direction. She had stepped off of the trampoline, but she still hovered behind the teacher, wiggling her fingers together.

"Oh, that one's not bad. Some of the kids bite themselves. I've got one student who's only four years old, and she has horrible scars on her hands because she won't stop biting them, no matter what we do."

The children weren't reacting to each other like normal children would. In fact, they weren't interacting at all. They were each involved in their own game, in their own world—separated by a lack of understanding and communication. I had to concentrate on Julie's kind eyes to keep from turning and bolting from the room.

Julie bent down and looked Marie in the eye. "Would you like to come and play with me so your mom can go to a very important meeting with other moms and dads?"

Marie shook her head.

"Are you sure? There're lots of toys to play with. And there are some other kids here who would love to play with you. Kids who have brothers or sisters just like your sister."

"There are other siblings here?" I asked.

Julie nodded. "Sure."

I looked down at Marie. "What do you think?"

Marie wrapped her arms around my leg and looked up at me, her eyes begging me not to leave.

Julie turned and called, "Veronica, would you like a new friend?"

A pretty little girl with black hair and dark skin, a baby doll in her arms, ran to Julie's side. She looked like she was about five years old.

"This is Marie," Julie said.

"Hi." Veronica smiled.

"Hi," Marie said. Her grip on my leg eased.

"Want to play dolls?" Veronica extended her toy to Marie, who took it gratefully and smiled up at me, just to say she was okay.

Julie and I watched the girls run away and disappear behind a group of children who sat on the ground tearing wrappers off of several crayons.

"We'll watch your girls. Go and meet the other parents." Julie smiled.

As I walked across the hall to the library, I couldn't help but feel disappointed. Part of me had hoped Marie wouldn't want to play with the kids so I could have someone at my side, or an excuse to leave.

I crossed the hall to the library and slipped into a seat near the back of the room. The other parents filtered in; some seemed strong and happy, while others looked how I felt—scared and unsure. Many mothers came in by themselves. Others came in with a husband close behind.

A tall, blond woman started the meeting and introduced the speaker. The library was almost full.

The speaker was a speech therapist for the school, and she held up a binder with strips of Velcro on the cover. She went on to describe the small pictures she stuck onto the strip of Velcro, making sentences like "I want bathroom." I paid little attention to what she was saying, though I thought the idea was a good one. Kaye might recognize pictures easier than mere words.

After the speaker finished, the parents separated into three different groups, each with a counselor. I was almost ready to go home, but one of the counselors stopped me. He was probably close to my age, not much taller than me, and he looked Middle Eastern. He had an employee ID hanging around his neck which read Theo Kaleel.

"You're not missing the best part, are you?" he asked.

"Is this the best part?"

"I think so. It helps to be able to express your concerns and ask questions. We're here to help you. Take advantage of that."

He looked so sincere, I couldn't turn my back on him. But I sat in the seat closest to the door so I could make a discreet exit if I felt the need.

The parents all sat in a circle so they could face each other. Theo took out his pad of legal paper and started the catharsis. "Who would like to go first?"

A petite woman with a white scar across her cheek raised her hand. "I'll start." She sighed. "I need a new way to deal with my son in the grocery store."

Several other parents groaned. Apparently, difficulty shopping was a side effect of having an autistic child, and parents besides me suffered from it.

"I am so sick of people staring at us! Trenton insists on putting cereal in the cart. I can handle getting him out of the cart and letting him do that—he calms down while he's loading box after box. The problem is that he has a fit when I get him to stop. He could fill the cart if I let him. I always go down the cereal aisle very last so we can keep the screaming to a minimum. But even then, people stare at us all the way out the door."

"Us too," a heavyset woman near the front of the room spoke up. "One time, Cameron screamed so loud, I swear the whole store stopped everything to turn and look. I told the cashier that my son was autistic, and the cashier looked so embarrassed for me. I'm not embarrassed. He's my son, and I love him. No, I'm not embarrassed. I'm angry."

The group nodded. A short woman sitting next to Theo spoke up. "Sometimes I wish my son had a physical disability, so people could tell just by looking at him that he was disabled. Then they wouldn't have such impossible expectations for him. Not only is he struggling, but he's got the stigma of having a mental illness, and that hurts my other children, too."

Everyone agreed, and I thought of Marie.

"So," Theo said, "any suggestions for these women? From what I hear, dealing with autistic children in public situations is one of the most difficult things you face."

A tall man with sharp eyes raised his hand.

"Yes, Dan."

"I've got a friend who runs a T-shirt printing shop, and I had him print shirts for my wife and me that say 'My child's autistic, what's your problem?'"

The parents laughed, and I couldn't help but join in.

"I'll order more, if anyone here wants one. I think ours were fifteen dollars."

Several parents raised their hands.

"Another thing you could do," Theo suggested after the clamor had died down, "is take several pamphlets from the school and hand them out to people. I think the key is education. If people know more about the disorder, they are more likely to be understanding of it."

It seemed to me that people should be less judgmental in the first place. I saw complete strangers every day, and didn't have to know about their personal lives in order to keep myself from staring at them. I felt like I shouldn't have to publicize Kaye's diagnosis in order for her to be treated with kindness.

"How is Trenton dealing with the divorce?" the heavyset woman asked.

The woman with the scar on her face sighed. "Trenton isn't doing well. We've been trying that PECS program Elly was talking about, and Trenton keeps saying 'I want Dad.'"

Everyone let out a sympathetic groan.

Trenton's mother sniffed. "And it would be fine if I had a fortune, but now I've got to work and support him by myself. Sometimes it feels impossible. If it weren't for this school, I don't know what I'd do."

Heads nodded as the whole circle murmured their agreement.

"Well," Theo said, "just remember that any of you can come talk with me at any time. One free session a month."

I wondered if visiting with Theo would help. I pictured his office with a couch, dim lights, and a ceiling fan. No matter what I imagined his office to be like, no matter what I imagined he would be like, I couldn't imagine me opening up to him and telling him about my weaknesses, faults, and fears.

More than ever, I wanted Adam with me, and if I couldn't have him at my side, I at least wanted to be home, where he lived. I snuck out of the room and went to get Marie and Kaye. We drove home as quickly as I could safely go, and I felt a rush of relief, then a twinge of fear as I saw his Saturn in his parking space. He'd just started the night shift; he shouldn't have been home.

When we entered the apartment, Adam was on the phone. He looked up at me with red eyes.

"I know, Dad. I wish you would stay here." He shook his head. "I want you to stay here. No. Jen and I can sleep on the sofa bed."

"Your parents are coming for a visit?" I whispered.

Adam held up one finger to ask me to wait.

If his parents were coming for a visit, something major must have happened.

"Billy wants me to call everyone else in our family, Dad. Yeah, I'd better go."

I hoped they were just planning an impromptu family reunion.

He hung up the phone and put his arms around me. I felt his breathing stop for just a moment.

I backed away, knowing by then that something was seriously wrong. "Adam?"

"Olive had a heart attack today, Jen." He wiped his eyes. "She's gone."

My legs seemed to give way under me, and I sat hard on a kitchen seat.

"Her funeral is Tuesday, so everyone can have a chance to get here. I invited Mom and Dad to stay with us." Adam held the phone loosely in his hand, looking tired and shocked.

I stood up again and put my arms around him. I wasn't sure it would help us to have his mother under our roof, but she was family, and I knew it was important to Adam to have her come to Olive's funeral.

"Olive said she'd get your mom in an LDS chapel." I chuckled, though nothing felt funny. In fact, I felt as though life was pushing in on me, and there would be nothing to keep it from enshrouding me in darkness. Adam was all I had left. I held him close to me. For some reason I couldn't cry, but Adam could. His tears wet my hair, and he kissed my head.

"Do you want me to make the phone calls?" I asked.

He took a deep breath and shook his head. "I'll do it. I just need a minute."

I let go and he sat at the kitchen table.

"Will you pray with me?" he asked. We prayed together almost every night, and basically said the same thing in every prayer. But I consented and sat at the table with him. He took my hand and bowed his head.

He prayed for strength, for understanding, and for the ability to see and follow God's will. Many of the words were familiar, but his tone of supplication was so intense that I had to open my eyes and look at his face. His eyes were shut tight, and he furrowed his brow. Olive's death had hurt him at a time when we were already suffering. In his pain, Adam turned to God.

I wanted to turn to God too, but I wasn't sure how. It was as if the pillars of my strength had fallen between Him and me, and there seemed to be no way to erect them. I felt unstable, like a roof with no crossbars, a tent with no support.

We ended our prayer, and I tucked the girls into bed and sang with them. Only after I was alone in my bed, listening to the sound of Adam's voice as he broke the news to his siblings, did I feel hot tears in my eyes. Oddly, Kaye seemed extra happy that night. She giggled in the dark until Marie cried in an exasperated voice for Kaye to be quiet. It made it worse to have Kaye apparently so happy. I had to remind myself that she just didn't understand.

Neither did I.

Chapter 17

VIEWING

Monday afternoon, Adam's parents showed up at our back door driving a rental car. Blanch wore a delicate scarf over her short brown hair and tied beneath her chin. She loosened the tie at her neck as she entered the house, greeted me coolly, and looked me up and down.

"Well, I see you're eating well."

"Hello, Blanch. How was your drive?" I asked cheerily, and I put on my brightest, fakest smile.

"This happens with every vacation. Tim rents a convertible and takes the top down. Makes for a horrid ride. Do I have bugs in my teeth?" She flashed an exaggerated smile. Her teeth were aging a little, but they were probably whiter than mine.

I shook my head. "No bugs."

"Hallelujah."

She walked past me and set her suitcase down in the middle of the kitchen floor. Then, it was time for inspection. I half expected her to put on a white glove. Blanch walked to the sink and turned on the water, apparently just to make sure it worked. Then she opened the cupboard where my storage containers were kept. Luckily, I'd expected it and spent the day before straightening everything and scrubbing floors and carpets on my hands and knees.

"I like what you've done with the apartment, Jen."

She must have seen the surprise on my face.

"Well, I know there's only so much you can do in an apartment unless you want to forfeit your deposit."

I bit my tongue.

"So, did you pass?" Tim, Adam's father, asked. He walked through the door with his suitcase and a garment bag in hand. His face was rough and sun-worn, but kind. His green eyes glinted as he took off his sunglasses and slipped them in the pocket of his shirt.

"I think so," I said.

Tim threw his arms around me. "It's good to see you, Jen."

I hugged him back. "It's good to see you."

Adam joined us in the kitchen and picked up his parents' bags. "Hey, you guys. You're early."

"I think your father went ninety the whole way here." Blanch glared at Tim.

Tim led me to the window to look at his borrowed toy. "Wouldn't you go ninety in a car like that?"

Adam nodded and mouthed the words, "Yes! At least ninety!" when he was sure his mother couldn't see.

"Where are my granddaughters?" Blanch called as she ventured into the front room. "I only see pictures of these girls lately, and I need to kiss them!"

"Marie, come kiss your grandma!" Adam called up the stairs.

Marie bounded down the stairs and stopped near the bottom step, a quizzical look on her face. I wondered if she thought we meant my mother instead of Adam's.

"Oh, there's a big girl. Is this my Marie?" She beckoned for Marie to come into Grandma's waiting arms. Marie came slowly, and when Blanch finally got hold of her, it took two seconds before Marie's cheek was covered with brick-colored smudges.

She set Marie down and looked up the stairs. "And where's little Kaye?"

I looked at Adam.

"I'll go get her," he said.

I moved the suitcases to the corner of the room where they wouldn't get in the way and wondered if I should prepare Adam's parents for the news of Kaye's diagnosis. I wasn't sure how they'd take it. I hadn't taken it well, so I couldn't expect them to.

Adam came down the stairs with Kaye in his arms. I'd put her hair up in pigtails, but she'd pulled them out and her long hair was frazzled. It needed to be cut so badly, I could barely see her eyes. She was only wearing her diaper.

"Did she just wake up?" Blanch said, looking right at me.

"Um, no," I said. It was the middle of the afternoon. Normal kids Kaye's age might be getting up from naps around that time.

"Well, why isn't she dressed?" Blanch asked.

"She doesn't like clothes," Adam said cheerfully.

"Well neither do I, but you don't see me running around in my underwear."

"Blanch, please," Tim said. "She's just a baby." He tried to take Kaye from Adam's arms, but she squirmed away from him and headed toward the laundry room.

"Looks like you need to teach that one some manners," Blanch said to me, raising her penciled eyebrows.

I cleared my throat and looked at Adam. "Yeah. She doesn't listen very well."

"She's autistic, Mom." Adam went straight to the point. I had to admire him for that. At least he wasn't dragging it out.

"Autistic?" She looked at Adam. "No, she's not autistic." She turned away from Adam and headed into the front room, patting her starched hair.

"Could you get me something to drink, Jen dear?" she asked as soon as she was comfortable. "Do you have any diet soda?"

Adam had bought a six-pack just for the occasion. "Yeah. I'll be right back." I was grateful to have an excuse to leave the room.

"Spend some time with her, Mom. You'll see it." I heard Adam's insistent, quiet voice from the front room as I clinked ice cubes into a glass and opened the soda can.

"I've seen autistic kids on TV. They're retarded. My granddaughter's not retarded."

"Blanch!" Tim scolded.

"What? A kid has a couple of bad behaviors and people say they're autistic or they've got ADD. It's an excuse. She needs discipline, that's all. I bet it's because you dote on her too much. You spoil her." Her voice dropped to almost a whisper, but I could still hear her. "That wife of yours isn't organized enough. I told you not to marry her, didn't I?"

At least I knew where Adam got his directness from. I tossed the empty pop can in the recycle bin just a little too hard and it bounced against the rim and out to the floor. After picking it up, I plastered that fake smile on my face and took Blanch's drink to her. I was tempted to pour it on her, but I handed it to her instead.

"There you go."

"Thank you, dear." Her face was flushed, but she acted as if she hadn't slandered me only moments before.

"Jen met with a child psychologist a couple of weeks ago, Mom. I can show you his diagnosis if you'd like."

"A lot of good that would do. You know I've never believed in psychology."

"Gee, no wonder we all could use some therapy," Tim said.

I loved that man.

Blanch scowled at her husband. "Quit trying to be funny, it's not your forte."

Tim looked at me with his mouth hanging open and I grinned, just enough that he could see, then I looked pointedly at my shoes.

"Mom, I'm sure some kids are diagnosed when they don't need to be, but Kaye really is autistic."

"How can you tell the difference? A few years down the road, she starts reading and talking like normal, so you just decide the doctors were wrong? Don't be naive, Adam. If something like that happens, you've still got that 'diagnosis' on her permanent record and she'll always be treated like she's retarded."

"Will you stop saying that word?" Tim pleaded.

"Come on, call a spade a spade," she retorted.

I stared at Blanch, but she avoided looking back at me and focused her eyes on Adam. "He's gotten so politically correct lately."

I looked at Adam as if to say, *You invited them here. You deal with them.*

He caught my expression and shrugged.

"Well," I said. "I think I'll get started on dinner. It'll be easier to eat before the viewing rather than after."

"I'll help," Tim said. He rose from his seat next to Blanch and joined me in the kitchen.

"I'm sorry about Blanch," Tim said when we were alone. I heard Adam in the next room, listing Kaye's symptoms and behaviors, and telling Blanch about the testing Kaye had been through.

"It's okay," I said. "I'm not sure what to think of all this either. I'm not sure she's autistic, to tell you the truth."

"What makes you doubt?" he asked.

"Well, she's so cute when she wants to be. The other day, she was watching Marie dance around the front room—I was playing a CD with a bunch of children's songs on it—and Kaye was laughing and clapping her hands. She snuggles with me and with Adam, especially when she's tired. She gives us kisses at night. From what I've heard so far, a lot of autistic kids aren't affectionate. I don't know, Tim. She seems so *aware* of some things."

"But unaware of other things?"

I nodded. "She screams. A lot. Sometimes it's like having a newborn. She screams and we check her diaper. If that doesn't work, we try to feed her. If that doesn't work, we put in a movie. It's all trial and error. One time, she screamed and screamed until I finally gave up. I turned around and saw that a picture on the wall was crooked, so I straightened it. She stopped screaming."

Tim raised his eyebrows.

"Yeah. How am I supposed to keep up with that?"

"I don't know, Jen. That's definitely a tough one."

I started pulling tomatoes and onions from the fridge and took a Kosy Kitchen knife from the wooden case in the corner of my counter. I sliced the tomatoes thin.

"You're pretty good at that."

"I did cooking shows, a long time ago."

"Before the autism?"

"Yeah. In my life, everything is either before autism, or after autism—B.A. or A.A. instead of B.C or A.D."

Tim chuckled and washed his hands so he could help me prepare dinner. "Well, for me everything is before Blanch and after Blanch. Don't ask me which I prefer, or I'll get myself in trouble. Sometimes I wish Catholics supported divorce." He grinned to let me know he was exaggerating his misery and kidding about divorce.

I laughed. I knew for certain which phase of my life I preferred.

After we set the table and helped the girls into their seats, Adam bowed his head to pray. Blanch sat with her head upright until Adam was done, then she put the palms of her hands together and said, "Bless us, oh Lord, for these Thy gifts, which we are about to receive. From Thy bounty through Christ our Lord, Amen."

Tim whispered a quiet, "Amen."

I looked at Adam.

"Amen," Adam said aloud. "Now we're twice blessed. And we can use all the blessings we can get." Adam passed the salad to his mother.

She took the bowl with a slightly disappointed expression, as if she were hoping her prayer would cause contention and Adam's gratitude had foiled her plans.

"We have some good news," Adam said.

"Oh, good," Tim beamed. "I could use some good news."

"We're expecting another baby." Adam looked at me from across the table and smiled.

Blanch stopped in mid-bite and looked at me. "Really?"

I nodded.

"How are you going to deal with a baby and an autistic daughter?"

I looked at Adam.

"We'll deal with it just fine," he answered.

Blanch grunted and started shoveling food into her mouth again. She spoke before she was done chewing. "Don't get me wrong, I'm all for big families. We would have had more children if we could have, but Adam tore my insides apart."

Tim shook his head. "Not at the dinner table, dear."

"I just worry that if Kaye is autistic, you won't be able to handle the demands of a large family." Blanch looked right at me.

"Adam is wonderful with the girls. You should see how much they love their daddy." I tried to praise her by praising her son, hoping that would take me out of her line of fire.

"I'm sure. But Adam can't shoulder all the responsibility, can he? I wouldn't want you sending my son to an early grave."

"Mom, stop it," Adam said. "We're a partnership, and we will do just fine with as many children as the Lord sees fit to bless us." Adam reached beneath the table and put his hand reassuringly on my knee. "Now, how about I read the talk I'm giving at the funeral? You can give me pointers."

I was grateful for Adam's diversion, but my appetite had fizzled. I picked at my food while everyone finished dinner, then I cleaned the dishes as Adam took his parents to the front room. I didn't say a word the rest of the afternoon and avoided eye contact with Blanch unless it was absolutely necessary.

I refused to let her see me cry.

* * *

Adam held Kaye in his arms and I held Marie's hand as we walked toward Olive's stake center. The parking lot was full of people who loved Aunt Olive—friends who had hiked with her, students she'd had for physical education, as well as the extended family. One man showed up wearing leather and riding a Harley, a long ponytail cascading down his back. It seemed that Olive got along with everyone except her own sister.

Tim helped Blanch from the passenger seat. She clung to his arm, looking extremely uncomfortable, and made sure the gold crucifix around Tim's neck was outside of his shirt. "I want the Mormons to know you're taken." She gave Adam and me a sidelong glance.

I remembered that Olive had said she'd get Blanch into a Mormon church before she was "six feet under." I chuckled as Blanch entered the building just ahead of me. Olive had officially accomplished her goal.

"Adam," I whispered. "What really caused the rift between your mom and Olive? Was it just because you joined the Church?"

Adam shook his head. "It started long before that. Olive was raised Catholic too. In fact, she and my mom were really close. She met Scott at an NCAA basketball tournament, and they fell for each other and kept in contact through the mail. Olive came to BYU to finish her degree. She ended up joining the Church and marrying Scott. I think my mom felt betrayed by their relationship—it was like Scott took her away in every way he could."

"And then the same thing happened with you."

Adam nodded. "She's not very fond of Mormons and missionary work. She thinks we're out to take over the world."

"Well, we're out to convert the world. There's a difference. Besides, everyone has their own choice, no matter what. We don't exactly *like* it when people become Mormons for the wrong reasons."

Adam shrugged. "She just doesn't understand."

I watched Blanch ahead of us as she continued to cling to Tim. She glanced around her at the lines of people, then said something to Tim that I didn't catch. Tim patted her hand, and I heard him say, "We won't stay long. But you need to say good-bye."

"Tim, there's Martha!" Blanch patted Tim's arm as Martha, Adam's older sister, ran to Blanch with her arms open wide. "Martha, I had no idea you were coming!"

"I couldn't stay away, Mom. I knew you'd be here, and Daddy and I decided I'd surprise you."

Blanch looked at Tim with moist eyes. "You sweet thing!"

Tim shrugged.

"Hey, Martha," Adam said.

"Hey, little brother." There was a pause. "Jen." She gave me a curt nod. I was sure she'd heard so many negative comments about me from Blanch that no matter what I said or did, I would be unworthy.

"Hi, Martha. It's good to see you again." I extended my hand and she took it with a weak shake. Martha was a carbon copy of her mother, but a little more contemptuous, if possible.

"Expecting again, are you?" She looked at my belly.

I was barely showing. In fact, she was the first person to say anything. For a moment, I wondered if she was trying to offend me in case I was just overweight. "This will be our third," I said, and I watched her face for a look of disappointment.

Instead, I got a look of surprise. "Already? How long have you been married now? Six years?"

I nodded and looked her in the eye. "Six years this month. I figure, why waste time? Life is short."

"Look, there's Billy," Adam said, relief audible in his voice.

Billy was Olive's son, and since he was Adam's age, he'd been an integral part in Adam's conversion. In fact, Adam was the first person Billy had baptized. Billy stood near the door to the room where Olive's casket was laid out. He made sure people signed the guest book, and he embraced many people as they shared their condolences. His magnanimous smile put everyone at ease, and the guests ended up crying more than he did. He had an aura about him. He was comforting—the kind of person you wanted to be around and missed as soon as he walked away. He was a lot like Olive.

"Adam!" Billy walked toward us with outstretched arms. Adam handed Kaye to me so he could accept Billy's embrace, but I wasn't ready for her. She squirmed from my grasp and slipped through the crowd, wiggling between Tim and Blanch toward the viewing room.

"Oh, Kaye," I muttered.

She was small, and she found a way through the tall legs and the skirts that surrounded her.

"Excuse me," I said as I inched past the crowd, focusing on Kaye and praying silently that she wouldn't do anything crazy. I caught Blanch glaring at me, but I turned away from her, deciding she could think what she wanted to think. I was doing my best.

Between the shoulders of the people waiting in line, I caught glimpses of Kaye as she reached the casket. Her blond head was inches away from the foot of the dark-stained wood. She stretched out her little hand and touched the shiny surface.

My heart seemed to stop right then, and I held my breath. What if she tried to climb on it, or climb through the stand that held up the coffin?

She didn't scream, and she didn't laugh—the other two inappropriate things I expected her to do. Instead she began to walk slowly up the length of the casket, keeping her hand against the wood. Then, when she reached the head of the casket, she turned around and walked back toward the foot. I was almost to her. I'd have to pick her up and take her kicking and screaming from the room. Then her little face turned up to the white satin lining that puffed out where the casket was open.

Kaye was crying. Not screaming the tearless scream that so often drove me insane, but crying real tears, as if she were in pain. I stopped and stared at her, trying to remember a time when she'd cried for an emotional reason. It had been quite a while.

Kaye pressed her other hand against the casket and continued to look up at the satin. Her face twisted with sadness, and tears wet her cheeks.

Adam stopped at my side and we stared at her together.

"She knows what's going on," he said.

I couldn't explain it, but everyone around her stopped to watch the scene. It was as if the child before us was showing all the grief the adults around her felt, but couldn't express. Uncle Scott walked up to Kaye and lifted her. She let him. She didn't squirm or fight to get away.

"Do you want to say good-bye, Kaye?" Scott said. He looked at Kaye with wonder as she gazed into the casket at Aunt Olive's still face for a moment, and her tiny sobs sounded through the virtual silence of the once noisy room.

She looked at Olive and said, "Juice, juice, juice." Then, she wiggled her fingers in her line of sight. She stopped wiggling and looked up.

Kaye was looking straight at Blanch, whose nose had turned red.

"Juice," Kaye said.

Then, just as suddenly as it had happened, it was over. Kaye stopped crying and squirmed from Scott's grasp. She ran away from him, toward an open door that led out to the parking lot.

I hurried after her and caught her before she reached the sidewalk. Adam and his cousin Billy weren't far behind.

None of us could say anything. I picked Kaye up and held her close, and Adam held both of us. Her moment of connection was over, though, and she kicked against us until we put her down.

"Is this the autistic one?" Billy asked.

Adam nodded.

I couldn't stop crying. It was as if Kaye's simple act of crying over our aunt had unstopped the emotions I'd bottled up since Adam had told me the news. In an instant, I remembered my last phone call with Olive, the last hours we spent with her, her love for us, and her incredibly timely words of wisdom. I wondered if somehow she'd known her days were few. I wondered if Kaye understood what she'd done in that room—if she had some sort of connection with Aunt Olive that I couldn't see or understand. Kaye was amazing at that moment, and I looked at her with wonder.

"Well," I said, "now we know what 'juice' means."

* * *

We met Adam's parents in the parking lot. Kaye was already strapped into her car seat, and Marie was playing on a patch of grass in front of the car.

Tim came straight for me and put his arms around me. His kind face was still wet. "I don't care if she's autistic or not," he said in my ear, "that was the most beautiful thing I've seen in years."

"It was, wasn't it?" I smiled and looked over Tim's shoulder at Kaye. She seemed so content there, hugged by the straps of her car seat. I had a different view of her then. Adam's father had been touched in a way that he might not have if Kaye hadn't gone to the viewing, and for the first time in months, I was glad I'd taken Kaye somewhere.

Blanch barely looked at me as she got in the Mustang. She tied her scarf around her hair and strapped on her seat belt.

"Dad, is Mom okay?" Adam asked.

Tim looked at me, then at Adam. "Who knows? No one expected that. It was almost like Olive was telling Blanch she loved her, don't you think?"

Adam's face brightened, and he nodded.

"I doubt she knows what to think about it," Tim said. "She hasn't said anything since you chased Kaye out of the room."

I wasn't sure, either, what to think about what had happened with Kaye, or about Blanch's reaction. Blanch looked almost afraid—avoiding my eyes as she looked around, waiting to leave.

We drove home, feeling much better about things with Olive than we had earlier that day. We were sad about losing her, of course, but talking to Scott and their children had filled us with hope and comfort. And seeing Kaye react the way she had made me feel like Olive had somehow helped to show us something in Kaye we'd never seen before—a potential I'd given up on. I felt so good that night, I was even okay with the thought of Kaye being autistic.

That night in the canyon, Olive had sat on the ground next to Kaye and eaten our picnic under the stars. As I thought of that night, and the way Olive was willing to go to Kaye when Kaye wasn't willing to go to her, I felt a deep sense of gratitude for the aunt who had shown me how to love my daughter. Maybe Olive was still watching over us—like an angel—trying to guide me, and trying to help Kaye in ways that I couldn't.

When we got home, Tim and Blanch were waiting for us in the parking lot. As soon as the back door was unlocked, Blanch zipped past Adam and felt along the dark hallway for the stairs that led to the bedroom.

"Hey, Mom, need a light?" Adam flipped the living room switch.

Blanch ran up the stairs without looking over her shoulder.

Tim followed her at a much slower pace.

"Dad, what's going on?" Adam asked.

"She wants to stay at a hotel."

Adam held his hands out plaintively. "Why?"

"She says she's uncomfortable here."

That wasn't enough for Adam. He pushed past his father despite Tim's cautions. In moments, Adam and his mother were yelling at each other, and Kaye was screaming at the contentious air. Blanch hurried down the stairs with her bag partially packed.

"I just want to stay in a hotel, alright?"

"This is the first time in almost a year that you've even seen my children, and you want to leave so quick? What did I do to offend you, Mom? Tell me so I won't make such an *egregious* mistake again."

"Don't get sarcastic with me. You're always talking about a Plan of Happiness. 'The gospel is the Plan of Happiness. The gospel makes me happy, Mom. Betraying you makes me happy, Mom!'" she sassed.

"I didn't betray you! I've never betrayed you! I just chose to live my life differently."

"You left me." She nailed Adam to the wall with her eyes. "You left me when I needed you, and you didn't even ask about us, you didn't even . . ." She took a deep breath and closed her eyes. Then she turned her anger on me. "You married that thing so she could ruin your life. And now she's ruined your children."

The words stung, and listening to Kaye scream as Adam and his mother fought hurt just as badly. "You're upsetting her," I warned, glaring pointedly at Blanch.

"Well, she's upsetting me." Blanch pushed past Tim and headed for the back door. She set her suitcase down and flung the door open, then picked up the luggage again and left the door ajar.

"How is Kaye upsetting *her*?" I asked Tim.

Tim shrugged. "I'll find out. I'll get back to you." He touched Kaye's head gently, then followed Blanch through the kitchen.

"Kaye, it's alright," I soothed. But she wouldn't hear me. I felt the tension too, and such anger that I wanted to lash out at Blanch and ban her from any contact with anyone I loved. What had I done to hurt her? To calm Kaye, and hopefully calm myself as well, I started singing, "I Am a Child of God."

"You are such a coward!" Adam followed Blanch as she stumbled up the stairs for more of her things. His voice cracked as he shouted at her. "You felt something at the viewing. You back away every time you feel something you can't explain. You can't even tell if what you're feeling is good or bad! If it's new, you won't take the time to try to understand it."

"Don't you tell me how I feel," Blanch yelled back. I rolled my eyes, imagining what the neighbors were thinking of our public family drama. "I know how I feel, and I am unwelcome here." She pushed past him again with her makeup bag and purse.

"Well you are *now!*" Adam bellowed.

Blanch left the house and slammed our gate behind her. Tim stood at the back door with Blanch's suitcase in hand, and he looked at me apologetically. Then he looked at Adam as he walked out. "You're just like her, you know. That's why you never got along."

I picked Kaye up and tried to sing softly into her ear. I rocked back and forth with a screaming, crying Kaye in my arms, and Marie huddled close to me, trying to sing the song too.

"I'm nothing like her! My mother's insane and my father's whipped!" Adam yelled at the closing door.

His expression was so angry that I felt a twinge of fear. He looked at me and melted before my eyes. Soon our family cried in each other's arms, feeling alone again, and misunderstood.

Eventually, Kaye calmed down. We sang several songs as we tucked the girls into bed that night, and the music helped all of us.

We shut the girls' bedroom door and went to bed. Adam seemed weak and exhausted. We turned out the lights and lay in the dark. I was almost asleep when Adam whispered, "I can't believe her."

I couldn't believe it, either. Mostly because I couldn't understand it. "What did I do to her?" I asked.

"It was one thing for me to get baptized," Adam said, "and it was one thing for me to go on a mission. But when I married you in the temple—in a place where she couldn't even go—it was like my fate was sealed. She knew it wasn't a phase. She knew I wouldn't back out. She lost me, just like she lost Olive. Maybe all that today was about the connection we had with Olive. I mean, even our autistic daughter understood it, and the one word that Kaye says regularly has a connection with Olive. Maybe she saw that we have something she doesn't—something she denied herself." He sighed.

"I think you're right. But that doesn't excuse it."

Adam put his arm around me. "No, it doesn't. But know that I love you, okay? No matter what my mother says."

I nodded and thought of Trenton's mom at the support group. "I can't imagine life without you, Adam."

"Well," he said wearily, "you don't have to."

I kissed his arm. "Good."

Adam quietly rubbed my shoulder for a moment, then he spoke in a whisper. "Do you think Kaye could see Olive's spirit?"

The thought was comforting. "Maybe."

Adam was quiet, as if he were thinking. When he finally spoke again, his voice was barely more than a whisper. "I think she did."

Before long, Adam was drawing deep, steady breaths. I lay there thinking about Kaye, and the mystery she was. It wouldn't surprise me at all if she could see things beyond my sight. She often burst out laughing for no apparent reason, like she did the night Olive died, and she obviously saw an order to things that I didn't. It was also nice, and quite merciful, that she was blissfully unaware of the people who stared at her, judged her, and thoroughly misunderstood her. Maybe in her view, everyone was reacting to their own worlds the way she was reacting to hers—we were all in our own little bubbles, only interacting when it was absolutely necessary, like when our stomachs knotted with hunger.

Maybe Kaye had little to worry about, but the pain of reality was mine to bear.

Chapter 18

DEAREST DAUGHTER

Mom and I e-mailed each other every week. I tried to keep to the lighter end of things in an effort to save her from worry and distraction. There wasn't much she could do to help, anyway. I figured what I needed more than anything was a babysitter—an evening out so I could refuel. After I found out I was pregnant, I told her the news with all the excitement an expectant mother should have. Brienne had obviously told Mom the truth, because two days after Olive's funeral, I got a handwritten letter from Mom in the mail. Dad didn't write much, but he'd included a small piece of paper, which read, *Have Adam give you a blessing!*

Mom's letter was much more involved.

Dearest Daughter,

We hear our little Kaye is autistic. My heart aches for you and your little family, and the trial you must endure. But I must also admit that I am surprised you didn't tell me. And a little hurt. Brienne explained to me that you didn't want us to worry, but I'm not sure I understand. You've always been headstrong, and determined to do things your own way, but there are times in all of our lives when we must forget our own way and submit to God's way. There are times when we all need help. The adjustment is difficult, but God's yoke is easy, and His burden is light.

This mission has taught us so many things. Our earthly existence is so short. A mere blink of an eye in an eternity of growth. Pray, Jennifer. God will give you perspective.

Surely you see the way Kaye has blessed all of us. Remember the many times she sat on your father's lap and looked at books with him? Her sweet, gentle temperament was obvious even when she was very small. Remember how glad we were to get her? How welcome she was?

She is the same child you have always loved. The diagnosis has not changed Kaye. Don't let it change you. She is still your beloved daughter, just as you are mine. And we all are children of God. Hold to this fact in your times of trial. He is your Father. He loves you. He wants you to succeed.

Remember these things. And know that I love you. You are all in our prayers.

Love, Mom.

I read the letter, then set it on Adam's pillow so he could read it when he had time.

The words brought tears to my eyes, and for a moment I felt like I was young and secure in my mother's embrace. I tried to extend that embrace to Kaye, but she pushed me away. Thankfully, Marie was always ready and willing to hop in my arms and take the hug Kaye had refused. I often covered her face with kisses until she giggled. While I embraced Marie—touched to the core by how wonderful she was—I looked longingly at Kaye.

The letter on Adam's pillow prompted the thought that God might feel the same way about me—wistful over my negligence, over my lack of communication with Him. I wondered what the mist was that separated parent from child. Kaye was separated from me by something she had no control over. I was separated from my mother by space and responsibility. What separated me from God? That separation seemed to be something that Kaye could pass beyond, judging by her communion with Olive. I wondered how many veiled spirits spoke to Kaye through a language silent and foreign to me. How many spiritual experiences was she privy to that I had somehow locked myself out of?

I'd been taught all my life that prayer was the key. Prayer could bring me closer to Heavenly Father than anything else. Prayer could help me when nothing else could.

I fell to my knees and wondered what to say. There was so much in my heart. How would I begin? How could I dissipate the mist? My emotions rose close to the surface, and my nose began to ache. Maybe if I just cried and let my unspoken jumble of feelings flood my eyes, it would count as a prayer. Enos prayed all night. Would crying all night count?

Kaye pushed open my bedroom door and hurried to my side. She grabbed my hand and began tugging. I held my eyes closed and wished for more time. Kaye wouldn't have it. She tugged until I felt my finger pop. I rubbed my knuckle gently as I stood and followed her from the room.

Chapter 19

PAROLE

The rest of August crawled by. By the end of the month, Kaye was finally used to her dad's absence at bedtime. She only screamed and looked through the window for two minutes instead of two hours. She still woke up in the middle of the night, and that made Adam's homecoming difficult. He was ready to go to bed by then, and she saw him and was determined to play. Adam was tempted to stay up with her a couple of times, but we knew enough about autism by then that we understood doing something fun once might give Kaye the impression it was something to expect, which would give her an excuse to scream when she didn't get it. So Adam went to bed as soon as he got home, and I stayed up to watch movies with Kaye.

We attended church every Sunday and took turns in the hallway. I watched for Cathy, feeling a sting of guilt over the way I had treated her when she found out about Kaye's diagnosis and my pregnancy, but I didn't see her the whole month.

Brienne called after they had finished moving into their house. She was bubbly, as usual. They visited with Mom and Dad before they moved in, and Brienne told me how worried Mom was about me—creating that stress was the very thing I'd tried to avoid.

I thought of Olive often, but didn't talk about her. Adam seemed withdrawn after the incident with his parents, and I wasn't sure if he wanted to talk about his family at all.

It was an unusually hot August, and I was unusually alone. I ran my errands during the day while Adam stayed home with the girls and prepared to go to work in the evening. I fed the girls, sang them good night, and went to bed, all without Adam. We saw each other in passing, but lived our own, separate lives.

I knew it was wearing on me when he tried to tell me about his new job and all I could think of was the cute episode of *Sesame Street* that day. Elmo was a cutup.

Adam registered for school, and his classes started bright and early on August thirtieth. It meant, of course, that I saw even less of Adam. It also meant that the days of running my errands without two little girls in tow were over, at least for a while.

On September first, I got the call from the Behavioral Therapy School, where I'd been attending parent meetings alone for a month. A placement had opened for Kaye, and I was to bring her down and get acquainted with her teacher. I drove across the valley to the school and walked in. The receptionist in the office sent me to room twelve, where Kaye would spend most weekdays, from eight thirty to three, for the following school year.

I'd seen the other students at BTS, but they'd all been sharing chaos in the gym. I'd never seen them in the classroom. The student-teacher ratio was two-to-one, and the teachers focused on the children, mostly boys, with the greatest patience I'd ever witnessed. I couldn't believe how well-behaved the children were in the structured environment. Then, as if to shatter my newly formed positive opinion, a boy in one of the rooms screamed and started shaking a desk. Papers spilled from the desk, and the boy stepped back from them as if they were made of acid. Then he went to another desk and began shaking it.

The teacher, a heavyset woman with a southern accent, held the boy by his shoulders and tried to look him in the eye. "Austin, stop shaking the desk. Austin, stop shaking the desk, please. Austin, stop shaking the desk now." Her voice was firm, and when the boy didn't comply, she escorted him to a chair as far away from the desks as possible, and knelt in front of him, holding him in the chair by his legs.

I gripped Kaye's hand again, hoping she wouldn't come home and shake my furniture. It was bad enough that she climbed on it.

Room twelve was noisier than the other rooms had been. The children were playing a version of musical chairs, but there was a chair for every child. I was pleased to see Julie standing next to the CD player.

"Okay, the music's going to stop," she warned before she stopped the childish tune. "Everyone sit down!" The other teachers helped the boys find their seats. Kaye would be the only girl in that class.

Julie smiled at me as she remembered us. "Hi! This is Kaye, right?"

I nodded.

"Great! Come on in."

We obeyed.

Julie left her post at the CD player and walked to my side. "Today is Gene's birthday. We're celebrating. We'll have cake later. You're welcome to stay."

I nodded as Marie eyed the cake.

"I can't tell you how thrilled we are to have a girl. These boys are so active, it's hard to keep up with them."

As she spoke, one of the boys started rocking back and forth on his chair. The teacher next to him tried to get him to calm down and he slapped her. She grabbed his hands and pressed them to his chest, telling him, "No."

I looked back at Julie, and she must have seen my dismay.

"They behave a lot better when we don't have birthday parties."

"Then why do you bother?" I asked.

Julie smiled. "Because they're kids. Kids need birthday parties."

We watched as the teacher calmed the boy down, and when he was quietly sitting still, she praised him with a soft rub to his back. "Nice sitting, Trenton."

I remembered his mother was the one in the process of getting a divorce. I wondered if that was why the boy was acting out.

"We teach the children how to sit still in their chairs with their eyes on the teacher, their mouths quiet, and their hands in their laps. That's all we teach them."

"Wow. I'll be amazed if you can teach that to Kaye." I was doubtful.

"Autistic kids can learn. It just takes a little longer, and a little more repetition. In two years, Kaye will be a model student, you wait and see."

My eyebrows shot up.

"She may not be at grade level for kids her age, but she'll know how to pay attention. Then she can learn just about anything we can teach."

I'd never thought about needing to learn how to learn, but that seemed to be the primary goal of BTS.

"We go on field trips occasionally, and we very much appreciate parents who come with us. In fact, we'd like you to come whenever you can to help Kaye. We've found that when parents help, the kids take what they learn home. Plus, you learn some of our techniques and use them at home."

I was a little overwhelmed. The fidgets and howls coming from the boys made me feel like I'd been sitting too long in the middle of an aviary. Was that how Kaye felt when I tried to get her to settle down?

After a few more minutes, Julie suggested I try to leave Kaye there, just to see what she would do. I'd never left Kaye with strangers like that before, except for nursery at church, and that didn't go so well. I hesitated.

"It will be okay. She'll get used to us. Besides, you're not *really* leaving her today."

It seemed mean, and I thought back to the conclusion Adam and I had made about starting new habits with Kaye. I'd entered the school with Kaye and I'd stayed for a while. I wondered if Kaye would expect me to stay every time I dropped her off at school. If I pretended to leave, then came back, Kaye would always expect me to come back in just a few minutes, and when her expectations were unfulfilled, she'd scream.

"I don't think it's a good idea. She'll scream."

"We're used to that," Julie said with a smile.

That may have been so, but I wasn't used to purposefully making Kaye scream, in fact, I was used to doing everything within my power to stop her screams. I stayed in the doorway, and Kaye looked up at me. She came to me and tried to get out the door. She wouldn't let me pretend to leave.

"I guess I'm not going to leave her." I shrugged.

Julie smiled like she'd dealt with many hesitant parents. "It's okay. You can take her home today. But we'd like to get her started as soon as possible. She's already behind the other kids."

How could she be behind? They weren't studying academics. The kids weren't learning anything measurable that I could see. I was almost ready to back out, and not have Kaye attend the school at all.

Julie seemed to sense my concerns. "You see that little guy over there?" The boy she pointed at was small and pale and very quiet. "He started here last year. He's one of the lucky ones who will be in this program for three years by the time he graduates. He'll probably be mainstreamed. He didn't speak at all last year, and now he's using the PECS system to ask for what he wants. Imagine if Kaye asked for what she wanted."

The idea was appealing.

"I know this isn't easy, but this is the best thing for your daughter right now. I've seen so many kids here come such a long way. There's no reason why Kaye wouldn't make progress with the system of teaching we use. It will be good for her, but hard for you."

Everything was hard for me. "How about we try again tomorrow?" I asked hopefully.

Julie nodded. "Do you want to try putting her on the bus? They meet several kids at a few different places in the valley."

I couldn't imagine putting Kaye on a bus and watching it drive away. Would Kaye be big enough to see through the windows?

"There's pick-up information in the main office. And you can come down here anytime you'd like, to observe or to help."

I nodded my thanks and stopped by the office on my way out. The bus would stop in the parking lot of a grocery store five blocks from my house at 7:40 in the morning. They didn't have school on Fridays, but the rest of the week Kaye would be gone from 7:40 A.M. to 3:25 P.M. My stomach lurched as I thought of how long a day that would be for her. Then I thought of how long a day it would be for me.

* * *

I met the bus along with two other children and their mothers. I helped Kaye up the stairs, where a bus attendant took Kaye by the hand and helped her pick a seat near the front. The driver was a kind-looking woman with soft, blond curls and crisp, blue eyes. She smiled at Kaye, then at me.

"Is this her first time on the bus?" she asked.

I nodded.

"Well, don't worry. We'll take care of her." She looked back to see that all the children were belted into their seats. "Kaye, say 'I love you, Mommy.'"

Many of the children repeated the driver's words. Kaye just looked around at the large, brightly colored stickers lining the inside of the bus. I felt a sudden urge to take her back home, where she was comfortable. She was too young to be away from me all day. What if she needed me? Julie, as wonderful as she obviously was, didn't know Kaye. She didn't understand Kaye's way of communicating. She wasn't used to Kaye's screams and babble. My feeling of apprehension was worse than I'd ever experienced when leaving Kaye with a babysitter.

"We'll be back here around 3:20 this afternoon." The bus driver spoke quietly, giving me a hint to get off the bus, but doing it gently, as if she understood my dilemma.

Three twenty seemed forever away.

I blew Kaye a kiss even though she wasn't aware of me, then I backed down the stairs until my feet hit the pavement.

Marie and I sat in the Metro and watched the bus pull away, and I prayed for my baby on the bus.

We sat in the parking lot for a minute before I realized I had all day to run errands without worrying about Kaye screaming or throwing a tantrum. I thought of the furniture store we'd been kicked out of, the grocery store we frequented where the clerks stared at us from the time we got in the checkout line until the door closed behind us, and the hair stylist who invited us to leave because Kaye was a "liability." Marie sat quietly in her booster seat behind me. I turned to look at her, feeling like a convict who'd finally gotten parole.

"Marie?" I asked.

She looked up at me.

"Where would you like to go? Anywhere at all."

Chapter 20

OBLIVIOUS

Kaye's first week of school passed quickly. Julie wrote a message to me each day in a small notebook they kept in Kaye's backpack. In the messages, she told me how often Kaye screamed, hit herself in the chest, wiggled her fingers together—they began calling this "stimming"—squirmed away, or was non-compliant. The messages were long. Kaye kept taking off her clothes at school, and they told me to make sure I kept getting her dressed at home so that she would get used to clothes and eventually come to like them. They also sent home papers with dietary suggestions that could help Kaye control her behaviors. All the suggestions were a bit frustrating. We were having a hard enough time dealing with life as it was. Trying to implement changes like that seemed impossible.

I figured Kaye liked school, because she seemed to hate being at home. Friday was her first day that week without school, and she woke up at the same time I'd been waking her all week. She found her backpack and waited for me at the back door.

"No school today, Kaye," I said, hoping for a miracle that would help her understand what I was saying.

The miracle never came.

Kaye screamed, tried to open the door only to be hindered by the chain lock Russ had installed, and she hit herself for three hours. I didn't want to go anywhere, partly because I'd run all my errands during the week while Kaye was at school, and partly because I knew in the back of my mind that Kaye wouldn't be satisfied with going anywhere other than school.

During those three hours, I washed dishes, folded laundry, and cried.

The next day, Adam had an accounting conference at the college. When he left, Kaye was already waiting at the door with her backpack in hand. She wailed when he wouldn't let her out of the house, and Adam looked at me sympathetically as I cried almost as hard as Kaye screamed.

Thankfully, Kaye didn't scream as long that day. I put in one of her videos and turned up the volume until she was distracted enough to leave her backpack by the door and come into the front room. I hid her backpack in the coat closet.

Kaye still didn't want to keep her clothes on, and in an effort to stick to Julie's guidelines, I chased her around the house picking her clothes up as she threw them on the floor so I could dress her again, just to hear her shirt and pants flop to the floor as soon as I turned my back.

The nutritional pamphlets advised a strict diet—no sugars or dyes, but lots of meats and complex carbohydrates. So I fixed cheesy scrambled eggs for breakfast. She left them sitting on the table going cold, and sat in front of the refrigerator screaming instead. I tried to be strong, to not give in, but eventually Marie came up to me with tears streaking her face, asking why Kaye was sad.

By ten in the morning, I'd given up. She was too hard to deal with. Having her in school had given me a taste of what life would be like without having to worry about Kaye. It wasn't that I didn't love her anymore, or that I wanted her out of my house—that was unthinkable—but I wanted things to be different. I wanted her to either learn how to deal with her frustration in an acceptable manner or . . . What was the alternative? There wasn't any medical recourse—no pill she could take to heal her.

It wasn't long before I consented, and Kaye walked around the house with a baggie full of chips and a juice box. Her clothes were on the floor and a cartoon played on the television. I lay on the couch staring at the chaos around me and feeling like a horrible mother. At that time in my life, I was supposed to be hosting play groups with four or five children who loved me and were dear friends with my children. I was supposed to be the neighborhood benefactress. I was supposed to be everything I wasn't.

Adam came home from his conference at two in the afternoon. I was half asleep, and Kaye had climbed to the top of the side-by-side washer and dryer in the laundry room and she was pacing back and forth across them, singing. Adam peeked at her, then glared at me.

"I still don't think that's safe," he said.

"You know how good her balance is. She's been up there all afternoon."

"Her diaper is sagging to her knees." He set his briefcase down and lifted her from the dryer, holding her away from him so she wouldn't leak on his clothes. He laid her on the floor and went to get a diaper. As soon as he walked away, Kaye stood up and took off for the laundry room again.

"Could you help here, honey?" His voice was strained.

I got up from the couch, feeling weak and tired. It only made it worse that he was so obviously upset with me. I felt like I was doing my best.

He chased Kaye to the laundry room and brought her back. He laid her down on the floor and I pinned her shoulders to the carpet while he changed her diaper. It took almost all my strength.

"I thought the teachers told you to keep getting her dressed so she wouldn't get used to being without clothes."

I nodded. "Yeah, well I got her dressed twenty times today."

"But she's running around in her diaper right now." He found her clothes on the floor and started dressing Kaye. As soon as he was finished she ran toward the laundry room again, stripping.

I raised my hand and pointed at Kaye as her diapered bottom disappeared around the corner. "Twenty-one."

He glared at me, picked up the clothes, and followed Kaye.

I plopped back on the couch and whispered, "Twenty-two."

Adam reappeared from the laundry room, avoided looking at me, and went to the kitchen. I heard him open the fridge. I remembered, with a dull ache at the base of my skull, he'd expected me to make him a sandwich so he could eat before he went to work. I'd forgotten. Or, maybe I'd blocked it from my mind. I'd forgotten to buy lunchmeat, and if I'd packed him a lunch, I would have had to go to the grocery store first. I didn't plan on taking Kaye to the grocery store ever again.

Adam stood in the doorway between the kitchen and the front room with his hands on his hips. I glanced at him, hoping he wasn't looking at me with expectation. Worse than looking at me, he was scanning the messy room. Kaye had spilled a juice box in the corner, and though I'd tried to clean it up, it left a red stain on the carpet. Toys and books were strewn across the center of the floor since the kids liked to read and play in clean areas but they conveniently forgot how to pick up after themselves, so they moved from one area of the carpet to another until you could hardly see carpet at all. I watched his eyes move from one pile to the next, waiting for him to look at me and accuse me of sitting on my tush all day when I should have been doing *something*. But he didn't look at me. He didn't say a word. He just turned and walked into the kitchen.

Guilt sprouted again, like a thorn in my side. Soon I was bothered enough that I pushed myself from the couch and dragged my feet across the front room. When I stood in the doorway, I saw Adam rolling up his sleeves and standing in front of the sink. He started organizing dishes so they could be washed, then turned on the hot water.

"What are you doing?" I asked.

"I'm washing dishes."

The thorn in my side grew and dug at me. He'd been out all day, trying to get his foot in the door to a good career, and I hadn't even washed the dishes from the night before.

I sighed. "I'll do it."

"You go lie down. You look like you need it."

"You're home for two hours a day besides the six hours you sleep. I'm not going to make you clean while you're home."

"You're not making me do anything," Adam said, and he squirted dish soap in the hot water and swirled it around as it started to foam.

I went to his side and tried to push him out of the way. "Go sit down."

"Jen, I'm fine. I can wash a couple of dishes."

"It's my job. I should do it."

"Why is it your job? I can do it just as well as you can."

"That's not what I meant." I threw a dish in the sink a bit harder than I intended to. The soapy water splashed up and soaked Adam's shirt and tie.

He backed away from the sink.

I turned my back to him and plunged my hands in the hot water, scrubbing at the crusty dishes.

"It will be easier if you let them soak," Adam said with a quiet voice.

I didn't say anything because if he heard my voice he'd know how hard I was crying. He probably knew anyway. Instead, I scrubbed the dishes until my fingers hurt.

He stood there stubbornly behind me. I wished he'd just go away and leave me in the pile of work I'd neglected all day. I couldn't concentrate with him there. But he didn't go away. He stepped up close behind me, put his arms beneath mine and reached into the soapy water. His chin rested on my shoulder so he could see what he was doing as he pulled a plate from the water, took a corner of the rag I was using, and scrubbed as much of the plate as he could.

"Oh, I can't quite reach," he said, and he pushed me close against the counter and reached deeper into the water for another dish. We'd washed dishes that way when we were newlyweds, but we didn't get many dishes clean before we abandoned the job.

I held the giggles in for as long as I could until they exploded in a burst.

He stepped back as I turned around and slapped at his wet shirt playfully. "You geek, can't you let me be depressed?"

"Absolutely not." His face was serious, but he had a twinkle in his eye. "You're too happy of a person to be depressed."

I shook my head, looking at him with uncertainty.

"Come here, wipe your cheeks on my shirt." He put his arms around me and pushed me back against the sink again. I wrapped my dripping arms around his neck and did as he'd told me to. It felt like I couldn't hold him tight enough. His strong hands felt so good against my back. I wished we could stand like that forever.

Kaye came up behind Adam and pulled on his pant leg. She grunted and looked at the fridge.

"I guess she wants a drink," Adam said.

"She's had five juice boxes today, counting the one she spilled. I read the label just to double-check, and this brand of juice adds sugar. She shouldn't be having them at all." I sighed and wiped my cheeks with the backs of my hands. "We need to make her point to what she wants, or try to get her to ask for it somehow."

"She is asking for it, in her own way." Adam went to the fridge and pulled out another juice box. Kaye stood on her toes and grunted, her eyes glued to Adam's hands as he slipped the straw in the tiny hole.

He handed the box to her, her grip squeezing it enough that the juice squirted from the straw and dribbled down her bare stomach, leaving a red streak.

"Oops," Adam said.

"Yeah, I always take a sip before I give it to her."

Kaye walked on her toes and headed back to the laundry room.

"How does she get up there anyway?" Adam asked.

Our laundry room served as a half-bath—using the square footage of our apartment as efficiently as possible. "She stands on the toilet," I explained, "then pushes herself up onto the washer.

"And she's been up there all afternoon?"

I nodded. "I'm a terrible mother."

"No you're not," he said, but I didn't believe him. He smoothed his wet tie against his chest and chuckled.

I turned back to the dishes. My life was worse than a roller coaster. The rise and fall of my emotions were too close together to qualify as hills and valleys. It was more like a continuous valley with an occasional spike of happiness, over as quickly as it came. I focused my thoughts on the few moments of happiness I'd come to live for—Marie and Kaye playing in their sleeping bags near Mount Timpanogos, Kaye's blissful expression as she walked along the curb outside the church on a bright summer day, her fond farewell to Olive.

Adam started massaging my neck. "Your muscles are all knots," he said, and massaged in earnest. I had to stop washing and let his fingers work their magic.

We stood like that until Adam's fingers started to cramp. He rubbed gently down my spine with the palms of his hands.

"Thank you," I whispered.

"I think you need a real massage, from someone who knows what they're doing."

"I don't know. That was pretty good." I willed my hands to wipe the dishrag across the plate in my hand. The dried-on food had soaked enough that it came off easier than it had before.

"I'd better get ready for work," Adam said. His footsteps retreated across the linoleum, and I turned to see his back as he left the room. I didn't want him to go. Those moments with him and his gentle, familiar touch kept me sane. I realized that I thought of him all day, and wanted nothing more than to have him with me to help me bear the burden and make it all seem worthwhile.

I cried again, though I tried not to. My head ached, and I was exhausted. I wanted to sleep, but even that didn't feel like it would be enough of a release. At the end of a night's rest waited another morning and another day of not being what I wanted to be.

When the dishes were washed and drying on the counter, I started back to my place on the couch. Then the thought came to me that I should check on Kaye. She wasn't singing.

She'd pulled the lid from my tub of laundry detergent, and she had one hand in it. She was licking tiny blue crystals from the fingers of her other hand.

"Kaye, no!" I rushed to her and yanked her hand from her mouth. As I pulled her from the top of the dryer, her leg knocked the detergent to the floor. Blue crystals spread everywhere, but I was more worried about Kaye and how much detergent she'd eaten. I washed her hands and tried to wash out her mouth. "Adam!" I yelled. "Adam, I need you!"

Adam's feet pounded down the stairs. "What's wrong?"

"She's been eating detergent," I said, and the tears started again.

Adam lifted the empty tub from the ground and read the label.

"Should I make her throw up?" I asked.

"No. It says to have her drink lots of water and call poison control."

I groaned. Just what I needed, a stranger who knew I'd let my daughter eat laundry detergent.

"How much did she eat?" Adam asked.

"I have no idea. I was washing dishes and I guess I'd tuned her out." I couldn't stand the guilt. It seemed like guilt was my primary emotion lately. I did everything wrong.

"I can't believe she got this lid off, Jen. You've asked me to open this for you before."

I knew the lid was tight, but it obviously didn't matter. Kaye was so different from other children, I realized it was time I stopped thinking of her in the same way I thought of Marie. Kaye needed different rules, more supervision, more discipline, more structure. All I had to do was scold Marie, and she backed off of whatever she was doing. I could bribe her to do basic chores around the house, and she complied without hesitation. Kaye was a different story. If I scolded her, all she picked up on was the tone of my voice, not the meaning of my words. And if my tone was strained or contentious, she started screaming.

I filled a tumbler with water and tried to make Kaye drink it. She didn't like water, and she screamed at me. I held her arms tightly against her chest and tried again to get her to drink. The cold water dribbled down her chin and onto her bare chest. She squirmed and screamed again, but I didn't stop tilting the glass. She breathed at the wrong time and got a breath of water.

"Oh, no," I said, and I dropped the tumbler.

Kaye coughed until she finally did throw up, and the vomit was slightly purple from the red juice she'd been drinking all day and the blue laundry detergent. I held her over the toilet and cried. The water from the tumbler I had dropped mixed with the detergent on the floor and I stood in a slippery, soapy mess. I sat down in the mess and cried some more, resting my back against the wall. Kaye wiped off her mouth and ran away, leaving a trail of soapy footprints on the carpet in the hall.

I sobbed and covered my face with my hands. I hated my life.

Adam stood in the doorway with the phone in his hand. "Where's Kaye?" he asked.

I could barely see him past the tears in my eyes. "She's gone," I said in despair.

Adam walked away in the same direction I'd heard Kaye go. I looked around me at the soapy floor.

Great, I thought, *something else to go to the store for.* Then I wondered if Adam had been on the phone with poison control. He should tell them she'd thrown up. I tried to stand, but my feet slipped and I landed hard on the floor. I crawled slowly to the hallway and stood up when I had carpet to help me get good footing. I had suds dripping down my legs and from my fingers, but I followed Kaye's soapy footprints to her bedroom.

Adam sat on Marie's bed, talking on the phone. Kaye sat in front of her bookcase and pulled out the Disney books one by one. She looked at the characters on the cover, wiggled her fingers over them and sang to them, then pulled out a different book. She looked perfectly fine.

"Okay. Thank you," Adam said, and the receiver beeped as he hung up the phone.

"They said to keep lots of fluids in her and watch her for a while. She should be fine, but if she starts acting sick, we should take her to the emergency room."

I nodded. "She did throw up. I was trying to get her to drink."

"Well, if her throat doesn't seem irritated, I don't think that makes much of a difference. She must not have eaten much of it."

"No, I don't think she did. Her vomit wasn't even foamy."

"But you're foamy," Adam said.

I turned around to show him my wet backside.

He chuckled, but tried to hide it.

I would have laughed if my bottom hadn't been so sore.

"Hey, it could be worse," he said.

I waited for him to give me an example of how it could have possibly been worse. When he didn't say anything, I asked, "How?"

He shrugged his shoulders and laughed. "I don't know, I'm still thinking."

Finally I laughed with him. But it was halfhearted. Eventually I was crying again, and he walked over to hold me.

"Come on, sweetie. A few years ago you would have been laughing your head off at this." He wrapped his arms around me and kissed my forehead. "Please don't overreact."

I stopped and let my arms fall to his side. He was judging me, the way everyone judged me. Him, of all people. He should have understood. He should have just held me and kissed me and told me everything would be okay.

"You think I'm overreacting?" I asked.

"Well, yes. A little."

I pushed him away and went to the bedroom, then slammed the door. "No, Adam. Now I'm overreacting!" I knew my statement was true, but I'd had enough. I didn't feel like laughing and I wasn't going to be guilt-tripped into it.

"Jen, don't be so moody. You're going to set Kaye off."

I stripped off my wet pants and threw them at the closed door.

When Adam spoke, his voice was muffled as if he were standing right next to the door. "What did I do? Why are you mad at me?"

I shouted as I fished through my drawers for a clean pair of pants. "At least you get a change of scenery, Adam. You don't deal with this twenty-four-seven. You can afford to laugh at me."

"I'm not laughing at you. I'm trying to laugh with you."

I threw the door open, so angry then that my tears had dried. "I think you like being away from home. That way you don't have to put up with me and my mood swings. You don't have to go to the school and see Kaye put in a group with handicapped kids and fit right in, if it's possible for an autistic child to fit in anywhere."

"Jen!"

"And I don't fit in anywhere, either. I hate being home. I can't go out in public with Kaye. She screams and throws a fit and suddenly people look at me like I'm a white-trash, bad parent with an uncontrollable child."

Adam gripped my arms just below the shoulder and tried to look me in the eye. "Jen, calm down."

I looked at him and he nodded his head toward the girls' bedroom, where Marie was pretending to read books to Kaye. With a deep breath, I backed into the wall behind me and slid to the floor.

Adam looked down at me. "What do you want me to do?" His eyes were intense and his voice was barely controlled. My anger had rubbed off on him.

I searched his eyes. I knew what I wanted, but it seemed impossible. "I want you to heal her, Adam," I whispered.

He stared at me.

My emotions swelled as I drew breath, and I exhaled the thoughts that had been building in me since Kaye's diagnosis. "I want you to give her a priesthood blessing, and I want you to heal her. I want her to talk to me. I'm sick of her pushing me away when I want to comfort her. I'm sick of not being part of her life while my life revolves around her. I want her to tell me she loves me." I could barely speak the last words, but I forced them out between sobs.

Adam's eyes were wet. He looked hesitant, like he wasn't sure what to say.

He had an alarm on his watch to remind him when it was time to leave for work, and as he stared wordlessly at me, the alarm began to beep.

He sighed. "I have to go to work. Remember, I had to trade this shift so I could go to the viewing." He straightened his legs and offered to help me up.

I stared at him, stunned.

When I didn't take his extended hand, he let it fall to his side. "We'll talk about this when I get home, okay?"

I nodded.

He straightened his tie, which was almost dry by then. "I love you, Jen."

I nodded again and inspected a hangnail as fresh tears blurred my vision.

He headed for the stairs. "We'll talk when I get home."

I listened as he shut the door and started his car.

After he was gone, I cried again. It was the hardest cry I'd ever had, but I couldn't stop it, even though I felt Marie watching me. Finally, she came to my side and threw her arms around my neck. I wrapped my arms around her and held her small body close to mine.

"I'm sorry, Mommy."

I kissed her head. "Shh. Don't be sorry, baby. It's not your fault. You're my little angel, you know that? Mommy just needs loves for a while, so thank you for giving me loves."

She cried on my shoulder, and I cried on hers.

As we held each other in the hallway, I looked past Marie into her bedroom. Kaye sat on the floor, completely oblivious to the drama just a few feet away—the drama that she had inadvertently caused. I wished, for just a moment, that I, too, could be oblivious.

Chapter 21

WINDOWS

The door opened in my dream, but Adam was leaving instead of coming home. I begged him to stay, but saw myself turning into Trenton's mom—complaining to some young, idealistic counselor as Kaye shook desks and slapped Julie. I put myself in the time-out chair and screamed as loud as I could, slapping my chest and biting my hand. I felt a strange sense of wildness, like I could break out of my body if I wanted to.

In my dream, I was crazy. But Kaye had a calming effect on me, like Olive, and she put her finger gently on my mouth. Without moving her lips, Kaye whispered, "Olivejuice."

One factor common to all my pregnancies was my tendency to have bizarre dreams, and I remembered many of them after I woke up. It took a while for my vision to clear and for me to realize where I was when I woke that Sunday morning. I was still in my bed as the sun rose, and Adam was sleeping next to me. With a surge of fear, I wondered if Kaye had figured out the chain lock and slipped into the night.

The doors downstairs were locked, and the television was off. I sped down the stairs without looking in the girls' room—it hadn't dawned on me that Kaye might have spent the whole night in her bed. But when I finally peeked in, that's where Kaye was, buried in a bundle of blankets. I pulled a blanket back to make sure she was still breathing, and Kaye's eyes squinted at the sunlight coming through her bedroom window.

"You okay?" Adam asked when I returned to our room.

"She spent the night in her bed!" I marveled.

Adam smiled sleepily. "Good for her."

He didn't seem as surprised as I was. In fact, he seemed withdrawn. He talked to me, but didn't look me in the eye.

As we dressed for church, I kept trying to catch Adam's eye, but he was barely aware of me. I pulled on my favorite maternity dress. My belly was getting rounder every day it seemed, and I was starting to feel sound kicks in my womb. With the girls, the first day I had worn a maternity dress was a big deal—it was like revealing our secret. It saddened me that there were so many other issues to deal with that day.

"Let's get going so we can talk to the bishop before church starts," Adam said as he straightened his tie.

"Why do you want to talk to the bishop?"

"He hasn't called a teacher for Kaye yet. We need to go to all of our classes." Adam looked so determined that I didn't contradict him. I couldn't argue with his point, anyway.

When we got to church, Bishop Hean greeted Adam with a smile and a firm handshake. "I'm glad you're here, Brother Young. We've asked a sister to teach your daughter, but we'd like you to meet with her before we set her apart."

It seemed unusual. Most Primary teachers weren't cleared by parents before they were presented to the congregation. I wondered what was wrong with this sister.

Adam looked relieved, but I could tell he wanted to have it taken care of before our meetings started. "Who have you called?" Adam asked.

For a moment, I hoped the bishop would say Cathy's name.

"Her name is Gay Lynn Wills."

Adam shrugged. I wasn't sure who she was, either, but that didn't mean anything since I hardly knew anyone.

"She's been in the ward for about five years. She and her husband run a real-estate company."

"How is she with kids?"

"Why don't you call her and find out?" The bishop led Adam to the clerk's office, where they looked up Gay Lynn's phone number.

"I don't like the sound of this," Adam said as we walked away with the number.

"Well, they wouldn't call her to the Primary if she didn't like kids," I said to soothe him. But the bishop's reply, and the fact that we were meeting with her before the calling was officially extended, set up a strange scenario that unnerved me a bit too.

I took Kaye during the Priesthood and Relief Society hour, and we walked around the curb outside as usual. Dani didn't walk her ducks that day. I wondered if she knew I was outside already.

When we entered the chapel for sacrament meeting, Adam walked behind me with Kaye in his arms. "Keep going," he whispered when I walked to a bench at the back of the room.

"Where?" I asked.

He pointed to a pew almost at the front of the room. "Fourth from the front, on the side."

I went where he'd asked me to, and we put Kaye next to the wall. After I sat next to her, I looked around the chapel. It looked different from the front.

"We're going to sit here from now on," Adam said.

He had determination on his face. I got a little nervous as I looked at him.

We took the sacrament, then testimonies began. Since I didn't fast while I was pregnant, I hadn't been aware it was fast Sunday. Adam shot from his seat soon after testimonies began, with that expression still on his face. Knowing he'd already told Cathy about our woes, I wondered what he'd admit to the whole congregation. I felt myself blushing before Adam opened his mouth.

"Brothers and sisters, my name is Adam Young, and that's my family over there." He pointed at Kaye, Marie, and me. I looked down at my hands. One of my nails had broken, and I felt a sudden need for an emery board.

"The last few months have been the most difficult of our lives. I was fired from my job last June, then my daughter was diagnosed with autism, my wife's sister moved, my favorite aunt passed away, and we found out we're expecting another baby." Adam was counting the events of the past few months on his fingers.

My face was hot, and I wanted to leave the room so badly I almost wished Kaye would start acting up.

"We've been inactive ever since we moved into this ward, so few of you know us. But that is going to change. I've learned something in the last few months, brothers and sisters, and I'd like to share it with you."

I braced myself.

"I've learned that I need this gospel. I need to be here so that I can learn what God wants me to learn, and so I can renew my covenants." He leaned on the pulpit and I watched him get control of his emotions.

"Now, I've got to warn you that my daughter has some different behaviors. She screams a lot, and—" he looked at Kaye, "this is normal behavior for her."

Kaye was sitting on the arm of the pew with her back against the wall, wiggling her fingers together and singing. I looked back at the congregation as they turned to look. I wanted to sink down in my seat.

"She's different, brothers and sisters, and I'm still getting used to her and trying to figure her out. But we need to be here, so we're going to be here. We're going to sit toward the front so Kaye can focus on the speakers better. During sacrament meeting, we're going to stay in the chapel until we absolutely have to leave, because autistic children are all about habit, and I want church attendance to be one of her habits. I don't want her to get used to leaving halfway through the meeting."

I peeked back at the congregation again. Thankfully, they were starting to focus their attention on Adam instead of me. Some of them looked upset, some compassionate, and some indifferent. I spotted Cathy near the back of the chapel; that wide grin was on her face. Dani sat in a middle pew with Steven on her lap. She looked shocked—her mouth hung open until she leaned over and whispered into her husband's ear. I knew then that Adam's testimony would be the subject of conversation that night in homes throughout the neighborhood.

"I believe in the Lord," Adam continued. "I've had to sacrifice to be able to live what I believe, so I *will* live it. And I believe that as I live the gospel, the Lord will open the windows of heaven and bless my family. I also believe that if you live His gospel, you will help us— we will help each other—and all of us will be blessed."

He closed his testimony and returned to our bench. I was glad when he didn't look at me, because I was miffed. I didn't want everyone to know everything about us, and I certainly didn't want strangers talking about us.

After the meeting, several people came up to Adam and shook his hand. Some apologized for thinking ill of us, some offered help, some shared their experiences with autism. Adam accepted their attention and well wishes with gratitude and watery eyes. I wiggled past people as Kaye crawled under the bench and left the half-empty chapel.

Cathy was waiting for me in the foyer. She'd distracted Kaye with a book to give me enough time to catch up.

I sighed when I saw her, and tried to smile my apology.

"That was quite a testimony," Cathy said. "Gave me chills."

I shrugged. "It was his testimony, not mine."

"You mean you don't agree with him?"

"No, it's not that. I just . . . I like to keep my cards closer to my chest, if you know what I mean."

Cathy nodded. "Me too."

She didn't seem like the type to worry about her privacy.

"I'm sorry I missed our visit in August."

"No, I need to apologize to you. I've been terrible."

"Eh." Cathy waved away my worries as she grinned and shrugged. "I won't be able to visit you this week, either, and September is always busy for me."

"That's okay. Count this as talking to me." I felt mildly disappointed. I could have used a visit. But I was so grateful she'd forgiven me so quickly that the disappointment was hardly noticeable.

Kaye got tired of the book and dropped it to the floor, then stood and headed for the hallway full of classrooms.

"Well, that's my cue." I followed Kaye, then turned and waved at Cathy. She smiled again, and I smiled back. Kaye went into an empty classroom and started walking along the chairs. I stood in the doorway and watched the foyer for Adam

He left the chapel, talking to Bishop Hean. "I appreciate that, Bishop. Can you come at, say, five?"

The bishop nodded, then turned to another member who was vying for his attention. Adam had Marie by the hand. He looked up and saw me, then he followed me into the classroom.

"Do we have another appointment?" I asked.

Adam nodded. "But this time the bishopric is coming to our house."

I thought of our messy apartment. "Good thing they're not coming until five. The whole bishopric?"

Adam nodded. "They haven't visited us since we moved in. Plus, I've asked them to help me."

"Help you with what?"

Adam scooped Kaye into his arms and stepped out into the hall. "We're going to give Kaye a blessing."

* * *

I spent the rest of the afternoon cooking dinner, then cleaning the apartment. As I worked, I wondered what Adam was planning on saying in the blessing—or rather, what the Spirit would prompt him to say. Would Kaye be healed that afternoon? Did I have the faith for that to happen?

Adam prepared by reading the scriptures. He sat at the kitchen table, flipping back and forth between the Book of Mormon and the Doctrine and Covenants. Occasionally, he'd stop reading and clasp his hands together and close his eyes. I could tell he was serious about this blessing—he hadn't stressed like that over a blessing since he'd given the girls names as babies. I left him alone and let him study and think.

In the meantime, I debated on what to expect. If I expected Kaye to be healed, wouldn't that be a sign of my faith? I wasn't sure. I figured I'd be better off having no expectations so I wouldn't be disappointed if Kaye wasn't healed.

But I still hoped.

When the bishop came, Adam looked calm. I felt as if frogs were jumping in my stomach, and I knew it wasn't just because of our developing baby.

After we'd sat down and engaged in polite small talk for a few minutes, Adam pulled a kitchen chair into the middle of the front room. I headed for the stairs to get Kaye, but Adam stopped me. "I'd like to give you a blessing first, Jen."

I hadn't expected it, but I sat in the chair and felt the heaviness of four sets of hands on my head. I quieted my thoughts and concentrated on that heaviness, that energy.

Adam started the blessing, and it was pretty standard. He told me I was loved by the Lord and by my family, and he admonished me to keep the covenants I had made. Then he told me something that cleared my mind of all distractions. "The baby that grows in your womb will be a blessing and a comfort to you."

I felt the baby kick me happily, with a flurry of activity. Since I'd found out I was pregnant, all I'd been able to think about was Kaye. Even with the movement inside of me, I'd been indifferent. I suddenly realized that I was having a *baby*—another human being who'd change the dynamic of our family, who'd look up at me with unfocused eyes, and nestle his tiny head on my shoulder as he slept. And Adam had said this baby would be a comfort to me. Tears sprang to my eyes as I thought of the word—comfort. That's what I wanted, more than anything. And God was giving it to me in the form of another child.

As I thought about it, Marie was already a great comfort to me—and Adam, when he was home. In that moment, I saw my family as a great strength, not a trial at all.

Adam ended my blessing and said it was Kaye's turn. I went upstairs and brought her down. Kneeling at her feet, I held Kaye in her chair as I'd seen a teacher do at school. The men laid their hands on Kaye's head, and it was her turn.

Since Kaye seemed to have such a spiritual connection, I expected her to sit quietly and let the Spirit speak to her, but Kaye didn't. She squirmed and fought, and the brethren struggled to keep their hands on her head. The blessing was simple—it had to be, because Kaye wouldn't allow anything lengthy. Adam told her that Heavenly Father loved her, her parents loved her, and she was a very special child. Then he hesitated, as if he were deep in thought. After a moment, Adam closed the blessing.

Kaye sprang from the chair as soon as we let go of her. I looked up at Adam from my position on the floor, and he smiled. He looked pleased. But all I could think of was the fact that he hadn't healed her. I still felt the glow from the blessing I'd received, but I was disappointed.

After the bishopric had left, and we'd tucked the girls in bed, I sat next to Adam on the couch. He rubbed my swollen belly and cooed at our growing child.

"Adam," I ventured. He looked at me as if he knew what I was going to say. "You didn't heal her."

Adam nodded. "I know."

I looked at him, wondering why. But part of me knew before he told me.

"I don't think the Lord wants her healed. I wanted to heal her, Jen. I wanted to tell her to live a full, normal life with a husband and children, but I didn't feel inspired to tell her any of that. So, I didn't."

I rested my head on his shoulder, and he put his arm around me. "I'm sorry, Jen."

"Don't be sorry, Adam. If that's what God wants, then that's what we'll take." It was easy to say, but I felt my nose tingle and my eyes grow hot.

Adam kissed my head and whispered, "If we obey Him, the windows of heaven will be opened, and we will be blessed beyond our capacity to understand."

I wrapped my arm around his stomach and snuggled into his chest. Adam had faith. If the Lord had wanted to heal Kaye, I knew in that moment, He would have.

I tried to focus on my blessing, and the comfort that would come, but my thoughts distracted me. It wasn't enough. Maybe the Lord hadn't healed her because the answer was already available to me—I just had to find it. We could try the diet again, take her in to see the neurologist that Dr. Suriya had recommended more than a month ago, and I'd even heard of some parents at the support group who had begun taking their children to chiropractors and massage therapists for something called cranio-sacral therapy.

The resolution burned in me. If the Lord wouldn't heal her with a simple blessing, maybe I could find another solution. It wasn't a door opening to the answer, but maybe it was a window.

Chapter 22

TESTING

They sedated Kaye and laid her down on a sheet-covered metal slab that moved slowly into a tunnel. She slept as they took images of her brain, and all I could think of was how still she lay there—her jaw relaxed enough that her chin could drop, and her eyes still beneath their lids. I stood outside the room, looking over the shoulder of a technician at the images on the computer screen. I didn't know what any of it meant.

Then Marie and I sat in the recovery room, waiting for Kaye to wake up. She'd never been sedated before, and I wasn't sure how she'd react to the anesthetic. When she woke up, she sat up too quickly and threw up all over the white hospital blanket.

"It's okay," a nurse said. "This happens all the time."

That was enough to make Kaye lie back down and go to sleep for a few minutes longer. Her eyes creaked open a couple of times, and when she saw me sitting next to her, her little hand in mine, she drifted back to sleep.

"What's your daughter in for?" The only other parent in the recovery room asked me. She sat across the room with a large child—he had to be about seven years old—on her lap.

"She just had an MRI."

She nodded. "Mine too." The boy in her arms reached his hand up and placed it on her face. She looked down at him lovingly.

"What's wrong with him?" I asked.

"Oh, a couple of things."

With her oblique answer, it occurred to me that my question might not have been very polite. I turned my attention back to Kaye.

"He's got leukemia." She kissed his hand.

I watched her smile gently as her son patted her face again.

One of the nurses walked over to her with a hypodermic needle and a couple of vials. "Do you want to do it, then?"

The mother nodded. She stood with her son in her arms and gently laid him down on the hospital bed next to her. His body was long and frail, and his skin a sickly shade of white. The mother tied off her son's arm, and began pressing the soft skin at his inner elbow. Then she stuck the needle in and began to draw his blood.

I looked questioningly at the nurse.

"She works here, but that's her son."

"Oh," I said. I was grateful I didn't have to draw Kaye's blood.

"It's more comforting to him when I do it," the mother said, and she locked her eyes onto her son's as the second vial filled with the red, life-giving fluid.

The boy's eyes fixed on his mother's, but the pain registered on his face as his brow furrowed and his lips parted to release an uncomfortable scream—a stressed, non-communicative scream.

"He's autistic, too," the mother said.

Her eyes looked too complacent, too content for her to be dealing with so much at once. I couldn't handle autism, let alone leukemia. "How have you dealt with that?" I asked. "Mine's only autistic, and that's enough to drive me crazy."

She placed a bandage on her son's arm, then picked him up and cradled him again. "You know, it hasn't been as bad as I thought it would be." Her eyes were bright and sincere as she looked at me. "There are a lot of rewards, you know?"

I couldn't think of many. "You're a better woman than I am."

She shook her head. "I doubt that. I just decided I was going to treasure every moment with him. It's made all the difference."

I stared at Kaye's face and brushed her hair gently from her cheek. Every moment, huh? It was easy to treasure moments like this one, when she slept soundly and looked like an angel. I wanted to ask the mother how she treasured the moments when he was screaming and interrupting everyone around him. Did she have a public life? Or was she sequestered in her home for the duration of her child's illness?

A mother and father followed a nurse into the recovery room. Their baby couldn't have been more than two months old, and he lay there on the tiny hospital bed looking miserable—but not as miserable as his parents. The mother's face was red, swollen, and tear-streaked, and the father looked as pale as his baby.

Sickness pressed in around me, and I began to feel claustrophobic. It reminded me of the first time I entered Kaye's school. It was foreign to me, and I didn't want it to be familiar.

By the time I was able to pry my eyes from the weeping couple, the mother who had drawn her son's blood had left the room. Her tranquil expression stayed with me long after Kaye recovered enough to be taken home.

* * *

Our new neurologist went over the tests with me. She said the MRI was normal, whatever that meant. The EEG showed potential for a seizure disorder, which was fairly common in autistic children. This revelation opened a whole new box of possible problems. She confirmed Dr. Suriya's diagnosis that Kaye was autistic, but that's about all she did for me. I left feeling worse than when I'd come.

A week later, I took Kaye to a doctor who used cranio-sacral therapy as part of her treatment of autistic children. She had me lay Kaye down on the examination table, and she held Kaye's head in her hands. Kaye didn't like it, and squirmed and screamed until she was red in the face.

"If this is going to work, she has to lay still," the doctor said.

I lay my head on Kaye's stomach and looked up at her and sang her songs. She sang the notes back to me and played with my face while the doctor closed her eyes and pressed her fingertips against Kaye's scalp. Kaye got a wild look in her eye, as if the doctor were violating her somehow.

"The bones in her skull are moving, very slightly. She can feel it," the doctor said.

Hours later it seemed as if it did help. Kaye was happier all day, and slept deeply that night. But she was still autistic. It didn't heal her.

The next thing on my list of "professional help" was counseling. Since I only knew one counselor who was offering free sessions, I made my first appointment with Theo Kaleel. I wasn't looking forward to it, but two of Julie's aids volunteered to watch the girls for me, so I didn't have an excuse.

Theo's office looked nothing like I'd imagined. It was probably an old janitor's closet, and somehow they'd squeezed in a desk and two leather chairs. There was a lamp on his desk and a light hanging overhead with a dimmer switch near the door.

"Is the lighting comfortable?" Theo asked.

"Sure. But don't I get a couch?" I laughed.

"I wanted one, but we couldn't fit it in," Theo said.

"This will be fine," I said, and I sat in the chair against the wall. The leaves of the artificial tree in the corner tickled my arm.

He pulled a yellow legal pad from a stack on his desk, and a blue pen from behind his ear. "You're Kaye Young's mother?"

I nodded. "Jen."

He wrote my name on the top of the legal pad. "Okay, what would you like to talk about today?"

I looked around the room. "I'm not sure. I've never done this before. What do you usually talk about—sports? The weather?"

He grinned, then jotted something down on his paper. "We talk about whatever my patients want to talk about. Do you *want* to talk about sports?"

I'd barely opened my mouth, and he was analyzing me. I wasn't sure I liked it, and didn't know if I could stand an hour in that leather chair.

"I went to a Jazz game once," I said, feeling a little deflated. He jotted something else down on his paper. His right forefinger was badly bruised—as if he'd shut it in a door—and the fingernail looked like it might fall off soon. I wondered what hard work a psychiatrist would engage in to endanger his finger like that. Maybe one of the more violent autistic kids didn't like being analyzed either.

He crossed his right leg over his left, and rested the pad of paper on his lap. "So, how are you doing?"

"Well, my daughter's autistic. It's not at all what I expected it to be, but we're coping. Of course, most the time I don't know what to expect anyway. I cry a lot. How are you?"

He grinned. "You've made four attempts at humor since you came through the door."

"Attempts? Ouch, tough crowd."

"Five." He smiled at me, but made another mark on his paper. Was he keeping track of my jokes?

"I make jokes when I'm uncomfortable," I said with a shrug.

"You make jokes to distance yourself from your pain."

I thought about his analysis and straightened my back as if I were in a job interview. "I thought humor was healthy."

"It is, unless it's used as a means of avoidance. You aren't facing your pain."

"Excuse me?"

"You aren't facing your pain. You make jokes to separate yourself from your grief."

"What grief?" I thought again of Olive. I missed her, but I felt as though Adam and I had dealt with her loss fairly well.

"You're grieving the loss of your daughter."

"But I didn't lose a daughter."

Theo smiled. "Yes, you did. Tell me, did you have any expectations for Kaye's future?"

I thought immediately of Marie. I'd expected Marie and Kaye to grow up together, sharing everything the way Brienne and I had done. Memories flashed in my mind—of Brienne and I staying up late into the night on weekends, a queen-sized blanket pulled over our heads so our parents wouldn't see the flashlight we had shining on our high school yearbook as we talked about boys. We double dated to my senior prom. She was the first person I told when I got engaged. She witnessed the birth of Marie, and I witnessed the birth of her little Emily. Certainly I had expectations for Kaye. I expected her to have what Brienne and I had—what Olive and Blanch had in their youth. I expected Kaye to have relationships, love, life.

"Kaye cannot meet your expectations," Theo continued. "The daughter you planned on has, in a sense, died. You are a mother in mourning."

I'd never thought of it that way.

"Until you can deal with your grief, and come to accept the child you have, you will be unable to deal with your pain, and you'll continue to make bad jokes." Theo smiled.

I tried to smile back. "Now who's making bad jokes?"

Theo smiled again and jotted something else down on his notepad.

Feeling thoroughly exposed, I turned to my original purpose for seeing Theo—healing Kaye. "I have a question," I said.

Theo looked at me with his soft, dark eyes.

"Can you counsel Kaye?"

"I do. I meet with each of the children every week."

"And what do you do? I mean, how do you counsel them if they can't talk to you?"

"I usually sit in on sessions with the teachers and watch how they interact. Then I make my recommendations."

Just as Dr. Suriya had done with me. "So you really don't do much but give your 'professional' opinion?"

He laughed. "Nope. I really don't do much more than that."

I sighed. No wonder Blanch didn't like psychiatrists. He'd given me a lot to think about as far as my feelings and expectations for Kaye went, but he really didn't help me much. I stood to leave. "Are we done?"

"Apparently so." He extended his hand to me.

I took it. "Do you need to see me again?"

He shrugged. "That's up to you."

I let go of his hand and picked up my purse. I had the sudden urge to hug him, but I didn't. Instead, I said, "I'll let you know."

Theo opened the door for me, and I hurried to Kaye and Marie in Julie's room. The walls were decorated with Halloween things— witches and skeletons, and ghosts made with white footprint cutouts and each of the kids' names beneath them. Kaye sat in the corner of the room, looking at books. Marie flipped through the pages of another book, looking at the pictures and making up a story. She showed the pictures to Kaye, even though Kaye was pretty much unaware.

Julie was straightening the room, and she looked up when I came in. "How are you?"

"I'm okay. Were the girls good?"

"Good as gold."

Kaye glanced at Marie's book when Marie wasn't watching her. As I watched the girls, I thought about what Theo had said. Was I in mourning? Kaye was so beautiful. And Marie treated her so well. When the book was finished, Marie put her arm around Kaye and kissed her cheek.

I may have been in a kind of mourning, but I hadn't really lost her. My expectations weren't dead, either. Kaye was getting out of her life what I expected her to get—she had relationships, she had love, and she certainly was full of life. My expectations weren't dead, they were just . . . different.

I went into the corner and sat on the floor next to the girls. Kaye looked me in the eye for just a moment and smiled as she looked away.

"Hi, Kaye," I said.

Marie climbed up on my lap. "We read books, Momma."

"I see that. You're a wonderful storyteller."

"Uh-huh." Marie nodded and smiled gratefully.

Julie approached us, straightening desks as she came. "We're really getting to know Kaye now."

I looked at her and chuckled. "Really? I'm still getting to know her. What have you found out?"

Julie smiled. "She likes numbers. Eventually, she'll probably be quite the math whiz."

"Really?"

"Oh, yes. She's starting to sign numbers. In fact, it encourages us to use ASL with her—she may start using it as a means of communication."

"Sign language?"

Julie nodded. "She's also been using PECS, which is a form of communication with pictures. She actually likes that better than sign. At the next parent meeting, we're going to talk more about PECS and we'll make folders with all the basics in them."

"Cool." The thought of Kaye being able to communicate with me, even a little bit, excited me. "What else have you learned?"

"She loves her family, that's for sure."

"How do you know that?"

"Remember at the beginning of the year, when we had you send photocopies of your scrapbooks?"

I nodded.

"Whenever Kaye does something wonderful, we give her that book as a reward. She loves it. Makes her happy for hours." Julie smiled.

I liked the thought that Kaye considered pictures of her family a reward.

"Did you have a good talk with Theo?" Julie asked. "Not that it's any of my business, but I just want to know you're okay."

I nodded. "Theo's good."

Julie agreed.

As we drove home from the school, Marie drifted in and out of sleep. Kaye watched passing headlights with wide eyes. I thought about Theo. He was right in some ways, and wrong in others. I wasn't avoiding my pain through my jokes—I faced my pain every day when I got out of bed, not knowing what I'd endure that day. My pain was not knowing what to expect, and yet I kept going. Maybe I was more like Kaye than I wanted to admit. She stressed out when her routine was interrupted, and the whole point of routine was to give her the comfort of knowing what would come next. I guess I liked routine too. And despite my step toward accepting Kaye the way she was, I still wanted her to be healed.

The only thing I learned from the medical community—traditional and non-traditional, psychological and biological—was that every child was different, and what worked for one child wouldn't necessarily work for another. Trial and error. Time. No one could offer me a quick fix. In a way, it was good, because through the special ed. programs, her teachers would give her the education she needed—everything would be on her terms. Every parent wants their child to have an education that fulfils their child's needs. I'd been guaranteed that for Kaye. On the downside, no one could take away our pain.

Other parents told me there was hope—some people experienced remarkable improvement, so remarkable that it seemed like a cure. Intensive therapies retrained an autistic child—remapped their neural pathways step by slow step. Private schools continued the behavioral treatment and structure that Kaye was getting at BTS. Experimental medications—unapproved by the FDA and therefore not covered by any insurance program—helped children calm down and focus on their surroundings until they were finally able to process stimulatory information. All of these treatments required one thing I didn't have—money.

Once again, my mind raced to come up with ways to make lots of money, but all of them required capitol, babysitters, and time and energy I didn't have.

Hope for healing was gone. Healing became a word I barely remembered—buried somewhere in the recesses of my mind. The light at the end of the tunnel was as dim as a distant, dying star.

This knowledge filled me with a dread unlike anything I'd felt since the initial diagnosis. People told me to take life a day at a time. And I tried. But it wasn't a short enough segment of time for me to deal with. A day seemed like an eternity. I woke in the morning, dreading the unknown, and I went to bed worrying about the day to follow. It was a painful, lengthy existence, and it seemed as though there would be no end to any of it. It seemed as though there would be no salve for me—no comfort. My prayers were frustrated, voiceless, and very short.

I wondered if God heard me at all.

Chapter 23

WITHOUT A PATTERN

It was so hard to get out of bed, but my heightened sense of smell—another side effect of my pregnancies—propelled me before my alarm went off. During the night, Kaye had taken off her diaper, and it was obviously dirty before she'd taken it off. She'd gotten some mess on her fingers and rubbed it on the wall next to her bed in four dark streaks, then she'd kicked the diaper out of her way so she could go back to sleep. The heels of her feet were filthy, and she'd left tracks along the sheets. I'd never seen—or smelled—such a mess in my life.

I had to clean Kaye first, going through several wipes before she was clean enough to put in the tub. After she was scrubbed and smelling better, I got her dressed for school. Then, I spent the next hour cleaning her bed and wiping down her walls with an anti-bacterial cleanser. By the time I was done, the mattress had been shampooed, the sheets and blankets were churning in the washer, and the walls were spotless. But my hands didn't smell entirely clean. No matter how hard I scrubbed, I couldn't get the smell to go away. It bothered me so much I couldn't rub my nose without holding my breath. But I couldn't hold it for long because I had to get Kaye dressed again before we left for school.

We missed Kaye's bus, so I drove across town and took her into Julie's classroom just before their lunch break. Julie asked if I was okay, but I told her "no" with one look.

Because we'd digressed from the routine, Kaye expected to leave with me when it was time for me to go, just as she had done the first time I'd visited her school and every time we'd come for parent-support group. Julie held Kaye tightly while Kaye screamed and tried to claw her way out of Julie's grasp. I led Marie away as tears dripped from my eyes. It was a horrible morning.

And my day wasn't over.

Marie had taken to preschool like a bird to flight. Usually I dropped her off at the school where Brienne had paid a year's tuition, then read a squeaky-clean LDS romance novel while I waited for school to get out, but I felt so sick to my stomach that day, I decided to go home and rest—put my feet up. I woke up to the ringing telephone, and heard Marie's crying voice on the other end of the line.

"Mommy? Are you coming to get me?"

I looked at the clock. Marie's class had been over for ten minutes.

Her teacher, Mrs. Orion, took the phone and spoke with a stern, alto voice. "Mrs. Young. You're ten minutes late to pick up Marie."

"I'm sorry. I fell asleep."

"I warned all the parents on the first day of school that they had a total of twenty minutes maximum to pick up their children. If you're not here ten minutes from now, I'll call child services. I have a short lunch break, Mrs. Young, and I don't have time to babysit your daughter just because you're a little sleepy."

I sighed. "I'll be right there. I'm leaving right now."

"We'll be in the classroom." She hung up the phone.

I hoped we were getting Brienne's money's worth. If Mrs. Orion had as much skill with teaching as she did with compassion, Brienne had flushed a whole bunch of money down the toilet.

As I waddled to Marie's classroom, dull pain pulsed in my lower back and I felt a stitch tug in my abdomen. My little one was giving me enough pain that I thought of going back to the doctor to find out what was going on.

Marie sat at a table near Mrs. Orion, who sat munching on a salad. Marie's little face was tear-streaked, and her lip quivered.

"Marie, I'm so sorry honey." I rushed to her and took her in my arms. "I fell asleep, baby. Mommy's been so sick lately, and I fell asleep." I pushed her back to look at her face. "I didn't mean to. It won't happen again."

Marie nodded and hugged me tightly.

Mrs. Orion shoveled salad into her mouth and glanced up at me.

I forced myself to have a calm voice and dry eyes as I spoke to Marie's teacher. "We could use a little compassion right now. I don't appreciate your threats."

She pointed at me with her fork and swallowed her food. "You're the one who's neglecting her, Mrs. Young. Not me. Besides, I was lenient. I gave you twenty minutes to come and get her. I have every legal right to call child services when children aren't picked up. And if this happens again, I won't give you a wide open window."

Her words stabbed my heart. Neglecting her? I wondered if she was right. Had I been neglecting Marie? My life had been so wrapped up in Kaye and all my struggles with her, that Marie had kind of been left on her own. The thought of someone taking her away tore at me. That would be too much to bear.

I wanted to pick Marie up and carry her out of the room, but the pain in my back barely let me bend over to take her hand.

"Thank you for keeping her company and not calling them," I mumbled.

Mrs. Orion grinned. "You're welcome."

The look in her eye intimidated me, and I rushed from the school as fast as Marie could run. After Marie was strapped in, I sat in the car and took several deep breaths until my heart had slowed back to its regular beat, and the sharp pain in my back had eased, then I looked at Marie. She had calmed down, but she was very subdued.

"Is Mrs. Orion nice to you, Marie?" I asked.

"Yes. We played dolls, and she let me eat her roll."

I nodded. "Well, that's good." At least she only showed her disapproval to me. I didn't want Marie suffering at school. Things were bad enough at home. And if Mrs. Orion treated Marie as badly as she treated me, I would pull Marie out of school and tell Brienne to complain and get a refund. After all, we were talking about my daughter. She was far more important than money could ever be.

"I love you, Marie."

She smiled. "I love you too, Mommy."

We waited longer than usual for Kaye's bus, and when they dropped her off, Kaye was screaming. I tried to hug her, but she pushed me away, and she didn't calm down until she was strapped in her car seat. I let myself cry all the way home, because I knew if I held it in, I'd feel even worse.

Adam's car was in the parking lot, and he peeked out the kitchen window when I pulled up. I'd never been so happy to see him.

After we'd helped the kids out of the car and into the house, I spilled every detail about my day. Adam listened intently, groaning in all the appropriate places.

Adam kissed my hand and smiled sympathetically. "I don't have to be to work till seven tonight because they're training people. Let's go to McDonalds, okay? Give us both a break from cooking."

I didn't need much convincing. "It's a deal."

Kaye heard the word "McDonalds," and she ran into the kitchen with her shoes in hand. It was the one word she understood perfectly.

We went just before the dinner rush, so Marie and Kaye had a few minutes at the playground without any other children. I loved it when we were the only people there—I didn't have to worry so much about what Kaye was doing. Gradually, however, people lined up to order dinner, and kids filled the playground. The noise was getting to me, and we were just about to leave when Kaye slid down the red plastic tube wearing nothing but her diaper.

"Oh, great," I said.

"Did she have her clothes on when she climbed up there?" Adam asked, looking around on the floor for her clothes.

"Yes, she had them on. I saw her climb up that tube."

The playground was a system of tubes winding around each other, leading to platforms with large plastic-bubble windows and padded bars to climb on. Halfway up one of the tubes was a net, which the kids could climb like a rope ladder, or lay in like a hammock, or look down at other children playing below them in the ball pit. At the top of the tube was a room, which led to the twisty slide Kaye had just slid down. I figured her clothes were somewhere in the tubes divided by the net, or in the room just before the slide.

Kaye ran around the dining area wearing nothing but her diaper, and McDonald's patrons stared at her and laughed as Adam followed and scooped her into his arms.

"Marie," I said. "Honey, climb up that tube and find Kaye's clothes."

Marie nodded and disappeared in the tube. In a few minutes, she popped out of the slide with empty hands.

"Marie, where are Kaye's clothes?"

"I couldn't see them, Mommy."

I knew Marie couldn't see things even when they were right in front of her. It seemed to be a common trait for everyone in my family except for me.

Adam's face was strained as he held a squirming, naked Kaye in his arms. "Let's go," he said, then he gritted his teeth.

"Let me get her clothes."

"I'll meet you in the car," Adam growled. He put on Kaye's shoes, then slipped her coat on over her bare skin. Kaye knew something was missing, and she tried to take her coat off. Adam zipped it quickly and threw her over his shoulder. Marie hurried to go with her Daddy.

I went into the tube headfirst, hoping no one was watching me, and hoping the clothes were closer to the bottom of the net than they were to the top. The tubing was tight, but I fit through. I figured I could shimmy out as easily as I was shimmying in.

The clothes weren't anywhere on the bottom landing. The angle of the tube wasn't very steep, but the top of the tube was at least five feet from the ground. I tested out the net to make sure it would hold my weight before I started to climb—a fall from that height was the last thing I needed. When I was almost to the end of the net, where it connected again with the tube, I caught a glimpse of Kaye's shirt. I let the net curve around my belly as I reached ahead and clasped Kaye's clothes, then, when I had my prize, I thought of how I would get out.

I couldn't see behind me, and because I was so round, I couldn't begin to bend or roll over in the tubing. I'd have to go down the net backwards and blind. I was almost to the end when my foot slipped and my shoe went through the net.

Yanking it out wouldn't work. I tried with all my strength to pull my foot free of the net's grasp, but using my muscles that way caused a spasm in my abdomen. The last thing I needed right then was to

send myself into premature labor. Bending over was impossible—
once again my belly got in the way. Stretching as far as I could, my
ankle was just out of reach.

Panic began burning in my chest, and the emotions of the past
few weeks flooded back to me. Was my life meant to be one horrible
thing after another? One disappointment, one embarrassment, one
failure after another? I didn't know anyone in the dining area—Adam
and the girls had already left for the car. I was completely alone and I
had no solution to my problem.

It seemed to be a definition for my life—no solution. I wanted to
cry, hit myself, shake any furniture nearby, bite anyone within range
of my teeth. My breath came in short, painful gasps, and I wondered
if I was about to have a panic attack.

Help! I prayed. I'd studied the gospel enough to know that the
Lord had said He wouldn't test us beyond our abilities to endure. I
felt as though I had reached the edge.

Help came when a young voice sounded near my feet. I couldn't
see the child, but she obviously had parents who hadn't taught her to
be polite. "Mom, there's a fat lady stuck in there!"

In a flash, I pictured how it must have looked from her angle, and
I couldn't help but chuckle. She may not have been polite, but at least
she was honest.

"What do you mean, there's a fat woman stuck in—oh." The
woman's voice got louder as she peeked up at my round bottom. She
choked back a snicker.

"A little help, please," I said, trying to decide whether to laugh
or cry. It had been a horrible day, and what a horrible way to end
it. It would be even more embarrassing if they pulled me out of the
tube and I was crying uncontrollably. I focused on what I must
have looked like from the child's point of view, and I chose to
laugh.

"What can I do?" The woman's voice sounded sympathetic now.

"My shoe is stuck." I wiggled my leg to show her how the net had
wrapped around the heel of my tennis shoe.

"Oh, okay." I felt a pair of hands on my ankle. "Yeah, I'm just
going to take off your shoe."

"Okay," I said. Then I laughed as I said, "Thanks."

With deft fingers, the woman untied my shoe through the net, and held the shoe as I pulled my foot free.

"Okay, you can come out," she said.

I stepped in a different area, and wriggled backwards until I was able to escape. I felt my face grow red as I backed out of the tube, with Kaye's clothes in hand and one bare foot.

"Here, I'll get it." The kind woman, who was much thinner than I, climbed in and wrestled my shoe from the net, then handed it to me with a smile.

"Thanks," I said, and I dropped the shoe to the floor and slipped my foot into it without bothering to tie it again. "I'm going to go now. Got what I went in there for, so—thanks."

The woman smiled. "You bet."

I heard a few people snicker as I left the dining area, and part of me laughed with them. The rest of me burned with embarrassment.

"What took you so long?" Adam asked when I got in the car with Kaye's clothes.

"I got stuck in the tube."

"What?"

"I got stuck in the tube. I climbed up there to get Kaye's clothes, and I got stuck. A woman had to help me out."

"Are you okay?" Adam eyed my belly with concern.

I laughed. "Yes, I'm fine. I'm thoroughly embarrassed, but I'm fine."

Adam smiled. "You really got stuck?"

"Oh, yeah." I raised my eyebrows and laughed until I shook.

Then I shook until I cried.

Adam focused on me. "Are you okay?"

I nodded, though I felt my face contort as I tried to keep it all in.

Adam put his arms around me, kissed my wet cheeks, and smoothed my hair behind my ears. "You okay?" he asked again.

I nodded. "I'm just stressed, I guess." My stomach felt tight, as if a contraction could start at any time. I took a deep breath and rubbed my belly gently.

Adam massaged the nape of my neck and I took another deep breath.

"I'm okay," I said.

After we got home, I dressed Kaye again and Adam got ready for work. My adventure in McDonald's playland may have been funny, but I didn't want to experience that again. And I didn't want a repeat of that morning's adventure in cleaning either. I had to figure out a way to keep Kaye's clothes on her—just as Brienne and Russ had figured out a way to keep Kaye in the house at night. There may not have been a solution to Kaye's disorder, but there had to be something I could do about that little problem.

Was it possible to lock someone into her clothes? She needed something like a straightjacket. I doubted they had patterns for things like that at the fabric store.

When we got home, I watched Kaye undress again, and I began formulating a plan. She couldn't undo the snaps at the crotch of her bodysuit, so she stretched the neck and slipped it off around her shoulders. She needed an outfit she couldn't take off over her head, or slip down—something that snapped closed at the neck and at the crotch.

"Adam, watch the girls. I'm going shopping."

"What are you going to get?"

"I don't know how yet, but I'm going to make an outfit that Kaye can't take off. No more streaking for her." I smiled and grabbed my purse.

"Okay. Be back before I have to go to work."

I went to Deseret Industries and bought some overalls and a turtleneck, then I went to the fabric store and bought a seventeen-inch zipper and some large safety pins. With the tools in my hand, it wasn't hard to picture the solution to my latest problem. Of course, picturing it was one thing. Sewing it without the aid of a pattern was another. I'd never sewed without a pattern before.

First I sewed the turtleneck into the overalls at the neckline and shoulder straps. Then, I cut down the back of the turtleneck and the overalls, and sewed in the zipper. From the front, it looked like a two-piece outfit.

I tried it on Kaye, but she pulled it down around her shoulders, and the zipper unzipped until the outfit fell off. It was too stretchy for the high neck to make a difference. Adam had an old pair of jeans that he never wore, so I cut a strip of denim off the hem and sewed it around the neck.

I tried it on Kaye again, and though she couldn't stretch it around her shoulders, she didn't have to pull very hard before the zipper gave way again. So I threaded a safety pin through the eye of the zipper, and fastened it into the denim strip.

Kaye tugged at the clothes. She pulled the turtleneck and fiddled with the safety pin, which she couldn't see and couldn't figure out. She pulled at her crotch, as if she was trying to pull the outfit down over her shoulders, but the seam held firm.

I was so excited to finally solve something, that I barely slept before Adam got home. When he did, I led him into the girls' room to show him my handiwork.

"How do you like Kaye's new straightjacket?" I whispered.

"Her what?"

"Her straightjacket. She won't be able to take this off—she'll be locked in her clothes." I smiled with satisfaction.

"I don't know if I like you calling it a straightjacket," Adam whispered.

"Why not? It's funny. If she were crazy, it wouldn't be funny. But she's not crazy. She's smart." I folded my arms across my chest. I had to gloat a little over my first victory in months. "But she's not as smart as me—yet."

Adam smiled. "That is cool. You sure she can't take it off?"

I shook my head. "She's been wearing it all evening."

It felt so good to solve a problem that I began wondering what had changed in me. Why was I able to think clearly enough to find a solution for the first time in months? Was it because I chose to laugh when I had every reason to cry? Was it because I had prayed for help while I was stuck in the tunnel?

"What are you thinking?" Adam asked.

I realized I'd been staring into space. "Just trying to figure things out. I feel great right now, but this little outfit isn't really that big of a deal. I've solved one problem, but give Kaye some time, and she'll present a new problem for me."

"Isn't that what life's about?"

I didn't really want to live my life one problem to the next, waiting for occasional moments of happiness. I wanted to be prepared for everything. I wanted to be made of Teflon, or steel, or something that would be unaffected by life's difficulty and undamaged by life's storm. Instead, I felt like a little ship moved by the tide's ebb and flow. I wanted to be the kind of mother who treasured every moment with her children, but I was too busy getting seasick.

"Adam," I said, "all my life, I've wanted everything planned and perfect. I'm not a last-minute type of girl—someone who can throw things together and do just fine. I panic if things don't go according to plan."

Adam nodded with a grin on his face.

"But Kaye doesn't fit with my plans." It felt strange to say it, but it was what I'd been thinking.

Adam turned his thoughtful eyes toward Kaye. Finally he spoke with a quiet, contemplative voice. "I don't think life is supposed to fit with your plans, it's supposed to fit with God's."

He turned to me, looking so resolute—so faithful.

I sighed. "But I don't know His plans, Adam. How could I possibly have prepared for Kaye? How can I prepare for her future? I don't know what to expect, so how can I prepare for it?"

"You just have to have faith. Even if things don't fit with your plans, somehow they fit with His. No offense, but His plans are better than yours."

"I know that," I said. "But I wish He'd give me a clue before He gave me a trial."

Adam smiled and kissed my cheek. "He does."

He left the room without elaborating.

Chapter 24

TEACHERS

I'd agreed to meet Kaye's potential Primary teacher at the church with the Primary president. With my newfound determination to tackle Kaye's condition one problem at a time came a set of expectations for Kaye's Primary teacher. Adam was at work, of course, and the two women were already seated when I ushered Marie and Kaye into the classroom. I set my heavy diaper bag on the floor, and Kaye proceeded to empty its contents.

The Primary president, Sue, was a plump woman with black hair that twisted down her back to her waist. She started the meeting with a word of prayer, then with introductions. "Gay Lynn, this is Jen. Jen, this is Gay Lynn."

Gay Lynn's short, white hair waved easily around her clear, open face. Bright green eyes and smooth skin made her look much younger than her hair led me to believe she was. She couldn't be more than fifty years old. She had a bright smile, too. Her hand was small, but strong, and surprisingly cold.

Her gaze flitted to Kaye. "Is this Kaye?"

I nodded.

Gay Lynn looked Kaye up and down—apparently sizing up what she would be getting into if she accepted her new calling. "She's wiggly."

That was an understatement.

"I have to warn you, I've never really liked children." She smiled again.

I felt my jaw drop as Sue chuckled. I wondered if Gay Lynn was kidding, but her expression was too truthful—not a hint of a grin. I'd never met a Latter-day Saint who admitted they didn't like children, and I wondered why the bishop had thought of extending a Primary calling to her. It didn't make sense.

"I had two kids of my own, before I divorced and remarried. They've grown into wonderful men with kids of their own, but I don't really like kids. I'm not patient enough, I guess."

"I don't think you'll like teaching Kaye, then," I said, feeling very defensive. Maybe this woman wasn't the solution to our problem with church. I was ready to walk out of the room.

Gay Lynn folded her arms across her nearly flat chest. "I thought so, too. I mean, all these years I've told the bishop he could call me anywhere but Primary. I *promised* that if he called me to the Primary, I'd turn him down. But when the bishop suggested I teach Kaye, I had a feeling it would be a good thing for me to do."

Maybe good for her, but what would it do to Kaye? "What exactly don't you like about kids?"

She sighed. "The noise. The fighting. The rivalries. The immature rudeness." She looked up at me and must have seen my barely disguised alarm. "I guess that's a brash way to introduce myself, huh?"

I nodded.

"Well, let me ask about you. What's autism?"

I had thought Cathy was upfront, but this woman amazed me. No small talk, no polite, awkward introduction. She headed straight for the question I wasn't sure I could answer because I was still asking it.

"Um, autism is a developmental disorder. And Kaye can't talk. I'm not sure how much she understands. She stimms a lot."

"What does that mean?"

"She plays with her fingers—wiggles them together. Her teacher says it probably helps her concentrate."

"Okay. I can understand that. I have to rub my feet together to calm down so I can fall asleep at night. Kind of like a cricket, but I don't make noise." She laughed.

This woman was weird.

"Jen," Sue said after she'd stopped laughing herself, "can you give us any suggestions as to how to go about teaching Kaye? I wanted to have this meeting for my benefit, as well as Gay Lynn's. What are your expectations?"

Since I'd been thinking along those lines, I knew just how to answer. "We expect to be able to attend our meetings on a regular basis—no more inactivity, no more spiritual vacuum."

"Okay, so you don't want us to come and get you if Kaye acts up." Sue wrote it on a piece of paper.

"Well, Kaye acts up a lot, so if you came to get me every time, I'd miss all my classes so there would be no point. But there are a few things you can do to calm her down. She likes walking along the curb in the parking lot. She likes books, and Disney videos."

Gay Lynn couldn't take her eyes off Kaye.

Sue's pencil was poised over her notepad. "Okay, so you want her to be entertained? Do you want us to play videos for her every week, or what?"

I thought about it, and it didn't seem quite right. She was doing well in school—the notes I got from Julie every day showed progress—so I knew Kaye had the ability to learn, albeit slowly.

With a shake of my head, I turned to Gay Lynn. "I don't want you to babysit. I want you to be her teacher."

Gay Lynn nodded and turned her face to Kaye. "She's not like other kids, is she?"

I thought of how different she was from every child I'd ever watched. "No."

"But she likes pictures?"

"Yes."

"What if we put big pictures of Jesus around the room—taped them up on these walls. I could tell her the stories behind the pictures every Sunday, and eventually she'd memorize them, right?"

I nodded. "Eventually."

"She's probably like the rest of us—repetition is the greatest teacher, right?"

"Exactly. And she likes routine, so if you establish a routine with her, she'll be more attentive," I agreed.

"So the first little while will be hard, but things will get better?" Gay Lynn still hadn't taken her eyes off of Kaye, but she finally had a touch of a grin on her face. "Look at her. She's doing a pattern."

Admittedly, I hadn't been watching Kaye. I'd been wondering what could have pointed to this strange woman as a potential teacher for Kaye. But, as I changed my focus, I began to see why Gay Lynn was smiling.

Kaye had a book open in her lap to a picture of a princess. The princess, dressed in a flowing pink gown, extended her hand to the prince, who was just out of reach on the next page. Kaye stimmed over the princess, then the prince, then the princess again. It was almost as if she were trying to coax the pictures together—trying to tell the prince to move it and take the hand that reached out to him.

"What's going on in that little head of hers?" Gay Lynn asked. She shook her head and looked at me as if she'd woken from a trance and everything was suddenly clear. "We'll establish a routine, so she can get comfortable. Every Sunday we'll tell the same stories with the same pictures. And after she's used to me, we'll integrate her with the other Primary kids a little at a time—as Kaye will allow. Add as much to her routine as she'll let me."

"Sounds interesting." My heart lifted as I thought of it—Kaye learning how to interact with the Primary children, and the Primary children learning how to interact with her.

"What about sharing time and singing time?" Sue asked.

"Kaye loves music, but I'm pretty sure she'll get nervous before too long," I replied.

"That's okay," Gay Lynn said. "We'll go for as long as she can stand it, then we'll go back to her classroom. I won't mind taking her back to the classroom anyway, away from the noise. I bet we both get overstimulated."

Julie had mentioned that overstimulation often caused Kaye to stress out. "You'll get pretty tired of doing the same thing every week, won't you?" I asked, mentioning the one glitch I saw in the near future. The best teachers always burned out. Also, many adults tired of the kind of repetition Kaye needed.

"I don't know. It might be nice. Besides, you need help. And I'm willing to help. Plus Kaye and I will get along like peanut butter and jelly. I can tell." Her green eyes crinkled at the corners as she smiled at me and gave me a half hug.

She had no idea how grateful I was to hear those words.

"Should I start Sunday?"

I searched my feelings about this odd woman, and felt a sense of calm. "Sure," I said.

It seemed like the woman who didn't like children was the perfect teacher for my little Kaye, and I smiled as I led the girls out to the car. I'd be able to attend my meetings on Sunday without worrying about where the girls were. The calm spread over me, and I knew all would be well.

* * *

The Primary president assigned a room for Kaye and Gay Lynn. When we brought Kaye to the room the next Sunday morning, Gay Lynn had a stack of pictures on the table, a television in the corner, and a Disney sing-along hiding in her bag.

"I'll pull this out if we get desperate," she said as she turned her back to Kaye and showed me the sing-along.

"Great idea! You seem prepared," I said.

"Well, as prepared as I can be, based on our talk the other day."

"You know where we'll be if you need us." I looked at Kaye. She was already flipping through the pictures on the table.

Gay Lynn ushered us out the door. "It will be fine. We won't need you."

Adam and I separated for Relief Society and Priesthood, and I listened to a nice lesson about finding peace in the gospel. I could see why the word of God was referred to as a balm—I felt as though the searing pain of my wounds was lessened, at least for a time.

Brother Arnold, the man with deep dimples and dark hair, taught Gospel Doctrine again. He opened his Bible and asked us to do the same. "I am so grateful to stand before you today, brothers and sisters. I learned a lot preparing for this lesson, and hopefully you will glean some of that learning from me.

"First, let me ask you this: Does Jesus Christ have the power to heal us?"

My stomach tightened. The lesson was already hitting painfully close to home.

Many voices throughout the room said, yes. Some with solid conviction, others with quiet resolution.

"Of course He does," the teacher continued. "Don't raise your hands, but think about this. Have any of you ever been healed?"

There were fewer responses in the room. I remembered a time when I was about eight years old, and I had such a horrible fever that I was delirious. I felt my father's hands on my head, pressing heavily on me. When he took his hands away the pressure disappeared and I slept soundly. The fever broke later that day, but it still took two days for me to feel better. Did that count as a healing? I might have gotten better without Dad laying his hands on my head. I wasn't sure if I'd been healed or not.

"How does the Savior heal us anyway?" Brother Arnold continued. "Can any of you think of an example of a healing in the scriptures?"

A man on the front row with a military-style haircut and a goatee raised his hand. "There are several examples of healings, especially in the New Testament."

"Give me one," the teacher said, still looking at the man on the front row.

"Well, there's the woman who touched the hem of His garment and was healed of an issue of blood."

"Several blind people were healed," a woman next to the wall chimed in.

"Lepers too," said the man next to her.

"All of these people were healed of physical ailments, correct?" Brother Arnold asked.

The class agreed.

Brother Arnold set his open book on the podium and clasped his hands behind his back. "Are we healed in any other ways?"

"We're forgiven of our sins, so our spirits are healed." A kind-looking, white-haired man on the other side of the room spoke up.

"Thank you, Brother Smith. He heals us of our spiritual infirmities. Take the case of the woman who washed His feet with her tears in the house of Simon the Pharisee. He said to her, 'Thy sins are forgiven . . . Thy faith hath saved thee; go in peace.' These are miraculous ways of healing us," Brother Arnold continued. "But is that all? Does He always take away our infirmities?" Several people shook their heads, including me.

"Can He heal us without taking away our infirmities?"

No one answered his question.

"I'd like you to turn to Mosiah 24:15."

I heard the raspy sound of thin scripture pages turning, and I opened my Book of Mormon with everyone else. If He didn't take away our infirmities, was He healing us? I'd never thought of healing as anything but taking away sickness or injury.

"Who'd like to read that for me?"

Adam raised his hand and read the verse. "'And now it came to pass that the burdens which were laid upon Alma and his brethren were made light; yea, the Lord did strengthen them that they could bear up their burdens with ease, and they did submit cheerfully and with patience to all the will of the Lord.'"

I glanced at Adam and smiled. He was braver than I was. I wouldn't volunteer to read.

"Thank you, Brother Young. So," Brother Arnold continued, "sometimes the Lord strengthens us and helps us endure our trials. Is this a type of healing?"

He looked at the class thoughtfully. A few people nodded their heads in agreement. Some people didn't seem to agree so readily.

"It's better to be given the strength to endure than to be left alone! Also, we learn more from having trials than from having our infirmities lifted, don't you think? I think the Lord heals us this way more often because He wants us to learn from our infirmities so that we can have compassion for others who suffer."

Brother Arnold walked to the blackboard and wrote the points he had covered, along with scripture references. "Okay, so He heals us by taking away our infirmities, taking away our sins, strengthening us, and . . ." He wrote a number four on the board. "Please turn to John 14:27."

The scriptures rustled again. A thin woman sitting in front of me raised her hand, volunteering to read.

"Please." Brother Arnold motioned to her.

"'Peace I leave with you: my peace I give unto you: not as the world giveth, give I unto you. Let not your heart be troubled, neither let it be afraid.'"

Brother Arnold looked at the class with a slight grin. "Is this a form of healing?"

A few people whispered in agreement.

"Sure it is," he said. "He sends the Comforter, the Holy Ghost, to take away our fear and give us peace." He turned and wrote, "comforts us" on the blackboard.

"How does He do all this, brothers and sisters? Please turn to Isaiah 53:4 and 5."

I leaned over to Adam while the pages were rustling. "He's a good teacher, isn't he!"

"It's a good subject," Adam whispered.

Brother Arnold read the verse. "'Surely he hath borne our griefs, and carried our sorrows: yet we did esteem him stricken, smitten of God, and afflicted. But he was wounded for our transgressions, he was bruised for our iniquities: the chastisement of our peace was upon him; and with his stripes we are healed.'"

He paused and looked up at us with wonder in his eyes. "He heals us through the power of the Atonement. He had such a great love for us that he suffered the incredible pain of being scourged and then the agony of dying on the cross. As I contemplated that suffering while preparing this lesson, Gethsemane came powerfully to mind and I received the strongest impression. I am supposed to say these words to this class today. 'The Atonement will heal you.'" He paused and lifted his glasses to dab at the corners of his moist eyes.

"If you take notes, write these words down. If you aren't into taking notes, burn these words in your heart, 'The Atonement will heal you.'" His voice was full of conviction.

Everyone could feel it, the energy of the room was charged with his testimony. My scriptures were still open to the verse in John. In the top margin I wrote "The Atonement will heal me."

"He may not heal you in the way you expect, but He will do what is best for your welfare. Trust Him, have faith, and He will heal you according to His will."

He ended the class, and someone said the closing prayer. As people started leaving the room, I stayed in my seat. I didn't want to leave. My mind had been opened in that class, and I'd been given a different way to think about things I'd read about since I was able to read. The feeling of enlightenment—the warmth of the Spirit was too rare in my life for me to willingly stand up and shake it off. I didn't want to go back to Kaye and the struggles we had with her. I wanted more of the feeling I had sitting there in that chair.

Brother Arnold locked his eyes on mine and smiled gently, as if he thought I was the reason he'd taught that lesson that day. He looked away as a young, teenaged girl with dimples just like his came and pulled him from the room.

I looked down at my scriptures, where I had written the little note to myself. Then I gathered my things.

* * *

That night, I had another vivid dream. In my dream, I slept soundly in my bed and woke to Kaye screaming. I didn't want to leave the comfort of my covers, but I did. Darkness surrounded me, and an eerie red glow emanated from downstairs. At first I thought it was the television, but as I descended, I found the family room flooded with lava. Kaye sat on the couch, looking frightened and confused. She didn't look to me for help, but kept her eyes on the burning red rock around her. I called her name, but she wouldn't look at me.

The heat from the lava melted picture frames on the walls around me, and the portraits of my children stretched and dripped. I looked at Kaye. Her image was distorted by the heat, as if she were merely a mirage—all waves and swirls. I called to her again before the lava engulfed her.

Soon my screams were all around me, ringing in my ears, burning in my throat. I ran down the stairs and walked across the hot coals, barely aware of my singeing soles. It took an eternity for me to cross the room—long enough for the heat from the lava to lessen, and the family portraits to stop melting and solidify like cooled candle wax on the walls. I knelt next to where Kaye had once been, and plunged my fingers into the black, cooling coals. I broke them apart, and Kaye shot out of the ash like a ray of light.

Kaye stood before me then, a grown woman dressed in white. Her denim eyes locked onto mine, and she wouldn't turn away from me. She still didn't speak, but she reached her hands out and held my face—so gently that I could barely feel her touch. Her lips twitched in a gentle, knowing smile.

I woke from the dream and went to Kaye's bedroom. She had the covers pulled up over her head and was snoring loudly. Her feet stuck out from beneath her covers. With a smile on my face, I closed her door quietly and went back to my bed. The rest of the night's sleep was sweet.

Chapter 25

OH, BOY

"Do we want to know the sex?" Adam asked me.

"I already do," I said with a calm grin.

Adam looked at the doctor, who shrugged. "I don't know, so it must be mother's intuition since your baby was being modest for the first ultrasound." She squirted cool gel on my bare, distended stomach.

"Okay, what do you think? Tell me now so I can tease you if you're wrong." Adam winked.

It was so good to have him with me—I'd become used to being alone. I didn't like the life I was used to. "It's a boy."

"A boy?" Adam grinned and got a proud-papa expression.

"Should we see?" Dr. Rimes proceeded to give the ultrasound. She pointed out the baby's head, both hands with ten perfect fingers, both feet with ten perfect toes. His heart was perfect, with just the right number of chambers and beats per minute, and his face was shaped like Adam's—he had the same chin.

"Well, I hope it's a boy, 'cause that baby looks like Daddy," I said with a laugh.

Adam grinned.

Marie looked at the picture, trying to see what we saw. "I can't see him, Mommy. Where's his hair?"

I laughed. "He doesn't have hair yet, sweetie. It's kind of hard to tell what we're seeing, isn't it?"

Marie lost interest in the picture and reached for her dad to pick her up.

"It's definitely a boy," Dr. Rimes said. "He's showing his stuff just so we know for sure." She laughed.

I sighed. "I like things I can plan on."

Dr. Rimes gave me a towel to clean my skin. "Well, you can go buy a ton of blue clothes without keeping the receipts."

I looked at Adam, and he grinned. His eyes moistened as he kept staring at the picture frozen on the monitor.

"We're going to have a boy," I whispered.

Adam spoke to the doctor as she was heading for the door. "Oh, Dr. Rimes, before we forget—Jen's been having some pain lately, in her lower back."

She turned to me. "Oh?"

I nodded. "And I feel all tense, like I could have a contraction at any time."

"Well, everything looks good. Back pain is common for a third pregnancy, and you could be having some early labor. Are you going through any stress at home?"

I glanced at Adam. "Yes, our other daughter was diagnosed with autism four months ago."

"Oh. Well, that will make one stressed! You're, let's see, twenty-six weeks along now. You could be having some Braxton-Hicks. Just make sure you take it easy as often as possible, and try not to let the stress get to you." She smiled, as if it were as easy as it sounded.

Marie couldn't stop talking about her little brother all the way to the car. She clutched the printout of the ultrasound in her hand and skipped along. "Let's name him Mark!" Marie said.

"We've already got an M in the family, *Marie*." I laughed.

"How about Albert?" Marie suggested.

"Already have an A, too."

Marie looked quizzically at me.

"Daddy's name is Adam, remember?"

"Oh, yeah."

Adam laughed.

"How about Scott?" I suggested.

"Like Uncle Scott?" Adam asked.

I nodded.

Adam grinned and agreed. "Scott Young. What about a middle name?"

I shrugged. "Does Uncle Scott have a middle name?"

Adam shrugged. "I don't know. But plain Scott's good."

As Adam helped me into my car, he bent down and put his lips next to my rounded belly. "I love you, Scott. Be good to your Mommy, you hear?"

He kissed me and went back to school.

That night, while Adam was working, we had another parent-support group meeting. Once a month they had a special speaker share ideas or new research findings about autism. After I found my seat on the back row, I looked up with dismay at Dr. Suriya.

I may have been shooting the messenger, but as I looked at him, my stomach tightened. He was the bearer of ill news, like the superstitious signs my mother-in-law feared—he was a ladder, a black cat, and a broken mirror wound up in one. My gaze caught his for just a moment, but his eyes lacked the slightest hint of recognition. I was probably one in hundreds of victims he'd left at the roadside, struggling to find help.

His face was void of emotion. People greeted him, and he didn't smile when he took their hands. He answered questions curtly, but honestly, without a grin or a twinkle in his eye.

"Some of the best doctors are detached." Trenton's mom, the thin woman with the scarred cheek who'd recently divorced her husband, put her arm around me and spoke quietly near my ear.

I turned to look at her. "Well he must be the best doctor in the state."

"Some say he is. He diagnosed Trenton too."

"Trenton's in Julie's class, isn't he?"

"Yes. Julie's great."

"I like her too." I wondered where Trenton's mom got her long, white scar. Her eyes were a light hazel, and her dark brown hair was streaked with gray.

"I started having kids late in my life. Trenton's my only one. I can't believe you're having another." She pointed at my round belly.

"Well, I got pregnant before Kaye was diagnosed. He's a bit of a surprise."

"You're Kaye's mom? She's so cute. She's in Julie's class too."

I nodded.

"Do you know this one's a boy?"

"We found out today."

"Well, I hope he's not autistic too. They say it's at least partly genetic, and it's more common in boys."

I'd never thought of it, but the fact that Kaye was the only girl in a class of nine children was an obvious indication. I rubbed my belly just as Scott stretched, and imagined going through the past four months all over again. I felt congested—like I had a bad case of bronchitis. By the time Dr. Suriya stood in front of the crowd, I could barely breathe, and I pushed my way past impatient people and their knobby knees until I rushed into the hall.

My life was hard enough with one autistic child. I couldn't bear the thought of two. I reminded myself that Scott would be a comfort to me. Adam had said so. He couldn't be autistic and be a comfort to me.

I thought of leaving early, but I had to talk to Dr. Suriya. I had to know what my odds were. During the ultrasound, I'd admitted that I liked to know what was ahead. This was no different. If Scott was going to be autistic, I wanted to nip it in the bud. I wanted to know before he was born, and have the neurologist and the pediatrician informed. We could catch it early and treat it, and maybe he'd never show an obvious sign. This time, I would be prepared. This time, I would be perfect and no one could blame me—not even myself.

Sharp pains in my abdomen made me sit down in a child's chair in the hall. No matter how prepared I thought I could be, it wouldn't be enough. I knew what was wrong with Kaye, and by then I knew a few ways to deal with her tantrums. But it wasn't enough. I still cried when she got so sad and frustrated that she wouldn't let me comfort her. I still had to put myself in time-out when she screamed for hours for a mysterious reason. I worried about Kaye's past, present, and future, and the thought of having another child like her sapped the energy out of me until my ears buzzed and I thought I would pass out.

I put my head between my knees and took the deepest breaths I could, but since Scott was preventing me from breathing in that position, I sat up again and leaned my head back against the wall. Silent prayers formed in my mind—prayers with panicked feelings but no words. By the time the meeting had ended and the parents had separated into their therapy groups, I could see clearly again. Dr. Suriya left the library, and I called to him.

"Yes?" He turned and looked at me. "Are you alright?"

"I'm fine," I lied. "I need to ask you, though. What are the odds that I'll have another autistic child?" I ran my hand across my belly.

"Is it a boy?"

I nodded. "We found out today."

"Since it's a boy, you have about a thirty percent greater chance that he will be autistic, and that's if the child who attends this school is a boy."

I shook my head. "She's a girl."

"Well, the odds could be higher then. We're not sure why there are more autistic boys than there are girls, so the numbers can't really be accurate. But, we know that families with autism are more likely to have additional children with the disorder. It has some genetic link."

I nodded and felt myself getting light-headed again.

"But you can't really tell until he's about eighteen months old. There are some theories that diagnose the children earlier, but there's so much development that goes on before a child turns two, and since all children develop at different rates, I'm cautious to diagnose before eighteen months. Treatments may get better by the time he's that age, though. We're learning more all the time."

I leaned against the wall.

Someone else took Dr. Suriya's attention, and he left without another word to me.

I wasn't ready to pick up the girls, so I hovered just outside the door as the parents found their seats for support group.

"I know what you mean," Trenton's mom said. She was standing near the doorway with a Diet Coke in her hand, talking to another parent. "That's how I got this scar. Trenton's been pretty violent since he was two. He threw a pair of gardening shears at me, and one of the blades cut my cheek. Fourteen stitches."

I rubbed my belly and ran the words of Adam's blessing through my head until my vertigo went away.

Somehow, I got home that night and tucked the girls in their beds. I lay awake for hours, rubbing my belly and feeling Scott kick inside me. Sleep wouldn't come, and I tried to relax, to focus on something besides the feeling of panic building in my chest.

Finally Adam came home. I heard him shut the door and slide in the chain lock. He snuck into the bedroom and sat gently on his side of the bed while he took off his shoes.

"Scott's going to be autistic," I whispered to his back.

He spun around to look at me, his eyes were round and glowed slightly in the moonlight. "I thought you were asleep. What did you say?"

"Scott's going to be autistic," I whispered again in almost the same tone.

"Where did you get that idea?"

"Dr. Suriya spoke at the support group tonight, and he said there's a genetic link and it's more common in boys, especially if you already have an autistic girl."

"Whoa, slow down. Just because there's a genetic link doesn't really mean anything. Besides, we don't have anyone in either of our families who's autistic. I'm not entirely sure our case has anything to do with genetics."

"So it's my fault, then?" I asked as I pushed myself up in bed. My grandmother had Alzheimer's, and I had a cousin with learning disabilities. It didn't seem like Adam had contributed any traits similar to autistic characteristics. I started taking my prenatal vitamins later on in my pregnancy with Kaye. During those first few weeks of the pregnancy, I took walks near the medical research facility at the University. I had no logical reason to blame any of those sources for Kaye's autism, but I felt the need to blame someone or something. Blaming myself was the easiest thing to do. Besides, I was physically responsible for her from the moment she was conceived.

"Of course it's not your fault," Adam said. "Stop talking that way."

"Mrs. Orion said I've been neglecting Marie. If she grows up with problems, she'll be in therapy because her mother neglected her."

"I wouldn't call it neglect. Everybody's late once in a while. You've been doing the best you can."

"And all we do all day is watch television," I lamented.

Adam dismissed it. "Our kids multitask all day long. The television is background noise."

"I can't do anything right, Adam! Everything I do messes up somehow. Everything I hope for fails. Why do you love me?"

Adam rolled his eyes and shut himself in our bathroom.

His reaction hurt. "What, am I just overreacting again?" I called to him, as loudly as I could without waking up the kids. "You can't handle another crying girl in the house, huh? Well, then, why don't you leave? You're obviously happier at school and at work than you are at home. Even on Saturdays, you're gone all day. You don't have to go anywhere on Saturdays. So why do you leave, Adam? Don't you like being home?"

The bathroom door flew open, and Adam stormed out, looking straight at me. "No, I don't like being home!"

I stared at him and felt myself begin to shake—with fear of becoming single like Trenton's mom, and with anger. "So you like leaving your pregnant wife to deal with everything by herself, huh? You think that's fun, Adam?"

"Well, Kaye—if she's the problem—is gone most of the time anyway, so what do you have to complain about? And when I'm home, you make me do everything, so why should I enjoy being home? Do you know what it's like to come through the door after a hard day, and be greeted with a weepy wife and a 'honey-do' list?"

"No, Adam, I don't know what that's like, because I've never been able to spend the day away. You get a change of scenery. You get to talk to adults. You get to have a life!" The pain came sharp again, and I clutched my belly. But I couldn't stop yelling at Adam. It was his fault anyway, as much as it was mine. "I would trade you jobs in a second, and you wouldn't last taking care of the house and the kids. You'd be *begging* to trade me back in a day." By the time I finished my rampage I was doubled over. The contraction gripped me and wouldn't let go.

"Jen. Are you okay?" Adam knelt next to me and took my hand in his.

I tried to breathe, but the contraction wouldn't ease.

"Call Cathy," I said. "We need her to watch the kids while you take me to the hospital."

Adam ran from the room, and I concentrated on breathing. Finally, the contraction eased, but I was nervous by then. It was too early. I knew if I gave birth to Scott, he probably wouldn't make it. I prayed wordlessly until Adam came back upstairs.

"She wasn't home. Or, she didn't answer. Who else should I call?"

"I don't care, Adam. Just call someone before I lose this baby."

Adam ran downstairs again, and I went back to my happy place—a perfect yard full of happy, smiling children, and Marie and Kaye dancing around a tiered birthday cake.

"She's on her way," Adam said as he stepped into his shoes.

"Good." I rolled to a sitting position and put on my robe. Adam brought me my sandals and strapped them on my feet, then he helped me to stand.

I felt a slight spasm in my side and stood more slowly. "Who did you call?"

"You had a number on the fridge for Dani, so I called her."

I'd never thrown away Dani's number. I looked at Adam, my eyebrows raised. "You called Dani?"

He nodded.

"And she's coming?"

"She's on her way."

I sighed heavily. Knowing Kaye didn't have school the next day eased me a bit, but it also meant that Dani might have to deal with Kaye's wake-up ritual—a sliced apple, a Disney sing-along video, and a minimum fifteen minutes crying by the back door with her backpack on as she wondered why she wasn't getting on the bus.

"Did I make a mistake?" Adam asked.

I didn't know what to say. Nothing much mattered then. I couldn't think about offending Dani or wonder where Cathy was, or dwell on my argument with Adam. The only thing I could worry about was my baby boy.

Chapter 26

FAMILY

"I can't believe you called Dani," I said as we backed out of our parking space, and my mind had cleared a bit. Dani was waving good-bye with a condescending smirk on her face.

He tried to defend himself. "Well, I didn't know who to call. Besides, the girls are asleep."

"Yeah, for now," I whispered. "You don't remember her, do you?"

"I remember she watched the girls once."

"Yeah—*once,* while I did that cooking show at Bri's house." I waited for recognition to dawn on him.

"Oh, she's the bite lady."

"Yes. Kaye bit her son and she basically banned Kaye from nursery."

"Well, I think you may have read too much into that."

"Oh, Adam, stop. You're always blaming me."

"I am not."

"Yes, you are. And after this is over, you'll blame me for it too." I winced.

"I won't blame you for anything. No matter what happens." He glanced at my belly, showing a hint of the fear he felt.

Neither of us said anything as we traveled the rest of the way to the hospital, or as we walked to labor and delivery.

I hadn't had any sustained contractions like the one in my bed, but I'd had erratic spasms through the ride to the hospital, and some minor bleeding. The monitor they hooked me to still showed spikes—little contractions that made me worry. I tried to calm down, but Adam's presence in the room kept me on edge. It was strange. He usually calmed me.

"What time is it?" I asked.

"It's almost three thirty."

"Well, you should rest if you're going to class in the morning."

Adam stared at me. "I'm not going to class if you're in the hospital!"

"You could at least sit down. You're driving me nuts."

Adam flopped into a seat near the window, still staring at me.

I closed my eyes and concentrated on every movement Scott made inside of me. My belly bulged slightly as he stretched. "How's his heart rate?" I asked Adam.

He walked over to the readout screen on the monitor. "One forty. Is that a little high?"

"No, it's fine." I took a deep breath. "One forty's good." Thankfully, Scott didn't seem as stressed by the situation as I was.

Adam walked back to his seat next to the window. "I didn't mean what I said, about not liking life at home."

I took another deep breath, and kept my eyes closed. "Yes, you did."

"I love you, Jen. And I love our kids. I just . . ."

"You just don't like being with us."

"I didn't say that. I love being with you, just not at home."

I opened my eyes slowly and looked at him. "What's that supposed to mean? You only like being with us in public? Because I don't like being with Kaye in public. That's a lot harder than being with her at home."

"That's true."

I closed my eyes again. We'd tried all our marriage to only say kind words to each other, and that night, we had both crossed the line. Autism was destroying us, bit by bit. But I refused to end up alone. If keeping him with me meant caving first, I'd become a champion spelunker.

"You're right, Adam." I gazed up at him through tired eyes.

He looked at me. "Right about what?"

"I put too much pressure on you when you're home. But please understand that I need a break. I know Kaye's at school all day, but when she comes home, her behavior is even worse. Now she doesn't like being home either, because I don't have organized activities like they do at school, and we don't have the right toys. She cries most of the time she's home, and I'm completely helpless because she never lets me comfort her. I can't *mother* her, Adam." I felt myself getting stressed again, and I took a slow, deep breath.

Adam scooted the chair close to my bedside and held my hand. "I know you need a break. And I promise I'll work harder to give you one."

Relief helped me take another breath. He'd proven that he was willing to admit he was wrong too. As long as we were both admitting our own faults, I figured we were both willing to give each other some leeway. "Thank you, Adam."

He kissed my forehead. "I love you."

"I love you too."

* * *

Adam filled out the paperwork to admit me into the hospital—I was dehydrated and exhausted. The doctors put in an IV and gave me something to help me sleep. When I woke up again, sunlight spotted the white blanket across my lap. I turned on the television to find it was four in the afternoon. But more important than the time, I discovered that my belly was still round, and Scott was still wiggling.

There was nothing on, so I turned off the television. It was so quiet compared to home, but there was still noise. I listened to the hum of the monitor, the scratch of the graph that recorded my lack of contractions, the almost silent drip of my IV. A nurse in the hallway laughed as she left the nurse's station and padded down the hall.

My thoughts drifted to Olive. I hadn't thought of her in far too long. She'd touched so many people with her life, her love, her happiness. It seemed like she'd touched everyone but her own sister.

We hadn't heard from Blanch since the viewing. In fact, she wasn't even at the funeral—apparently, the viewing was enough of a good-bye. I remembered seeing Blanch touch the crucifix at Tim's neck and make some comment about warning the Mormons. Did she really think we were out to take Tim from her? She felt like Scott had taken Olive, and that was what started the whole separation of the sisters. How sad, that two sisters who loved each other so much would end up separated for the rest of their lives just because of different points of view. Blanch wasn't the only person at the viewing who wasn't a Mormon. There were several people there who didn't act or dress like the typical Latter-day Saint. So why did Blanch act the way she did? Couldn't she somehow form a relationship with Adam, and with me, despite our differences? Could two people who were so different ever be close?

Kaye and I were different, too, and I wondered if we'd ever connect. How I wanted to hold her when she cried, but she always pushed me away. All my life, I'd never imagined I'd be rejected by my three-year-old daughter.

Sleep coaxed me away from my thoughts, but I dreamed about sitting on the floor next to Kaye, inspecting the wheels of a toy car. It was a little blue car, with a black plastic chassis and a slightly bent axle. When I spun the wheel, its corresponding wheel spun just as fast, and the two wobbled slightly because of the axle. I showed it to Kaye. She looked me in the eye and spun the wheel just like I did. Her eyes were just like mine—the same stone-washed, denim blue. And just like me, she had an eye for detail.

* * *

"I figured out what you need," Adam said as he drove me home the next day.

The girls were sitting in their seats, and Kaye was still smiling and stimming at me. I'd been watching her as the miles between LDS Hospital and our West Valley home passed outside the window. I couldn't have asked for a better welcome than that look on Kaye's face.

"What did you say?" I asked.

"I said, I figured out what you need."

"Okay, tell me what I need."

"You need to open up more. You stress out and keep it all locked up, then it builds and builds until you explode."

"I tried that with Theo. I don't think talking helps."

"Of course it does."

I sighed. "But I talk till I'm blue in the face, and it doesn't change things. I think and I analyze and I plan. I get my hopes up for a solution, but there isn't one. There isn't a solution."

Adam glanced at me as he slowed for a stoplight. "Are we still talking about you dealing with stress during your pregnancy, or are we talking about Kaye?"

His eyes glinted with understanding. I looked out the window. "We're talking about Kaye. It's always about Kaye."

He reached out and took my hand.

It was easy for him to tell me to vent. He was good at opening up. In fact, he wore his troubles on his face, and he was terrible at telling people he was fine when deep down he was suffering. I'd been like him once. I hung around with a cool girl in junior high, and I told her everything, including which boys I liked. In eighth grade we had a dance, and this girl who I had thought was my friend leaked my secrets to each boy I thought was cute. Those boys stood together in a line near the door—looking like a row of delectable sweets set up before a diabetic. When I finally got up the courage to ask one of them to dance, they each turned their back to me, one by one. Later on that night, I saw my friend dancing with the boy I liked the most. They had their arms around each other, and she giggled as I walked past them. Apparently I wasn't cool enough for her anymore, and she severed our relationship with one quick, brutal blow.

I dated Adam for a year before I told him anything really personal about me, and the first thing I told him was that I hated dances. The second thing I told him was that I'd joined Future Homemakers of America because I wanted to be a wife more than anything. I saw how close my parents were, how they communicated with each other without having to say anything. I wanted someone I could trust that much, and until I found someone that trustworthy, I refused to open up.

"I'd like to open up to you, Adam," I said.

He glanced at me, then turned his eyes back to the road. "You can! You can tell me anything."

"No, I can't."

He scowled.

"Think about it, Adam. What were we just arguing about the other day? You already think I nag you."

Adam stared at the road.

"I can't complain to you every time I feel neglected, because you're already spending as much time with me as you can. I can't complain about Kaye because you're already maxed out dealing with your own feelings about her. We're going through the same thing, and we can't support each other when we're too busy trying to keep ourselves strong. I can't vent off steam to you about you, because you're already doing your best."

Adam's glance told me he understood what I was saying. I was right. He was just as stretched and frustrated as I was.

"I'm sorry my best isn't enough," he said.

"Yeah, well you're not alone. My best has never been enough."

Adam reached out and took my hand. "I love you, Jen. And I'm not going anywhere. We're partners, and we're going to ride this out together. Things will get better, I know they will."

I squeezed his hand. "I just wish they'd get better quicker."

We rode in silence for a while, still clutching each other's hands.

When we pulled into our parking space, Dani was waiting for us. She held a cake and wore a bright smile on her face. I eased myself out of the car, and after Adam took the cake, Dani threw her arms around me.

"Oh, I'm so glad you're okay. When Adam called me, I knew you must have needed me desperately. And I remembered his testimony from a few weeks back, and I just couldn't stay away." She took a step back and looked at me. "I hope you'll forgive me if I offended you after Kaye bit my Steven. Now I understand, Kaye was just being— herself." She hugged me again and cooed as if she were hugging a small child.

I got the feeling Dani was trying to be kind, but the way the words slipped from her glossed lips made me think she was trying to insult me.

Dani released me and clapped her hands together. "Let's go eat cake!"

Adam took down plates and forks and dished up a piece for everyone. Dani and I sat at the table, and Adam rushed the girls from the kitchen. "Here, we'll let you girls talk," Adam said.

"You have so much on your plate," Dani said. She smashed crumbs of cake with her fork and sucked them from the tines. "And I'm not talking about food. You have other children to think about. Some mothers would put their autistic child in a home, you know."

I glared at her.

"Well, it's not that bad of a suggestion. There's nothing wrong with it. In some cases, that's the best thing for the child and the family. Some autistic children can be quite violent."

I thought of Trenton and his mother's scarred cheek.

"Besides, I read that autistic children don't have feelings the same as you and me. Kaye probably wouldn't know the difference between you and one of the people who cares for the handicapped in homes like that. Just as long as her needs are met, it probably doesn't matter by whom. You need to think about Marie and your new baby and what they need."

My stomach lurched. She'd struck a nerve, and I wanted to strike back. I pushed my slice of cake away and glided to the door—a delicate sheen of self-control keeping me from grabbing Dani by the shirt and shoving her out onto the porch. "I think it's time for you to leave, Dani."

Dani's eyes fixed on mine. "What?"

"It's time for you to leave." I smiled. "Thanks for the cake. You can take the rest with you if you'd like."

Her mouth fell open. "Don't take it the wrong way, Jen. Should your other children suffer because you've got one child you can't handle? You can't be as good of a mother to them if you have such a hardship to deal with." She looked sincere, her eyes drooping with concern.

I opened the door. "Leave now, before I say something I'll regret."

Dani took a last suck on her fork. She picked up her purse and walked toward me. "Maybe you've already said something you'll regret, huh?" She walked out the door, her heels clacking on the pavement. "Keep the cake," she said.

Adam came in when he heard the door slam. "Well, that was quick. You didn't have much time to open up."

"You couldn't pay me to vent to her." I felt stress building in my chest again as Dani's words sunk deeper. For Dani to even suggest that I send Kaye away—I couldn't believe she'd say such a thing.

"So, what happened? What did she say?"

I shook my head. "Can't talk. Have to go to my happy place." I rubbed my belly and stumbled weakly toward the stairs. Adam followed me, with his hand pressing gently against my back.

Part of me wondered if Dani was right about one thing—was any of it fair to Marie? Or to little Scott? I'd seen Marie suffer and feel neglected. She'd been dragged to doctor appointments where she was expected to be the good, quiet little girl—and she filled the role perfectly. But she was suffering. I'd seen her at school—separate from the other children who played with each other outside of school and knew how to interact with kids their own age. Marie was often alone, even when she was surrounded by children.

In fact, we all were alone. Autism had isolated us from the rest of the world—given us experiences that no one else understood, worries that others couldn't comprehend. Even at the parent-support group we were all alone because each child had different behaviors and had to be treated in different ways.

And what if Scott was autistic too, as I feared? Marie would really be lost in the shuffle then.

I couldn't follow my thoughts where they wanted to lead—what kind of big sister would Kaye be? I caught visions of Kaye dumping Scott on the floor like she did her dolls, showing no interest whatsoever. Kaye wasn't violent, but with autism, I felt like I had no idea what the future might hold. It was too much to think about.

Instead, I thought of Kaye's expression all the way home from the hospital. She loved me. She might not have had the ability to tell me with words, but she loved me, and I knew it deep down. Dani was wrong about Kaye not being able to tell the difference between a care provider and me. There was more of a connection between us.

We were family.

When we reached the bedroom, Adam tucked the covers around me and sat on the edge of the bed. "I'm sorry about Dani."

"It's okay. I can't think about her right now, though. Tell me something funny. Make me feel better."

"Something funny. Well, I tried to do Kaye's hair this morning. That was funny."

I smiled.

"And after spending twenty-four hours alone with our daughters, I learned that your job is much harder than mine."

My eyes began to burn.

"What can I do to help you? You do so much for the rest of us, and you deserve so much more than I can give you alone."

I held his hand and sniffled. "That's not funny. You're supposed to tell me something funny." I smiled and looked at him through watery eyes.

"Oh, I'm sorry." He wiped the tears from my cheeks. "A Mormon bishop, a Priest, and a Rabbi go to a bar . . ."

I laughed.

"And the Mormon orders a root beer but complains that it's too fizzy."

I reached up and pulled his head down. "Just kiss me."

"That will make you laugh?" His kiss was little more than a peck. "Well, I'm offended." He smiled, then kissed me gently.

I focused on the softness of his kiss, and I held him there, making a good memory to draw on when I needed it. When I finally let go of him, I whispered, "It might not make me laugh, but it does make me feel better."

"Sleep as long as you'd like." Adam locked the bedroom door behind him so the girls wouldn't disturb me.

I'd done so much sleeping at the hospital I thought it would be hard for me to sleep again. But I remembered the feel of Adam's kiss, and the next time I opened my eyes, the sun had set.

* * *

It was dark, and a dank chill in the air told me it was snowing outside—the first big snow of the season. I peeked out the window to find the sidewalks blanketed, and cars swerving in the road. My robe wasn't thick enough to keep out the cold.

I climbed back in bed. It was quiet enough downstairs that I figured Adam had everything under control, and he didn't have to work that night, so I decided to take advantage of the solitude. Normally, it would have been a good thing—a few moments to decompress. But Dani's words echoed in my head, and I couldn't stop thinking about the possibility that my son would be autistic too. Maybe less severe than Kaye. Maybe more.

I'd become accustomed to the guilt over my contribution to Kaye's autism. I'd contributed some genetics at the very least, but my parenting style didn't seem to help things. Blanch was right. I was disorganized. And probably too casual about things like chores and consistent discipline. It seemed like regular discipline didn't work with Kaye anyway, and how was I to know the right way to do things when I was so new at being a parent anyway? Kids don't come with instruction manuals, though I wished Kaye had one.

Deep down, I knew I couldn't blame myself. I'd come to accept that this was beyond my control. I couldn't choose which genes I passed to my children. And I could only do my best—as far from perfect as it was.

There had to be a reason we'd been given Kaye. I'd heard of other parents of handicapped children and of how righteous and loving they were. I didn't fit that description. I believed in the gospel, but didn't consider myself very spiritual. Adam fit that bill.

So, why? I tried, rather unsuccessfully, not to feel sorry for myself, but I had to ask. If Kaye was autistic because of factors beyond my control, they were certainly in God's control. He had the power to make her the way she was, and He had the power to heal her.

The idea came to my mind again, tugging at me to the point of discomfort. He could heal her. But so far, He hadn't.

Why?

I remembered the Gospel Doctrine lesson we'd had on healing, and I opened my scriptures to the part where the child was healed of palsy. I read it and knew it was true. I felt it in my heart as sure as I knew Adam loved me. And I didn't believe for a second that God would perform a miracle for that family that He wouldn't perform for mine, if my faith were strong enough.

What did that mean? To have strong faith? Believing obviously wasn't enough. Hoping wasn't enough. It involved something more. Something I didn't have.

I flipped through the scriptures again, and turned to John 14:27. In the top margin, I had written, "The Atonement will heal me."

I paused as an idea struck me. Maybe it wasn't Kaye who needed healing.

I read the verse aloud. "'Peace I leave with you, my peace I give unto you: not as the world giveth, give I unto you. Let not your heart be troubled, neither let it be afraid.'"

Peace. That was what I needed. If I felt peace, I could deal with whatever was thrown at me. If I could look on Kaye with love and understanding—like the mother in the recovery room at Primary Children's, like Olive—I could see beyond the moments that were so hard to live through. If I felt peace, the healing would come from inside—nothing I could do would be as effective.

So I knelt down and prayed for peace, knowing this time that I had enough faith.

It came, soft and warm. That wonderful balm of the gospel of Jesus Christ was once again easing the sharpness of my pain. In a moment, I knew who Kaye was. She was that glorious woman in white who'd risen above the red, smoldering ground and touched my face. She was a daughter of God.

And so was I.

Adam began to tuck the girls in as I rose from my knees. He made his funny noises as he covered them with a blanket. His voice soothed their giggles until their tiny voices joined him. But something was different that time. Kaye was singing the words.

"Jen! Come here, quick!" Adam called.

I entered the room to find all three of them singing "I Am a Child of God." Kaye's voice was clear and sweet, and I knew just what she was saying. All those nights of singing together had paid off. The repetition had stuck in her mind, and she was showing me how well she could learn. It was as if the knowledge had been bottled up inside of her, and she chose that moment to give us a glimpse into her mind.

It was a miracle.

When they finished the song, Adam and I gazed down at Kaye and Marie with wet faces.

"Adam," I said. "Let's sing it again."

Chapter 27

CONNECTIONS

Kaye's progress, along with my spiritual experience, made the next few weeks much more bearable. Anytime I got frustrated, I just remembered that night, embraced that memory, and gained perspective. Things were definitely better. Not perfect, but better.

By the time Christmas break came around, I'd figured out that the best way to deal with weekends and vacations was to wake up every day at the same time we usually did, tell Kaye that there was no school, putting emphasis on the word "no," and go somewhere in the opposite direction of the school. The hard part was figuring out where to go, since we had very little money and public places with too many people made Kaye nervous. We decided the library was our best bet.

Kaye loved it there. Surrounded by more books than she could look at, Kaye stimmed at the book spines, rocked back and forth, and sang her signature note. Occasionally, she would break out in "I Am a Child of God," usually in full voice. A librarian gave me the evil eye once, but I didn't care. It was a miracle, and I was going to let Kaye sing as loud as she wanted to, as long as she wasn't bothering other patrons.

One morning, after spending a couple of hours bugging the librarian, we came home to find Adam cleaning. He was off of school for Christmas break, and I was delighted to have him home—but he only cleaned when he was nervous.

"What's going on?" I asked.

"Martha just called."

"Martha?" I asked. Adam's oldest sister had never called us before, and I wondered for a moment how she got our phone number. "Why did she call?"

"Mom had a heart attack. She's okay, but she's really hurting. They had to do compressions on her, and I guess they cracked a couple of ribs. She's still in the hospital so they can do an angioplasty, or something like that."

"Adam, I'm sorry."

"I can't stop thinking that we need to go see her." He wiped down the counter, which already looked spotless.

"We don't have the money to fly to Louisiana."

Adam nodded. "I know. We can drive."

"What about Kaye? Do you think she'll be able to handle it? Talk about digressing from her routine."

Adam shrugged. "All we can do is find out."

All I could think about was Blanch's behavior when we got home from the viewing. I couldn't imagine what would happen if we brought Kaye to Blanch's home. It could make things worse. "Do you want to go without us?"

Adam shook his head. "I want you with me. I don't want to go through this alone."

I couldn't say I'd blame him. If I were in his place, I'd want my sweetheart with me too. "Let's go."

Adam made arrangements with work, though they warned him he was skating on thin ice—he'd taken far too many days off since he'd started his job, and we were only a few months away from having another baby. It didn't ease the pressure on Adam's mind, but he had to see his mother, even if we drove straight through to New Orleans to do it.

Kaye wasn't very happy about all the things we were loading into the car, and the anxious look on her little face made me nervous, too. Back in June, when we'd tried the camping trip with Olive, Kaye had grown restless when she saw her blanket in the car. This was no different. It was only a matter of time before she'd be screaming and wanting to go home to her own bed and her routine. I thought of suggesting again to Adam that I stay home with the girls, but I didn't want him driving that distance alone, and we couldn't afford a last-minute flight. Besides all that, Adam wanted me with him, and I belonged at his side. I hadn't had any contractions or much pain in the previous two weeks, so I was sure everything was fine with the baby.

"It's okay. We're just going for a ride." I tried to look Kaye in the eye. Her eyes met mine for a moment, filled with panic.

"Adam, can we fit the bedding in the trunk?" I asked.

Adam let out a frustrated sigh as he moved things around again to fit Kaye's blanket and pillow out of sight. This seemed to relax Kaye a bit, but she glanced at her father.

"She can tell you're nervous, Adam. It's upsetting her."

"Well, I am nervous. What can I do about it?" He let out a quick breath. "I'm sorry. I'll try to calm down."

I touched his arm in an attempt to comfort him.

"I don't feel good about this, Jen. I don't know what's going to happen."

I knew just what he meant.

* * *

Early the next morning we drove to Denver in a cold, slippery mixture of rain and snow. I held my breath and tried not to brace myself on the door handle as Adam gripped the steering wheel until his knuckles turned white. The car was silent except for the occasional sound from Kaye, who looked out her window at the snow, and the thunder of water splashing up in the wheel well at high speeds. Normally, that sound grated my nerves like a fork scratching a plate, but I focused on Kaye and found that the storm didn't bother me so much. Weariness hadn't slaked Kaye's fascination with the weather yet, so she wasn't crying for home. Instead, she stared at the snowflakes rushing past her with an awestruck expression. Marie slept in her booster seat, her head lobbing from one side to the other.

The miles of I-70 passed slowly by, and when we reached Salina, Kansas, Adam's eyes were drooping. Kaye had fallen asleep, barely aware she had spent the day in the car. She woke up when I took the girls into a gas station for a potty break and diaper change. We grabbed a bite to eat, and I traded seats with Adam. It took him a few minutes to fall asleep, but he slept through most of Kansas as I drove on the nearly empty freeway—nothing but an occasional big rig and wide, brown fields as far as I could see. We had brought most of our collection of Disney books, and Marie proceeded to flip through all of them several times before we reached Topeka. I had lots of time to think, so I thought about Blanch.

It seemed strange to me that she would have a heart attack so soon after Olive's death from heart problems. I wondered if the two of them were tied to each other in some inexplicable way. It wouldn't surprise me. I was tied to Brienne, and very aware of the distance from New Orleans to Washington D.C. If we weren't already strapped for time and cash, I would have insisted we drive the extra miles so I could see Brienne. Glancing back at Marie and Kaye, I knew they were tied to each other despite their differences. For all I knew, Marie would be Kaye's only tie to the world around her, especially after Adam and I passed beyond the veil.

Marie read to Kaye, and Kaye stimmed over the book. God knew what He was doing when he gave us Marie. I watched the two of them together and felt wonderful.

Olive and Blanch must have been sisters for similar reasons. At that moment, I doubted any relationship was given to us by chance.

My stomach growled as we approached Kansas City near midnight. I pulled off the freeway and found a diner a few blocks away.

"Adam," I said, and I touched his shoulder gently to wake him.

He stirred and looked around. "Where are we?"

"Kansas City. I'm starving."

Adam nodded. "Okay. Let's eat."

"Kaye's been really good. I'm surprised, actually. I figured she wouldn't travel well."

Adam nodded again. "I'm glad."

He seemed quiet and distant, as if he had too many thoughts and feelings in his mind to be able to sort them out completely. We went in the diner and ordered our food, then ate in silence.

When we were finished eating, we pooled together our change, and Adam found a pay phone to call his dad and see how things were going. By the time he came back, Kaye had dusted the entire table with salt and pepper, and Marie was trying to clean up by wiping the spices into a pile in front of her. The waitress was giving me dirty looks, but I figured it was better than putting up with Kaye screaming if I tried to take the shakers away.

Adam barely noticed when he sat down and set his elbows in the white and black grains.

"How is she?" I asked.

Adam sighed. He had dark circles beneath his eyes. "She's home."

"Well, isn't that good?"

Adam nodded.

"So, what's wrong?"

"Dad says that Mom doesn't want me to come."

I leaned forward and grabbed Adam's hand. "Did you tell him we're more than halfway there?"

"Yeah. I heard Mom yelling in the background, and Dad bawled her out for yelling. He agrees with her—he says it's not a good idea."

Anger started building in me, and I leaned back in my seat. It hadn't been a bad drive, just very long and tiring. And if Adam had jeopardized his job by taking off work for ten days, just to be sent home, I wasn't sure I could ever forgive Blanch. Kaye tried to climb over me to get out of the booth, but I wrapped my arm around her and wouldn't let her out. "I don't understand why she doesn't want us to come. I mean, she almost died."

"I know."

Kaye tried harder to get past me and out to the freedom of the diner beyond our little booth. I pushed her back into her seat, and she let out a scream. "Did we come out here for nothing?"

"I don't know." Adam's voice was sharp. He ran his fingers through his hair.

I stood up and took Kaye into my arms, but that didn't satisfy her. She tried to get down. She was starting to hurt me.

"So what are we going to do, Adam?" I asked.

Adam stood and took Kaye from me. He gritted his teeth and gave me a look that made me wonder if he was angry with me.

"We see her anyway," Adam growled. "I came this far, and I'm not turning back." He balanced Kaye on one arm and handed me his wallet with the other. There wasn't a lot of money in there, but I tossed the payment for the bill plus a twenty-percent tip onto the salt-and-pepper-dusted table.

* * *

We stopped at a run-down Motel 6 for the rest of the night. Kaye had slept so much in the car that I stayed up with her until just before dawn, trying to get her to be quiet so Adam could sleep. We got up early to push through to New Orleans. The sky was clear, and it was warm enough that we took off our sweaters. The closer we got to the city, the better we could see the Christmas decorations on the homes, and the Nativity scenes in front of the churches.

The Young home wasn't quite a mansion, but it was larger than the home I'd grown up in. The double-wide driveway had one car parked in it.

"Looks like they've got a visitor. I bet it's Martha." Adam parked the car next to Martha's Accord, and he left the keys in the ignition. "Why don't you let me go in first, then bring in the girls."

"Just wave me in," I said. I didn't want to let the girls out of the car until I knew it would be okay to take them in the house. Otherwise, we'd be subjecting the whole neighborhood to one of Kaye's tantrums as I forced her back in the car.

While we waited for Adam, I pointed out some of the finer features of Grandma's landscaping. In front of the house, outdoor Christmas trees cast shadows across a park bench on a trellised porch lined with white-leaved hothouse poinsettias. The window box held some sort of vine with small red flowers, and icicle lights lined the roof.

"Mommy, can we go in and see Grandma?" Marie asked.

"She's sick, honey. Daddy just went in to see if she feels good enough for a visit."

"Oh."

Marie looked disappointed.

We waited in silence, watching the door for Adam.

Finally, he opened the door and motioned for me to come in.

Tim met us at the door with his finger against his lips. "She's sleeping. The doctor said to let her rest."

I told Marie to be quiet, but I knew it was too much to ask of Kaye. She'd been sitting in the car for almost twenty-four hours. Her eyes widened at the festive lights, and she stimmed in front of the white and red Christmas tree in the middle of the front room window.

"Kaye, quiet voice please." I touched her lips softly.

She sang anyway.

I approached Tim and put my arms around him. He held me for a long time.

"I know I complain about her," he said, "but I don't know what I would've done if she'd died."

"I know," I said, and I gave him a squeeze.

Martha came from the kitchen with an apron tied around her waist and a towel in her hand. "Everything's cleaned up, Dad."

"Thanks for calling us, Martha," Adam said.

Martha nodded and reached behind her back to loosen the apron. "I thought you'd want to know."

"I'm really glad you came, son." Tim's tender eyes never left Adam's face.

"I thought you didn't want me to come," Adam replied.

"I said I didn't want you to because Blanch said she didn't want you to. But rest assured, the fact that you're here anyway means more to both of us than you'll ever know."

Adam stared at his father.

"What do you mean, Tim?" I asked.

Martha stood behind her father. "He means it's about time Adam did something for Mom. It's about time he came home when she needed him."

Tim smiled sadly. "Easy, Martha. He just got here. Don't barrage him with guilt just yet."

Martha looked disgusted as she wiped her hands on the towel again and disappeared into the kitchen.

"If she has something to say to me, I wish she'd just say it." Adam looked almost as disgusted as Martha had.

"It's been a stressful time for us, Adam. Let it roll off your back."

Adam shook his head. "It's been a stressful time for me too. You talk like you two are the only ones affected by Mom's heart attack. I'm in this just as much as Martha is."

Tim shook his head. "Don't let Martha hear you say that. You live too far away to be in this as much as she is. She's been here all along."

"Great. Fall back on the same old arguments that make me a bad son. I live in Utah. I'm a Mormon. I'm at fault." Adam's tense voice showed how upset he was getting. I pulled him down to sit next to me on the couch, and I held his hand.

Tim sat across the room from us, and they looked each other in the eye. "I didn't complain when you became a Mormon. I didn't agree with it, but I know a boy has to strike out on his own when he becomes a man. I thought it would pass, and you'd return to the religion of your birth, but your heart is in your new faith. I see that now."

"Dad, I've been a Mormon for ten years. You're just now seeing it?"

"How would you feel, Adam? Wouldn't you hold out hope?"

Adam stared at his father, then nodded.

I squeezed Adam's hand and looked at Tim. "How's Blanch?"

He shrugged. "She's cranky. She must be feeling a little better." He smiled just long enough to give me hope that everything would be okay, then he hung his head again in worry. "We almost lost her. It was very . . . frightening."

I hesitated to ask the question brewing my mind, but I had to know. "Do you think this has anything to do with stress over everything that happened with Olive?"

Tim looked at me beneath his thick eyebrows. "That's been going on for so long. You have no idea how hard it was, even for her to go back to Utah for the first time in twenty-six years. That's why she was so hard on you. She was already hurting."

I thought of how I'd lashed out at Cathy when I was hurting and she said something I didn't want to hear at a difficult time. Then I wondered what would happen to me if I became estranged from Brienne, and she died suddenly. The thought made me queasy. It also made me realize I was a lot like Blanch.

"It's not just Mormonism that Blanch struggles with. That wasn't the only thing that divided her and Olive. Blanch spent a weekend with Olive at BYU. Did you know that?"

Adam shook his head.

"Enjoyed herself, too. No, it wasn't just Mormonism that came between Blanch and Olive."

"Then what was it?"

Tim looked at Adam and smiled as if it was something Adam should have known all along. "It was you. It was the way you treated us."

"I don't understand."

"Do you know why Olive invited you to spend that summer with her?"

"A graduation gift? To give me a new experience?"

Tim shook his head. "We should have told you, I guess. We should have let Olive tell you."

"Tell me what?"

Tim looked down at his hands.

Martha slipped back into the room, as if she'd been listening from the kitchen, and had seen her opportunity to let her presence be felt. "Tell him, Dad. It's time he knew."

"Tell me what?" Adam asked.

Tim leaned forward, his elbows on his knees. "I was an alcoholic. I spent that summer in rehab."

"You? But I never saw you take a drink."

"I worked hard to keep it from you. But your mother knew. She knew I was staying up late at night getting drunk in the bathroom. She knew I had a shot before I had breakfast. She didn't tell anyone anything—kept it all quiet and hidden. Until she couldn't take it anymore, and she told me to go to rehab, or she'd figure out a way to get me arrested. Right after you left, I checked in."

"And Mom handled everything alone," Martha said.

"Did you know?" Adam asked Martha.

"I figured it out. I cared enough to watch after them while you were gone."

"I didn't abandon her—she sent me away!" Adam defended himself.

"And you wrote her letters about how happy you were there with Olive and the Mormons. You thanked her for giving you the best experience you'd had in your life. What was she supposed to do? Ask you to come home?" Martha glared at Adam.

"Martha, hush." Tim held her hand and looked at Adam with compassion. "She didn't want you to see us while we were so weak. She didn't want Martha to see it either, but Martha has always been . . .

more involved than you have. She's our oldest. She's a woman. It's natural to her."

Adam hung his head.

"Things weren't the same when you came home," Tim continued. "We'd gone through this experience, and your mother had helped me so much. She helped me get sober, Adam, and I've been sober ever since. She brought me back to God. But you weren't part of any of it. And when you came home, all you could talk about was your new faith. You were always on the defensive, even when we weren't offending you. You seemed to always feel a need to explain your conversion. You were our son when you left, but you were a Mormon missionary when you came back."

I reached over and took Adam's hand.

"I never meant to hurt you," Adam said. "I'd just learned so much."

"And so had we. But we couldn't talk to you about it. We knew you wouldn't understand."

"I might have." Adam looked up at his father. "I'd been reborn too."

Tim stared at his son. "I began to realize that, but before I knew it, you were a missionary in Belgium. Then you went back to Utah and met Jen. The last thing we had to give you was your wedding, and we couldn't even attend the ceremony."

Adam looked down at my hand in his. "Well, if it's any consolation, I wanted you there."

"But your church wouldn't allow it." Tim's hurt expression tugged at my heart, but it didn't change how I felt about my marriage in the temple. One look at Adam told me he felt the same.

"My point is," Tim continued, "we sent our son to Utah, and he never really came home."

"And Mom blamed Olive for it." Adam didn't take his eyes off of our interlocking fingers.

Tim nodded. "And your autistic daughter has a connection with Olive that apparently extends beyond the grave, but Kaye doesn't even know her grandmother."

Adam looked up at his father. "I've still never come home, have I?"

Tim smiled. "Until now."

"But I haven't changed, Dad. I'm a Mormon, and I'll always be a Mormon."

Tim nodded. "I was born a Catholic, and I'll die a Catholic."

"Different, but the same," I said.

Adam and Tim both looked at me. I smiled. "And I'm a lot like Blanch—the kind of woman who insists on going through her most difficult times in life, stubborn and prideful and alone, hoping no one sees how imperfect she is."

I felt everyone's gaze. Instead of looking back at them, I watched my daughters explore their grandparents' front room. We should have visited them more often. That room should have been familiar and full of fond memories.

I stood and let go of Adam's hand. "I'll be right back. I have someone to say hello to."

Walking back to Blanch's bedroom, I wondered what I would say to her. One thing was certain—it was time I let our similarities pull us together rather than letting our differences push us apart.

I tapped on the door, then opened it. Blanch was lying in her bed, reading. She looked up when I entered the room. "I'm not well enough for visitors," she said, and she looked back down at her book.

"I know." I sat on the edge of her bed.

She glared at me.

"I just wanted you to know that Adam and I are here."

She nodded. "I told you not to come—waste of gas. I'm not dead, so you may as well leave."

I smiled. "Nope. I'm glad you're not dead. I don't want you to miss this opportunity to talk to your son."

"Something tells me you care very little about me. If I were dead, your life would be no different." She turned the page in her book.

"I care about your son. And speaking as one mother to another, I would think you'd be grateful to have an opportunity to talk to him. I mean, you almost died a few days ago. Isn't this your second chance?"

Her eyes flitted across the words on the page.

"We're a lot alike, but there is one very important difference. If I had a chance to talk to Kaye, I'd take it. I mean, here I have these two beautiful children, and one of them may never be able to sit down with me and carry on a conversation. Sometimes I think about that—all the things I'll miss with her. She won't tell me what she likes and dislikes, what her dreams are. She won't tell me about friends or boys or anything like that. For all I know, she'll never even have that kind of stuff, let alone be able to talk to me about it—at least, not in this life."

Her eyes stopped moving, but she didn't look up at me.

"I don't want you to turn down the opportunity when it's there, Blanch. It may not always be there. If you keep pushing him away, you'll lose him just like you lost Olive, and it will be no one's fault but your own."

She put her book down, but still didn't look at me, and didn't say a word.

"You know," I continued, "I've been alone for a while too. This autism thing has really thrown me for a loop. I hate relying on other people. It drives me crazy to leave important things in someone else's hands—what if they mess it up and I end up doing everything anyway? I'd rather do everything from the beginning so it's just the way I like it."

She straightened the comforter lying on her lap. "None of us can do everything."

"So I've learned. And your poor son has had to put up with me as I've begun to accept my own limitations."

"It's probably been good for him, to have to stick by you." I watched her bury her feelings again behind her book.

"It's certainly been good for me. He's a good man. Say what you will about him, but I'll defend him through the eternities."

She glanced up at me, just for a moment.

"Well, I just wanted to thank you for raising a good man. You know, in case you die and I don't get another chance."

Her glare could have melted ice, but when she saw the smile on my face, her expression softened.

I leaned over and kissed her cheek. It felt awkward, but I forced myself to do it anyway. I was setting the precedent—if I could change, so could she.

After the kiss, I stood and left Blanch's room, shutting the door behind me.

When I rejoined everyone else in the front room, Adam and Tim looked at me with curiosity.

"So, what did you say?" Adam asked.

"Oh, I just shared some thoughts—from one prideful woman to another."

Martha had gone to bed, and the rest of us were looking at a family photo album when Blanch came in the front room. She sat quietly on the couch, and watched Tim point at a picture and laugh.

"Come sit next to me, Adam," Blanch said.

Adam rose from the ground and sat next to his mother with the photo album still in his hands.

She kissed his cheek. "Now, what are you looking at here? Oh, yes. This is the picture your father took when his brother came home from Korea."

Adam watched his mother as she told the story of Adam's uncle. Kaye sat on the floor and played with a wooden Nativity set, and Marie recited the Christmas story to her little sister. We were warm inside as a cool rain pinged on the window. Connections were strong that night, and more was said with a glance and a loving smile than could have ever been said with words. I watched Kaye and wondered if words weren't all they were cracked up to be.

Chapter 28

CAREGIVER

It was the most wonderful Christmas I'd ever had, and after we came home, I was determined to change my life. I wasn't going to be a woman alone in a crowd anymore. Autism or not, we would live like a normal family. We would sit on the front row at church. We would go out in public—see movies, eat at restaurants, spend hours at a public pool. We would be active and alive.

The change would start with a few apologies.

Cathy had been attending Church, and I'd caught glimpses of her in the hallway between classes, or as she began her walk home. She seemed preoccupied and distant. Since that first month, she hadn't stopped by my home. I'd barely spoken to her since September, when we'd exchanged a soothing apology. I needed to prove that I was done striking out at her, so I baked her a cake and took it to her apartment on a crisp January morning.

She answered the door wearing grubby clothes. Her hair was tied back in a loose ponytail, and wisps of it curled along the sides of her face. The walls of her apartment were bare and boxes sat in rows in front of her couch.

"Cathy," I said. "You're moving out?"

"Jen! I meant to call you." Her eyes pleaded that I accept her apology, and I noticed they were red, either from crying or lack of sleep. "I've wanted to visit you the past couple of months. I've thought about you." She grinned, though her shoulders drooped and she cast her eyes to the floor. "I know it's not enough. I'm not usually like this. I'm usually very efficient."

"What's wrong?" I asked, knowing things must have gotten pretty bad for her, and feeling guilty for not noticing.

"My mother's got Alzheimer's. She's had it for a while, and my siblings and I have taken turns checking on her—making sure the house is clean and stuff like that."

Cathy had done so much for me, and I had no idea what she'd been going through. I hadn't even thought to ask. I'd been so wrapped up in my own world that I'd almost forgotten that the people around me were probably suffering just as much as I was—needing help just as much—and maybe just as reluctant to ask for it.

"A few months back," Cathy continued, "she started wandering out of the house at night. The neighbors took her back home, but I've been spending the night there a lot. Then, a couple of weeks ago, she put some hamburger on the stove to cook while I was gone, and she left it on until it started a grease fire. She wasn't even aware the house was burning. It caused thousands of dollars in damage, and if a neighbor hadn't seen the smoke, we may have lost her." She sighed and brushed her hair out of her face.

"Cathy, I'm so sorry."

She nodded. "Me too. You know, she doesn't even know me anymore. She remembers every detail about her first year in college—when she met my dad. She calls me by her best friend's name. It's like she never got married or had kids. It's all been erased."

"It hasn't been erased." I tried to soothe her. "It's just a file she doesn't have access to anymore."

Cathy smiled. "I know. And she may not know me, but I still know her."

"I know just what you mean," I said.

Cathy threw her arms around me. She was so much taller than me that I had to stand on my tiptoes.

"I'm sorry I wasn't a good visiting teacher."

"Don't say that, Cathy. You were just what I needed." It was true. She told me the truth when I didn't want to hear it, and if she hadn't been there, I might not have had Kaye tested for many more months, and she might not have made the progress she'd made to that point. "I was horrible to you. I hope you'll forgive me."

She shrugged. "I forgave you a long time ago. How's Kaye?"

"She sings lyrics to songs now."

"Really?"

I nodded. "And she said good-bye to me the other day when I put her on the bus for school. She even called me 'Mom.'"

Cathy grinned. "Every bit of progress is so wonderful, isn't it? That's the way it's been with my niece. I remember my sister cried for days after the first time she heard 'I love you.'"

"Well, we're not there yet."

"But you will be someday."

I nodded. "You know, I think we will."

She touched my belly tentatively. "And how is this going?"

I smiled. "It's a boy. We're going to name him Scott."

"A boy, huh? That will be different for you." She grabbed a stack of sticky notes she had on a nearby box and wrote a phone number on one. "Here's my mom's number. I'll be there most of the time. You'll call me when he's born?"

"I'll call. I promise." I hugged her again, and offered to help her pack, but she wouldn't let me do any work with my swollen belly.

It occurred to me as I walked away from Cathy's apartment how similar our experiences were, except Kaye would improve while Cathy's mother declined. We were on opposite ends of the same spectrum—bookends to the life of a caregiver.

As I drove home, I passed Dani's house and felt a sudden urge to call her, but I pushed the feeling aside. She'd left my house hurt and upset—almost as bad as I was. I realized she was just trying to help by telling me to put Kaye in a home, and I also knew that, depending on how things went, it might be the best solution for us sometime in the future. However, I'd keep Kaye in my home as long as possible, and the thought of handing her over to someone else was so painful that I'd lashed out at the suggestion, and I'd hurt Dani in the process.

Dani wouldn't want to hear from me anytime soon.

* * *

The second Sunday in January, Gay Lynn was waiting for us when we got to Church. She greeted Kaye with a smile and a big hug, which Kaye returned. Then Kaye went straight to the only small chair in the room, sat in it, and folded her arms.

"She's getting the routine," Gay Lynn said proudly.

"That's great. What do you think of it so far? You getting tired yet?"

"You kidding? Just between you and me, I think this is the best calling I've ever had. It's the first time in years that I've looked forward to going to church on Sunday, because I know I get to see Kaye."

It surprised me, after the way she'd introduced herself.

"We tried sharing time last week, and that didn't go too well, so I think we'll only stay for singing time this week. She sits still longer every time we go. Oh, and speaking of that, we'd like you to come into the Primary opening exercises sometime and tell the kids a little about Kaye so they know what to expect from her."

"Absolutely. Anytime." It warmed me to think they were doing so much to include Kaye.

"I think this will be great for all of them. You know, teach them how to love kids who are different from them. It's something we all could stand to learn."

I agreed.

After leaving Kaye in Gay Lynn's able hands, I slipped into Relief Society. Shauna Nulman was handing a clipboard to a sister on the front row. "We need some help for Sister Dani Stark, who was in a car accident on Thursday."

I felt my jaw drop. That was the day I'd taken the cake to Cathy's.

"Her van was totaled. Her son, Steven, had squirmed out of his seat belt when the accident happened. Dani was trying to get Steven back in his seat when she hit a patch of ice and slid into the median on I-15."

The sisters all groaned, including me.

"Dani's fine, but Steven has a brain injury. He's at Primary Children's Hospital. Dani will need some rides up there to visit while her husband is at work. He needs their other car for the long commute he makes every day and I've offered the Relief Society to help out. We'll be passing around a sign-up sheet during the lesson."

I couldn't count all the times Kaye had squirmed out of her seat. It could just as easily have happened to me. The sick feeling in my stomach intensified as I wrote my name on the list of people willing to help Dani. Kaye had been through her share of tests, and as wonderful as the nurses, techs, and doctors were, it was still a scary place for mother and child. Next to my name, I wrote, "I'll help whenever I can, and in any capacity." I was determined to give Dani what I had needed, but not received—a hand to hold.

* * *

Dani called me that night, but she didn't sound happy to hear me answer the phone.

"I really hate to ask this, but everyone else I could call is busy in the morning." She cleared her throat and continued. "I need a ride to the hospital. Steven needs some tests . . ."

"I'll be there," I interrupted. The reason she needed me didn't matter. "When?"

"Um, the first test is at nine tomorrow morning."

"Okay," I said as I thought of the schedule for the next day. "I'll have Marie with me—Kaye will be on the bus—so I probably can't come in with you. But you can call after the tests and I'll come back and pick you up."

"I'll try to make other arrangements to get home, that's fine." She seemed a little too quick to reject my offer. "It will be enough for you to take me there in the morning. I wouldn't want to put you out." Her voice stressed with thinly veiled sarcasm.

"There's no problem. I owe you." I did my best to sound as sincere as I felt. We'd had our disagreements, but they really didn't matter. What was pertinent at that moment was Dani and Steven.

She seemed to accept my apology. "Okay. I'll call you when the tests are done."

"What tests are they running, if you don't mind my asking?"

"Tomorrow they're running another MRI."

"Kaye's had one of those."

"Really? They did the first one right after the accident, and I wasn't there for it. When Kaye got hers, was it miserable?"

I remembered it vividly. "The worst part was the recovery. She'd never been under anesthesia before, and she threw up when she was coming out of it."

"Great," Dani groaned.

"But it turned out okay. She was just sleepy for a while." I hesitated, but since we were on the subject, I thought it might help Dani to talk. "How bad is his injury?"

Dani sighed. "He's been having seizures off and on since the accident. He had a bad concussion, and some swelling." Her voice cracked, and she cleared her throat.

"I'm sorry," I said.

"Thanks." Dani's voice was quiet. "I'll see you in the morning."

"I'll be there."

* * *

The next morning I dropped Kaye off at the bus, then went to pick up Dani. Her hair was barely in place, and dark circles shadowed her eyes. She looked thinner.

"Hi," she said, and she fastened her seat belt. "Thanks for doing this."

"It's no problem." I tried to be cheerful, but Dani didn't respond. She just stared out of her window.

The ride to Primary Children's was quiet, except for the hum of the road. When we reached the hospital, Dani requested that I just drop her off and she'd call me later. I did as she asked.

* * *

She called later and asked if I would pick her up after I'd dropped Marie off at school. I met her at the south entrance.

"Thanks," she said as she climbed into the car.

"How did it go?"

"Okay, I guess. He didn't have an adverse reaction to the anesthetic."

"Well, that's good."

Dani nodded. "They won't know the results for a couple of days. I have to come back tomorrow for the EEG. The swelling has gone down."

"Well, that's good, too. Need a ride tomorrow?" I asked.

She shrugged. "I don't know yet."

We were back on the freeway before Dani said anything else, and when she finally did speak up, her voice was quiet. "Did the tests help you with Kaye at all? I mean, is it worth it to get them? I hated seeing Steven lying there."

"The tests didn't help much with Kaye. They just confirmed that there was nothing wrong physiologically with Kaye. But the EEG told us there was a potential for a seizure disorder. That will help prepare us, but it wasn't comforting."

"I know what you mean." Dani's voice rose in volume as she turned to me. "I hate it when Steven has a seizure. He's had six in the past three days. Have you seen one before?"

I shook my head and looked at her with a sympathetic grimace.

"He kind of stares into space first, then he acts like he needs to throw up or something. Then his little body starts shaking and his eyes fix and his lips turn blue. I have to lay him down on his side, back away, and let him go. It's so scary."

I glanced at Dani. She kept playing with her wedding ring and blinking rapidly. I pictured Kaye the way Dani described Steven, and wondered if it would be something I'd have to deal with someday. "I'd be scared too."

"He stops breathing. Do you know what it's like to watch your child stop breathing and not be able to do anything about it? To just wait. Stand there watching, praying that he'll breathe again."

I shook my head and whispered, "Wow." I thought I felt helpless.

Dani looked out the window. "What am I going to do?"

I reached over and held her hand. "Just have faith. Everything will be okay. In fact, maybe things won't be as bad as you think." It seemed like little comfort, and yet I knew from personal experience that faith was the only thing that could heal us from the inside out— the only thing that gave us lasting peace. So, in a way, faith was the best I could wish for her.

She sighed. "Parenthood is hard. When you were growing up, did you ever think it would be this hard?"

"Nope. There's a surprise around every corner."

We got to Dani's house, and she reached for the door handle as soon as we'd stopped. Before she stepped out of the car, she turned to me with wet eyes. "I'm so sorry."

I could have acted like I didn't know what she was talking about, just to get her to admit what she'd done wrong, but I could tell she didn't apologize very often, and it was hard for her.

"It's alright," I said.

"No it isn't. I had no right to assume. No right to suggest. I mean, if someone said that to me! If someone told me there was no difference between me and . . ." The tears spilled from her eyes until her cheeks were wet, and salty water dripped from her chin.

"It's okay. You were right about some things."

Dani looked at me with surprise.

I shrugged. "It's not fair to my other kids. At least, it doesn't seem that way to me. But Adam says it's all part of God's plan, and I believe him." I looked at Dani, feeling a sense of calm reassurance, and as I told her I believed, my faith grew.

Dani shook her head. "Amazing."

"What's amazing?"

"Everything. That you're here with me right when I need you. That you have the experience to be able to help me with mine. That you care about me after everything I said to you."

It didn't seem too amazing to me. It seemed just . . . almost plotted out and planned by someone who cared for all of His children. If I could guide the lives of my children to have them help each other and learn from each other's experience, so that all of them could benefit, I would.

"Amazing grace," I said. And though I felt like my chest might burst, I didn't cry. I felt calm and certain.

Dani gave me a quick hug and a "thank you" before she climbed out of the car. I drove to Marie's school feeling really good—emotionally.

Physically, it was another story. I felt a dull ache in my back, and an odd pressure in my abdomen. Something was wrong.

As soon as Adam got home from school, he called Gay Lynn and asked her to babysit the girls. I tried to hold onto the feeling I'd had that afternoon with Dani—no matter what happened. It was all part of the plan. It was all part of His plan.

The nurses hooked me up to a monitor to keep track of the baby's heart rate and any contractions I might be having. Dr. Rimes was on her way.

Apparently, Dani would have to find someone else to give her a ride the next day.

Chapter 29

COMFORT

Dr. Rimes finally arrived, and she decided to take me for another ultrasound. As she spread the cool gel on my stomach, I held Adam's hand and looked up at his face. He, too, was lost in the moment—focusing his attention on the matter at hand, and leaving all our other worries up to God.

"Your placenta has begun to detach. I'm afraid we'll have to perform a Cesarean and get this little guy out into the world."

"I'm four weeks early," I protested.

"We deliver babies that early all the time. He'll be fine."

She gave me a calm smile, but four weeks early seemed like a lot to me. If I took bread out of the oven four minutes early, it was often doughy in the middle.

They gave me an epidural and took me to the operating room. A sheet hung across my chest so I couldn't look down and see them cutting me open, but I would be awake through the surgery. They said it was safer, but I wondered if it would be better for me if I slept through the whole thing. Adam stood at my head, dressed in surgical gear. He brushed my hair back from my face and kissed me through the mask.

A nurse fastened my arms out straight at my sides. He fastened a blood pressure cuff to my left arm, and a pulse gauge to my right forefinger. I tried not to think of how vulnerable I was—lying naked and sprawled with my life in someone else's hands.

"Can you feel this?" Dr. Rimes asked.

"Feel what?"

"Good. Okay, we're going to start."

I looked up at Adam. "Pray for us."

He brushed my hair from my eyes. "I already am."

At first, I had no idea what was going on—the doctor and nurses talked to each other in a foreign, medical language. Then I heard something splash onto the floor.

"Well, you've still got a lot of water in there," Dr. Rimes said. "That's good."

My body moved, though I had nothing to do with it. As they pulled our baby from me, Adam cooed in my ear, "He's here, honey. He's out."

But he wasn't crying. It wasn't like the birth of my girls had been—pain so sharp that all I could do was cry and push through it and think about the reward at the end of it all. It seemed like the girls had cried almost right after they were born, but when I listened for Scott's cry, all I heard was Dr. Rimes suctioning out his mouth. I willed my baby to breathe—I begged my Heavenly Father to let my baby cry.

The near silence went on far too long, and part of me began to think that my baby was dead. "Adam," I whispered, and felt my chin begin to shake.

Trust me.

I looked at Adam. He was watching Dr. Rimes, and his lips hadn't moved. I knew no human voice had requested my trust. I closed my eyes and felt tears tickle my ears.

I trust you, I thought. Instantly I relived many moments in my life—in the car with Dani, when I heard Kaye sing "I Am a Child of God," when I read that the Atonement could heal me, and when I knew who I was. They all streamed back to me in a reassuring calm, like sunshine breaking a storm.

Scott didn't cry. "Adam," I whispered again, feeling that my baby was gone. But I was grateful for having carried him. I was grateful for the comfort he gave me as he kicked and fluttered in my womb. He was my son, and I knew he was mine forever. If it was God's will that Scott should pass from my arms at that time, so be it.

The room was still, except for fevered suctioning. Then I heard the most beautiful and unexpected sound in the world—the low, raspy gurgling of Scott's first cry. Dr. Rimes suctioned him again, and he cried again—loud and strong.

"He's okay?" I asked.

Adam wiped his face with his sleeve. "Jen, he's gorgeous."

I turned my head to watch the nurses working on him. He was purple, and his thin arms and legs thrashed through the air as a nurse put another suction tube down his throat. She rubbed his back vigorously, and he wailed again.

"Adam," I whispered, quietly accepting God's will that Scott live. "We're outnumbered."

He laughed. "Kaye counts as two, so we've been outnumbered for a while."

We smiled at each other, and Adam gave me an upside-down kiss.

"Dr. Rimes," I said, "what are you doing to me?" My body was rocking, and I felt a pressure so intense it made me think she was pulling all my insides out.

"We're taking out the placenta. It's a good thing we did this, Jen. I think we saved his life today."

I looked over at Scott again. He opened his eyes and looked at the strange new world around him. The nurse wrapped him in a blanket and handed him to Adam.

"He's okay?" Adam asked.

The nurse nodded. "We'll have to watch him closely. He'll probably need to be on oxygen for a couple of days, but Mommy isn't going anywhere anyway."

Comfort had come, squalling. Adam held Scott near my face, and I kissed him. He was still a little purple, and he needed a bath, but his newborn eyes stared at me, and I forgot that I was lying on an operating table, naked, shivering, and nauseated. I forgot that a pile of bills was waiting for me at home. I even forgot that autism might be waiting in the years ahead. God was with us, and all was well.

Chapter 30

BLESSINGS

Adam brought the girls to the hospital to see their baby brother. Marie was so excited she could hardly contain herself, though she didn't like the oxygen tube taped to his face. She sat back in a rocking chair and held Scott in her little, five-year-old arms. He looked up at her, and she kissed his nose. Marie was already a pro at being a big sister.

Kaye was another story. She didn't look at Scott—she seemed detached and uninterested. What she wanted was to climb on my lap and play with the buttons on the hospital bed, but I was in so much pain I couldn't let her do that.

"It's okay," Adam said, "We won't stay long."

"I'm sorry, but I don't want her tearing out my staples."

Adam smiled. "I know. I was there. I watched Dr. Rimes put your staples in."

I grimaced.

It was Kaye's turn to hold Scott. Adam took him from Marie's arms and helped Kaye settle down in the rocking chair. Then he held Scott in Kaye's lap. She looked at him for the first time, and roughly pushed the blanket back from his face.

Adam used his free hand to show Kaye how she should handle the baby. "Soft," Adam said, and he touched Kaye's fingers lightly against Scott's skin.

Kaye touched Scott the way her father had shown her, then she began to wiggle out of the chair.

"Well," Adam said. "I guess she's done."

I smiled. It wasn't much, but with Kaye, we'd learned to take all the love we could get.

Aside from the painful recovery from my C-section, everything went better than I'd anticipated. Brienne came to stay with me for a couple of weeks during my recuperation. She helped fix meals, change diapers, get kids to and from school, and clean the house. I told her about my experiences with Mrs. Orion, Marie's teacher, and Brienne went in and scolded her after picking Marie up one day. It made me feel great, to have Brienne sticking up for me again. It was just like old times.

Kaye got used to Scott. She kissed him good night every night, and did it with an extra effort to be gentle. She didn't drop him on his head once, though I never left her alone in the same room with him—just in case.

When the time came to give Scott his name and blessing, everyone we loved—except my missionary parents—was there, including Tim, Blanch, and even Martha. Russ took a vacation from his big job in D.C. to join Brienne and their daughter Emily. Cathy came, and she brought her mother. Dani was there too, with her sweet little Steven. He still wore a helmet to protect his skull after the surgeries he'd had and in the event of a seizure. Dani, her husband, and Steven sat behind us every Sunday, near the front where there were fewer distractions. Uncle Scott was there, with as many of Olive's children as he could muster together. Even Kaye's teacher, Julie, was there. I'd never seen so many people who were so dear to my heart together in one room.

The men who held the Melchizedek priesthood stood in a circle, bouncing Scott in the middle. Adam once again blessed Scott that he would be a comfort to his mother.

I knew I had to bear my testimony that day. I hadn't borne my testimony in years, but I had to express my love and gratitude. I had to tell everyone what I was thinking.

When I finally forced myself to stand, my knees felt weak. I turned to face the congregation and saw the people I loved in front of me—and I seemed to love them more than usual at that moment. I took a deep breath. "Brothers and sisters," I sighed. "This past year has been . . . strange. Unpredictable. Stressful, wonderful, confusing—you name it! But I've learned so much in the past year. I guess that's how it works, huh? You learn the most when you're going through the most."

Gazing at the faces before me, taking note of those I knew, and those I didn't know, I realized that I loved them all. An elderly man near the front—the one who had moved to the opposite side of the chapel to get away from my noisy Kaye—pulled a small hearing aid from his ear and adjusted it. I wondered if he had moved away because of his hearing aid. Maybe it had nothing to do with Kaye after all.

I smiled at the congregation. "First off, I have to thank you all for your kindness. We've needed kindness. I think we all do." I had so many thoughts in my mind I wasn't sure how to express them all. What do you say when there is too much to say? When you've experienced the hand of God in your life, how do you express enough gratitude? I decided to open my mouth and let the words tumble out, as organized as the Spirit would make them.

"I used to feel like I had some level of control over my life, but Kaye took that control away. Or, autism took it away. Now I know that there is a distinct possibility that Scott will be autistic too. The thought of having another autistic child . . ." I stared at Scott in Adam's arms and suppressed a shudder.

"But I realize, as I stand before you today, that it doesn't matter if Scott is autistic or not." Adam looked up at me as I spoke, and I smiled at him. "It really doesn't matter. Because I believe that Kaye is the way God wants her. And look at what has happened to all of us because of her. Look at how we've been blessed so much by one little child who doesn't even know how to carry on a conversation." I looked at Gay Lynn, whose eyes were shining, and at Dani, who held Steven's hand.

"None of us are strangers to the Lord. He loves us all, and He gives us what we need, especially when we do our best to serve Him." Adam smiled at me, and Brienne wiped at her cheeks.

"So, if Scott is autistic," I took a deep breath, "I believe it's because God wants him that way. We almost lost Scott, but God let him live. There's a reason behind that, and whatever the reason, God will guide us to what we should do, because we are in His hands. He's in control." I smiled. "Not long after Kaye was diagnosed, I asked Adam to heal her. He couldn't. He laid his hands on her head and blessed her, but he didn't heal her. At first, I wondered why. I thought

I didn't have enough faith, or maybe I was doing something wrong. But the truth is I was asking for the wrong person to be healed. Instead of healing Kaye, He healed me."

I took a moment to collect my emotions. "One more thing, then I'll sit down. I know who I am. More importantly, God knows who I am. He knows each of us. And that makes all the difference in the world. Knowing who I am doesn't change the circumstances of my life, just like knowing Kaye had autism didn't change who she is. Knowing who I am changes me—it changes my perspective. So I handle things differently. Maybe that's how you know something is true—it changes you from the inside out. That's how God heals us. That's how He makes us stronger. He shows us who we really are, so we don't feel like strangers anymore. To Him, or to each other."

I closed my testimony and sat next to Adam again. He handed Scott to me, and I held my baby close and kissed his soft, downy head. Marie let Scott hold her finger in a tight grip, and she snuggled into my side. Kaye stood before me, sang a single note, and then stimmed over Scott's face. For an instant, she looked me in the eye and smiled.

——➤❈❈ About the Author ❈❈◀——

Amy Maida Wadsworth lives in Cottonwood Heights with her husband, Jason, and their four children: Maida Marie, Jessica Kaye, Russell Scott, and Kira Nerys. Amy studied English and Human Development at the University of Utah. She loves performing with the Sterling Singers, and watching her husband and children in dramatic productions. She is currently serving as her ward's Primary secretary.

When Amy's daughter Jessica was three years old, she was diagnosed with autistic spectrum disorder. Jason and Amy look back on this year of diagnosis as the most difficult in their lives to date. Jessica seemed like a normal two-year-old. She was learning how to speak and sang many songs with her musical family. Then, almost overnight and without apparent illness, she seemed to forget everything she had learned. While Jessica's disposition was always sweet, and her sister Maida was always willing to help and support her family far beyond the limits of her age, Jessica's frequent tantrums and complete lack of communication were often frustrating and discouraging. That year of trial—like most seasons of difficulty in a human life—shaped and molded the Wadsworths into the tight-knit, supportive family they are. That year also strengthened their testimonies. The themes of humility, forgiveness, spiritual identity, and learning to trust in the Lord are at the core of Amy's testimony, and writing this novel was an exercise in remembrance. When speaking of writing this novel, Amy says, "I feel privileged to have the opportunity to share my testimony in this forum. I hope this novel will touch many lives, and help us to know the importance of patience, love, and understanding in our dealings with each other."

If you would like to be updated on Amy's newest releases or correspond with her, please send an e-mail to info@covenant-lds.com. You may also write to her in care of Covenant Communications, P.O. Box 416, American Fork, UT 84003-0416.